When Galaxies Collide

1st Edition printed 2012: ISBN 978-1-927438-04-6

Note for Librarians: a catalog record for this book that includes Dewey Decimal Classification and U.S. Library of Congress numbers is available from the Library and Archives of Canada. The complete catalog record can be obtained from their online database at:
www.collectionscanada.ca/amicus/index-e.html

ISBN978-1-927438-04-6
Printed in the United States

Powell River Books
Powell River BC, Canada
Book sales online at:
www.powellriverbooks.com
phone: 604-483-1704
email: wlutz@mtsac.edu

10 9 8 7 6 5 4 3 2 1

When Galaxies Collide

Wayne J. Lutz

2012
Powell River Books

Books by Wayne J. Lutz

Coastal British Columbia Stories

Up the Lake
Up the Main
Up the Winter Trail
Up the Strait
Up the Airway
Farther Up the Lake
Farther Up the Main
Farther Up the Strait
Cabin Number 5
Off the Grid
Up the Inlet

Science Fiction Titles

Echo of a Distant Planet
Inbound to Earth
Anomaly at Fortune lake
When Galaxies Collide
Across the Galactic Sea

Cover Photos:

Front Cover – Arp 274 (NGC 5679) in Virgo, colliding galaxies approximately 400 million light-years from earth; image from Hubble Space Telescope.

Back Cover:

NGC 3314; These galaxies are not colliding, but are a trick of perspective as they overlap as viewed from Earth, while separated by approximately 25 million light-years; image from Hubble Space Telescope.

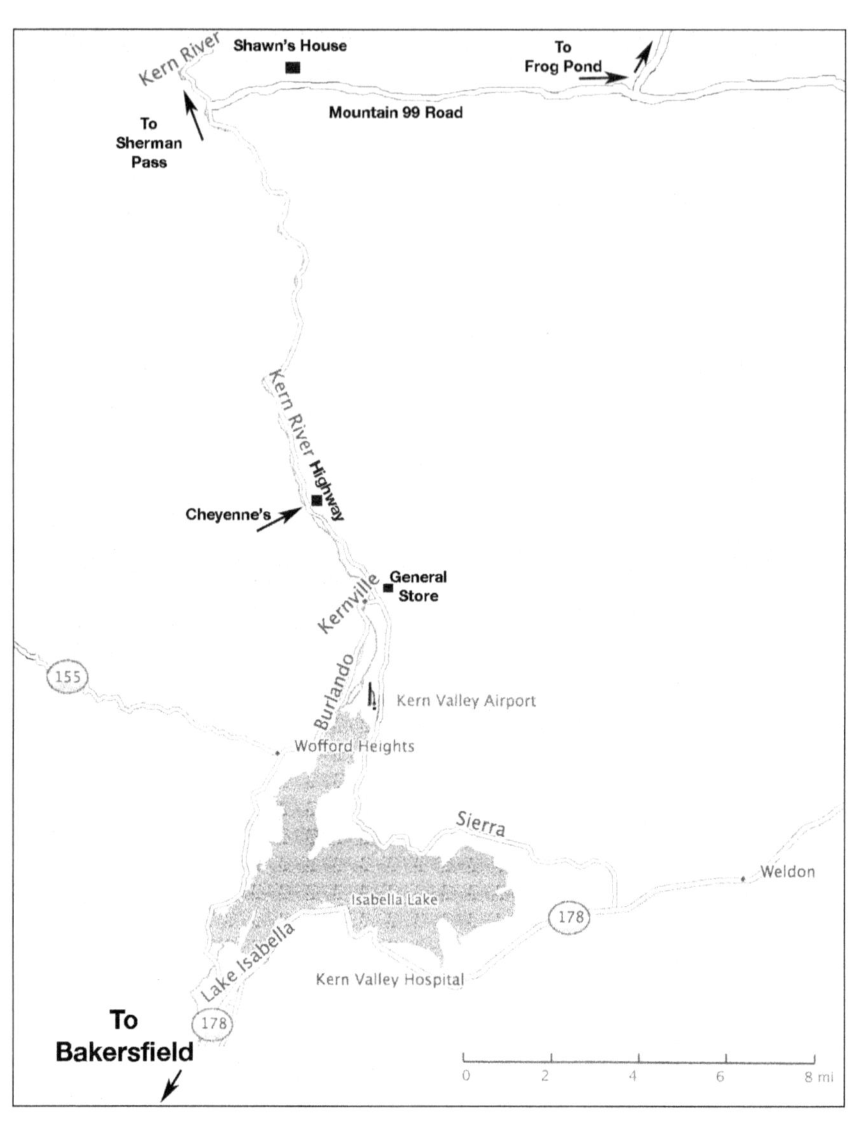

Kern River
Shawn's House
To Frog Pond
To Sherman Pass
Mountain 99 Road
Kern River Highway
Cheyenne's
Kernville
General Store
Burlando
Kern Valley Airport
155
Wofford Heights
Sierra
Weldon
Isabella Lake
178
Lake Isabella
Kern Valley Hospital
To Bakersfield
178
0   2   4   6   8 mi

Contents

Prologue

Andromeda and the Milky Way

At present, the Milky Way is in the process of colliding with a small galaxy called the Sagittarius Dwarf, a member of our local group of over 54 galaxies. Even as it occurs, you'd barely notice, since we inhabit a large spiral galaxy, and the smaller elliptical dwarf is losing the battle. Besides, collisions on this scale aren't as rough as you might imagine. Generally, most of the stars in both systems survive unscathed, although the distorting gravitational influence can trigger stellar formation. Stars are simply too far apart to make much of a cosmic mess, except when big galaxies hit head-on. Which will be the case when the Milky Way and Andromeda collide in 4.75 billion years.

This cosmic collision isn't a certainty, since measurement of galactic motions aren't yet accurate enough to predict, or for astronomers to agree on, such an interaction. However, a head-on collision is now considered the most probable scenario. When it begins to affect our planet in another 4.6 billion years, with "first touch" of the outer spiral arms of the two galaxies, the approximate year on Earth will be 4,646,927,019 AD. But on Planet Proteus in the Andromeda Galaxy, it will be 2050.

Planet Proteus

The Andromeda Galaxy

Chapter 1

The Amelia Glitch

July 2, 1937

They were looking for a flat sliver of land in the Pacific, a little over a mile long and only 1600 feet wide. To call it an island was an overstatement. Fred and Amelia were trying to find this tiny speck of land after dead reckoning in the morning twilight 800 miles from Lae, New Guinea, where their Bendix fixed-loop antenna on the Electra's belly had been torn off during an overgross takeoff. To make matters worse, they had cut off their long-wire antenna, the other part of their direction finder, to avoid the hassle of having to crank it back into the airplane every time they used it. In other words, they were flying blind, and looking for an infinitesimal patch of land sticking up only a few feet from the water.

"We must be on you, but cannot see you," Amelia radioed to the U.S. Coast Guard cutter *Itasca*, on-station at Howland Island to communicate with the Lockheed Electra. "Gas is running low. Have been unable to reach you by radio. We are flying at one-thousand feet."

Sixteen minutes later, at 7:58 am, Amelia Earhart radioed again: "Cannot hear you. Please send voice signals so we can try to take a radio bearing."

The *Itasca* heard this transmission, loud and clear, indicating the Electra was nearby, but they couldn't reply by voice on the frequency Earhart requested, so they transmitted by Morse code. Amelia immediately acknowledged receipt, sounding elated. But a few minutes later she broadcast once more in a more subdued tone, saying Fred Noonan was unable to determine the direction of the signal.

In a transmission that might have been her last, *Itasca* copied a broken sentence from Amelia that sounded like: "We are running on a line north and south."

The *Itasca* took this to mean Earhart and Noonan thought they were at the proper longitude, but were navigating up and down the meridian, looking for the low-lying island. The cutter fired up its boilers now, generating smoke to help the aviators find them. Scattered clouds near Howland cast dark shadows on the water under the low-angled morning sun, making island-like silhouettes on the water, indistinguishable from the real thing. The two famous aviators saw neither the smoke nor the low-profile island. They droned on for several more minutes, until suddenly Amelia exclaimed: "There it is!"

Fred Noonan, hunched over his chart in the back seat, where he had drawn a sun line running on 157–337, looked past Amelia and out the narrow cockpit windshield. Beyond the profile of Amelia Earhart in the left seat was a slim spit of land and a beautiful paved runway shining in the morning sun.

"God!" was all he could say.

* * * * *

As later research would reveal, until that day in 1937, there had not been a major glitch in the timeline on Planet Proteus. Certainly there must have been smaller irregularities earlier, as indicated by the minor differences in history that were already occurring, but none of them had a significant impact. Over a hundred years after the "Amelia Glitch," it would be determined that this deviation would have moderate impact on history, diminished by the fact that neither Amelia Earhart nor Fred Noonan went on to have any children. However, their fame provided a noticeable change in the timeline.

Amelia never flew another record-setting route, but she fostered the growth of the fledgling Ninety-Nines, an organization of women pilots that eventually led to the proliferation of females in the aviation industry.

Fred Noonan would return to Pan Am, and contributed significantly to its rapid expansion. However, the air carrier eventually faltered in a world of international pressures, which helped nudge time back on course.

It was little fits and starts like this that could bump the space-time continuum, as had happened since the creation of Planet Proteus. Compared to Earth, Proteus was slightly different, although it remained mostly the same.

Chapter 2

Up River Highway

June 4, 2015

Shawn Russell cruised up the Kern River Highway in his Ford Edsel, driving faster than he should on an evening in June when summer tourists were already beginning to arrive. The highway followed the twists in the river to his left, creating blind curves that could get your attention. Locals knew how to keep in their lane, but visitors might be gawking at their surroundings, maybe after one too many beers at Cheyenne's. Tourists wouldn't normally be this far north, but keeping a lookout for lights poking around the next bend was prudent self-defense.

The Edsel was a fine machine, one of several in the area. Shawn's was a gaudy fire-engine-red convertible, an older 2008 model, but still in excellent condition. He bought it fresh out of college, and the odometer now showed only 36,000 miles. He couldn't drive very far around here – mostly up and down River Highway to his home a little more than 10 miles north of Kernville, and an occasional 50 curvy miles to Bakersfield.

The throaty engine, converted to natural gas soon after the turn of the century, provided plenty of power for his needs. NG, although cheaper than traditional gasoline, was still a major part of his vehicle's operating cost, so he wasn't registering savings by speeding around these uphill curves, as he was tonight.

* * * * *

Shawn lived in a nondescript home just off Kern River Highway on Mountain 99 Road, which began as pavement, but switched quickly to gravel, and to dirt before reaching his house, where the power lines ended.

He was at the end of the electrical grid and the wired world of Internet as well. This was important for his home-based profession, a job no one knew about except his bosses and those few who shared his occupation. Shawn was a shaman, and few would understand.

If others knew what he did for a living, they might compromise his objectives, which would change a lot of things for a lot of people. Just like the original days of native shamans, his methods involved a world of good and evil realms, but not the kind found in apparitions and ghostly healing. Instead, his endeavors involved computers, astrophysics, and modern philosophies.

In Shawn's unadorned home north of Kernville, he worked as if he was semi-retired, plugging away at his computer and on the phone to distant parts of the world. It was a life much like a part-time writer or a financial consultant, except he lived his retirement-like existence at the early age of twenty-nine. Some of his friends and neighbors questioned this, but Shawn could back up his lifestyle with a good story.

One day at Cheyenne's, Farley asked: "Why do you need all those gadgets on your roof?"

"Well, as you know, I'm a writer," replied Shawn. "These days you need computers and phones to write books, especially e-books. And I'm my own publisher, so I need plenty of gadgets. Tax deductible, of course."

"Sure," replied Farley. "Whatever you say. But I don't know how you can afford it. Seems to me you'd eat up all your profits."

"Not me. I try to save money for the necessities of life. Just like you."

"Just like me? Who has an Edsel, an airplane, and an Energoe? To say nothing of those fancy antennas on your roof."

"The Cessna isn't mine, Farley. Three of us share the expenses. And the Edsel's almost ten years old."

"Well, a kid like you shouldn't have it so good. Just wish it was me!"

Farley was a great friend, smart and always straightforward, not a bad bone in his body. Maybe that's why he never asked much about where all of those e-books were going. If Farley had owned a computer, he might have checked Amazon, where he would have found only a single book title listed for "Shawn Russell," and that fellow claimed his home was in Rhode Island, and his age was 63.

* * * * *

While the sun was still rising behind the tall Sierras to the east, Shawn got out of bed and climbed down the stairs from the loft. His small home was cabin-like in size and function, but it was perfect for a fellow like him. The smaller the square-footage, the less to keep clean. He had plenty of electricity from the grid, and water from a robust well fed by a spring, along with a wood-burning stove that efficiently heated his small home. Sewage was through a septic tank, with a healthy leaching field. The nearest grocery store was 10 miles away in Kernville, and the airport only 3 miles farther south.

He seemed a long way from his original home in Los Angeles, but he could get there in slightly over an hour on clear days when he could fly point-to-point over the Tehachapi Mountains. Most of the time, he flew the marginal-weather route along the Kern River to Bakersfield, south to Burbank, and then east to Pomona. At other times, there was only the adverse-weather route, which meant you stayed home. Kern Valley Airport had no instrument approach, and its location in the north corner of a tight valley prohibited flights in bad weather or at night.

After a breakfast of oatmeal and toast, Shawn packed his off-road sack, and sat down on the old-fashioned couch with its tan flowers embedded on yellow cloth upholstery. The sofa came with the cabin, and like most of his furniture, he hadn't bothered to replace it. Shawn employed an easy-going attitude when it came to interior decorating. If it wasn't there when he arrived, he figured he really didn't need it.

Sitting on the old couch, he began dressing in the clothes he'd worn when he arrived from town last night. He pulled on his forest-green *River Rat* sweatshirt and tan knickerbocker-style pants, which were popular these days. It seemed everyone under the age of 30 was wearing the loose-fitting trousers, usually in bright colors. His cuffs were gathered mid-calf with a muted-blue elastic band. It fit the current style but not the colors. Then again, Shawn was nearly 30.

He pulled on thick wool socks and black low-cut hiking boots with zippers rather than laces. Once his boots were on, he pulled his thick gray socks up high enough that they met the lower cuff of his pants. Shawn's boots were so comfortable he wore them almost everywhere. Today he would need them for their all-terrain grip.

Then he headed out to the shed behind the house, where he kept his Energoe. It was a bright yellow model with four-wheel drive and differential lockers that could be engaged in tough climbs. His Energoe was manufactured by the company that initiated the concept, but many of the newer vehicles were built by upstarts that were just now entering the competition. Still, everyone call their all-terrain vehicles "Energoes," no matter who built it, since the company had monopolized the market for so long. His model was light enough for one person (a strong person) to lift two wheels off the ground when it was jammed into a tight spot, but Shawn's Energoe was tough enough to climb almost any mountain trail, and some mountains that didn't even have a blazed path.

After loading his sack of camping gear and emergency supplies into the rear storage box, he pulled out the choke, and used the thumb-activated starter to crank up the engine. The Energoe's motor was a basic hybrid, but the places Shawn took it usually required the power of old-fashioned gasoline. The electric motor kicked in only on flat or downhill stretches, but that was enough to prolong the range to over 200 miles. Ten miles, in the terrain he traveled, could take half of a day.

He slipped the choke back in, and shifted into gear. Off he went, headed east on Mountain 99, which Shawn called "Mountain Main," an apt name for a dirt road travelled only by logging trucks and the occasional Energoe. The trucks seldom ventured very far, since the terrain got rapidly steeper the farther east you drove. Still, loggers ventured into the area occasionally, when the government temporarily lifted the tree falling ban that had protected the forests in recent decades. These days, you'd be more likely to see an Energoe than a logging truck here, and a few miles farther east you could expect to find no one, for the Sierras plunged upward in a near-vertical ascent. The Pacific Crest Trail, not accessible from this "main," was only 10 miles away as the crow flies. Twenty miles farther east was Highway 395, on the other side of the Sierras, which seemed a million miles away.

His ride today would take him only 7 miles, the first four on Mountain Main, and the rest up a narrow trail Shawn had blazed himself, leading to the Snow Cabin. The first 4 miles would take only 10 minutes. The last three could take most of the morning.

When Shawn arrived at the turnoff to the Snow Cabin, he stopped to clear the branches he always placed along the side of the road to disguise the entrance to the trail. It wasn't meant to be a no-trespassing ploy, but he didn't want just anybody exploring the route. If they found the cabin, it might become popular, and so far, Shawn had never seen anyone else there while he was present. He hoped to keep it that way.

The cabin had originally been built by one of the big sawmills that harnessed the Kern River in the old days, using it as a snow survey location to help plan out mill operations for the spring. Snowmelt fed the river and the sawmill's turbines, which in turn produced electricity for the big saws. In years gone by, surveyors from the mill would hike up to the cabin, which was built by their co-workers, to measure the snow pack. The hike was so strenuous in the days before Energoes that it would take all day, requiring an overnight stay before starting back down. The cabin still sat there, maintained by hikers and Energoe riders like Shawn, and used by very few. It had become one of his favorite places, and a spot where a modern shaman could do his best work.

Chapter 3

Shaman

Shawn's appointed position as a shaman had come as a surprise. When he graduated from UCLA in 2008, he didn't even know modern shamans existed. Nor did many other people on Proteus know about such a thing. With a bachelor's degree in physics, Shawn didn't feel well positioned for anything, although it had been a fun ride so far. The primary problem was he didn't enjoy the math that came with the territory, although he'd always excelled in the subject. Only an advanced degree, preferably a doctorate, would allow him to progress in the field of theoretical physics, which meant a severe additional dose of mathematics. With merely a bachelor's degree, he would need to consider applied physics as an employment option. There were companies who hired physicists in engineering positions, which sounded even less exciting. So what should he do?

In Shawn's case, he decided to simply wait. He'd need a job to tide him over, until he could decide on a major to pursue in graduate school, maybe astrophysics, or to find a field of employment that actually interested him. In the meantime, he'd have a chance to travel and explore the outdoors, one of his passions. With limited financial backing available from his parents and a student loan deferred for two more years, he figured he could kick around for almost a year before getting serious about life. He couldn't do it without a job of some kind, but he was willing to work almost anywhere that would give him the financial freedom to explore the great outdoors.

In 2008, the economy was going through a bummer of a recession, what most financial experts referred to as a minor depression. But it wasn't minor for Shawn's graduating class – most of his classmates were having problems finding a job of any type. Open positions for physicists with a bachelor's degree were an even bleaker situation. That's when he heard about the GC Project.

He'd read about the project in *Scientific American*, and heard a little bit from one of his physics professors, who happened to be his favorite instructor. Dr. Feinem taught the only two astrophysics classes offered to undergraduates, an astronomy course for non-science majors, and a class in celestial mechanics. Shawn took both courses, although the basic astronomy class was, by far, the best. Although it didn't offer any degree credit for physics majors, he was enthralled by Dr. Feinem's classroom presentations in the big lecture hall. While his non-science classmates showed apathy to most of the topics, Shawn paid close attention, and enjoyed the course more than any of his required physics classes. Elementary it may have been, but it drew Shawn towards the field of astronomy in a mighty big way.

It was in the more-demanding celestial mechanics course in his last semester that Dr. Feinem had told his class about an email he received from the National Science Foundation regarding a new program called the Galactic Collision Project, a government-sponsored program to prepare for the much-touted event of the latter half of the century, the pending collision of the Heavenly Way with its sister spiral galaxy, Zeus.

Ever since Shawn could remember, the collision was a news item. Galactic collisions were a very slow process, at least as measured within the span of human life cycles. Over a period of 200 million years, the Heavenly Way and Zeus would undergo the collision process, generally causing little harm to any of the stars as the two large spirals merged into one giant elliptical galaxy. There was so much space between stars that galactic collisions were more a matter of grand camerawork by space telescopes than catastrophic events. Of course, if your star happened to be one destined for a direct hit (or even a gravitational sideswipe), it could get way too exciting.

In the case of Planet Proteus and its galaxy, the Heavenly Way, the collision wasn't projected to include a direct blow or even a near miss. Astronomical research became more refined over the years, and collision parameters were fine-tuned as galactic proper motions between the Heavenly Way and Zeus were more precisely determined.

A lot of funding had gone into astronomy in Shawn's short lifetime, just to reassure everyone they were safe and that future generations would not be threatened. Star formation and other significant celestial events would be triggered within the gravitational wake of two colliding spirals, but not a living soul would be harmed. Souls, that is, living many centuries in the future.

Astronomy grew by leaps and bounds in the early 1900's, with bigger and bigger telescopes, and enough data to explain that galaxies actually exist and we live inside one called the Heavenly Way. A nebula called Zeus, far bigger than any other fuzzy patch in the sky, was the first galaxy resolved into individual stars, shortly thereafter determined to be the twin sister of the Heavenly Way. And then the amazing astronomical leaps of the mid-1900's, when it was learned we were rapidly moving closer to Zeus. In fact, depending upon how you measured it, the collision was already underway. When you looked up there were two rivers of light, one called the Heavenly Way, the band of stars forming our awkward view, looking out through the plane of our own galaxy. Intersecting it in the sky was another galactic band, now nearly as bright – the almost open-faced spiral of Zeus heading directly towards us.

For eons before man knew anything about science, he had looked up and seen these two galaxies as they began their collision course, but didn't understand the significance. The two merging bands of white were called the Double Stream.

Now, after decades of headlines regarding the pending collision, the news seldom made the front page. How long can any media item capture the attention of the public? The event had been determined to be non-threatening, and would happen ever so slowly. Proteus' sun would be one of the many stars jostled out of its orbit within our own Heavenly Way, probably flung (slowly) to an outer region of the merged giant elliptical galaxy. But it would survive in such a way that future generations would barely notice the difference.

* * * * *

This was the image Shawn grew up with as he learned basic astronomy, first from his father and later from Dr. Feinem at UCLA. So when his favorite professor brought up the recently announced Galactic Collision

Project in his celestial mechanics course, Shawn was interested, and he paid close attention. The National Science Foundation was now hiring scientists and student interns to better understand the interaction of the Double Stream, and to better prepare for the kickoff of the grand event, now officially scheduled for 2050, only 42 years away.

To say a galactic collision would begin on a certain date was, as Dr. Feinem reminded his class, not exactly accurate in astronomical terms. The public needed a calendar to remind them when such an event began, but the merger would take place over 200 million years. In Dr. Feinem's own words: "To say it will begin in 2050 is like saying the human species was born on a specific date and time in anthropologic history. In reality, the merger is already well underway."

But Feinem supported the government's announcement of the GC Project, and Shawn was listening close as his favorite instructor described the program: "The public needs a specific date, and astronomy is here to serve the public. Scientists may view things differently, but we'll always need to bow to the interests of the people. For it's to humanity that we must remain committed. Besides, it's going to mean a lot of GS-12 government jobs for scientists. Maybe you'll want to apply for one of them."

Everyone in the class snickered, including Shawn. But with graduation pending, he thought about the GC Project. With only a bachelor's degree in physics, what were his realistic chances for such a job? Then again, what would it hurt to apply? The application procedures were already posted on the physics department bulletin board, right beside a similar NASA poster recruiting the next class of astronauts. In 2008, it was known that those with ambitions as an astronaut had a lot of challenges ahead. The Space Shuttle would soon be decommissioned, without a replacement vehicle on the horizon. So how far removed from reality was applying for a Galactic Collision position? Fortunately, there were two grades of jobs listed – project scientist and student intern. Project scientist was a stretch (GS-12), but student interns were on the opposite end of the spectrum, with an advertised pay scale equating to minimum wage and no GS grade at all. But an internship might meet Shawn's criteria for a temporary job with a lot of freedom. So just before graduation, he applied.

The application process was considerably more complex than he expected. First, he received a packet in the mail that required extensive background information and a signature on the dotted line for a complete security check. Meanwhile, he submitted applications to three prospective commercial corporations with openings in applied physics, which he considered "glorified engineering." As he waited for replies from these companies and the GC internship, he moved back in with his parents in Pomona. Lots of his classmates had been forced into the "return to the nest" syndrome. Economically, times were tough, and he had classmates who didn't even bother applying for a job. Instead, a common tendency was to move back home, and try to enjoy a few months of unpaid vacation, while waiting for a slot in graduate school. The only difference for Shawn was he wasn't ready for graduate work, so he really needed a job.

The Galactic Collision internship took longer to process than the other three companies, two of which provided almost immediate rejection letters. The third never bothered replying. So in October 2008, while settling into an extended recess between school and who-knows-what, Shawn finally received a reply regarding his GC application. He was scheduled for an interview, which made him realize two things: the internship selection process was more extensive than he had expected; and they seemed to be in no hurry to hire interns.

* * * * *

"So, Mister Russell, tell us about your football experience at UCLA," said the bearded man with the bright red shirt who sat squarely in the middle of the surprisingly young interview panel.

Shawn had been intimidated as soon as he walked into the room in a hotel near Los Angeles International Airport, expecting a one-on-one interview with a government bureaucrat. Instead, he now faced three informally dressed men and two women. One of the youngest men had a classic geek look, including thick-rimmed glasses and a pocket protector with protruding pens. It looked like a casual panel from the original cast of *Capcom Houston*, minus the white shirts and ties. But it wasn't their appearance or their numbers that intimidated him; it was their initial greeting:

"Sit, Mister Russell," said the bearded man in the center.

No "Hello" or even "Please have a seat." Just "Sit!"

As he took his seat in straight-backed chair, it reminded him more of an interrogation than an interview. Shawn considered his attire. He had spent money he didn't have on a new dark-blue suit, including the latest in expensive bell-bottom trousers. When he handed his credit card to the clerk, he remembered feeling confident this expensive purchase was in the best interest of assuring his internship interview went well. If nothing else, he would look professional. Now this — a panel of geeks with no common sense regarding interview techniques, and a first-question about football. Even in his college business management course, he had learned more about how to set a proper interview atmosphere than these bozos seemed to know.

"Well, I was a walk-on wide receiver, and I didn't get much playing time on a team like that. But I've always loved football, and it was a chance for me to test my skills. It was really enjoyable."

"What do you mean 'a team like that?'" asked the same bearded man.

So that's it — we start with a question with little meaning, and then see how I handle the pressure of an interview. At least they get credit for innovation.

"We were fifth in the PAC-12 the year I played, which wasn't too bad. So just getting some time on the field was something I considered an important accomplishment. In high school, I was a starting wide receiver, but at UCLA I barely got to play. That's how good they were."

"So did it make you regret trying out," said the young pocket-protector geek, sitting at the end of the table. "I mean, why bother?"

"Not at all. It was one of my most valuable experiences at UCLA. Practice was grueling, and it demanded a heck of a lot of dedication. So my studying time had to be focused. But I really enjoyed the total football experience."

The bearded man with the red shirt again: "You were on the team for four years?"

"Well, I'd tried out for the team in my first year, but I missed the cut. Same thing for the next two years. It wasn't until my senior year that I finally made it onto the team."

"Sounds painful," said the geek, seated off to Shawn's far right. He didn't look like he knew the shape of a football. "You said you didn't get much playing time. Exactly how much did you get?"

He might not know the number of yards on a football field, but he was paying attention.

"Well… Actually I got into a game only twice that year. I played five minutes against Stanford, just before the end of the game. The third-string quarterback threw a pass to me, but it went way over my head. I also played in the last few minutes of the USC game, when we were getting whipped something fierce. This time, the same quarterback was right on target, and I caught the ball in a stutter-step play angled towards the sidelines. I ended up losing a yard."

"Very impressive," said the bearded man. "I went to USC."

This kind of questioning, seemingly unrelated to anything involving astrophysics, continued for another hour. As the interview progressed, Shawn became more relaxed as he realized this group of five was sincerely interested in his attitudes towards life. Fortunately, they didn't ask him about his mediocre grade-point-average, although they already must have examined his transcripts. There were questions about his political orientation (which he described as "close to none, but hovering on Democrat"), his philosophy regarding global warming and the population explosion, and even his attitude towards death and the process of dying. They finished with a inquiry about his musical tastes. Not one question hinted at his knowledge of astrophysics.

* * * * *

"You've got the job," said the voice on the phone. "Of course, it's only an internship, but it has some benefits we didn't include with the job announcement."

"Great!" replied Shawn. "I can start anytime you say."

By the end of the phone call, Shawn was set for a meeting with a Galactic Collision representative, who would drive to Pomona to meet him. Together they were supposed to set up a work schedule and discuss additional benefits, which seemed a bit remarkable to Shawn. Bringing a GC employee to Pomona seemed excessive, since this was only a low-paying internship. The voice on the phone had explained these new GC jobs were handled under a special protocol requiring an initial "pre-employment overview meeting," and that would be the time to discuss all conditions of service, including "worksite selection."

It sounded more like the Peace Corps than a scientific project, and Shawn realized he didn't have the slightest idea what the internship entailed. He didn't even know where GC employees were based, but the fact that the representative would meet him in Pomona indicated there were positions on the West Coast. He had assumed he might have to move a long distance, and the financial implications were suddenly of concern, although he hadn't even questioned relocation requirements when he applied for the job. It was one of those shots in the dark that seemed a good idea at the time. Now it was clear he hadn't the slightest idea what he'd gotten himself into.

On the other hand, it was only an internship, so he could still get out of it. If the Pomona meeting brought up issues not easily resolved, he could still just walk away. And he might need to.

Chapter 4

Snow Cabin

The Energoe pushed its way forward, headed up the rugged trail from Mountain Main to the cabin. This early in the year, snow still sat along the sides of the trail, but these late spring patches could still transition into solid drifts blocking the route. Early June might be a few weeks too early, but the only way to tell was to give it a try.

The first mile was easily negotiated. Shawn stopped twice to cut fallen trees out of the way, using his chainsaw. The biggest problem was mud that reduced the Energoe's traction, but 4-wheel-drive solved most of the challenging areas. Twice he elected to engage the "Lockers" switch, which coupled his front tires together for increased traction. Shawn used differential lock only as a last resort, since it made steering difficult, and it only worked if you were willing to throttle-up nearly to the maximum. This was no place to let your bike go out of control. His satellite phone would bring a rescue team, but this was the kind of terrain where you could die in an instant, if you weren't careful. Riding alone, as Shawn often did, was something any rider should think about carefully before assuming it was worth the risk. The Snow Cabin was always worth it.

Stubby roots protruding from muddy banks had to be treated carefully. An Energoe's tires were tough, but it would be a long walk back if one was severely punctured. Shawn carried plenty of tools, including a tire repair kit for lesser damage and an air compressor that ran off his engine, and he was mechanically-minded enough to seldom get himself stranded. But he backed himself up with a sleeping bag, air mattress, tent, and a few days supply of food, just in case. Plus, the sleeping bag and food would be essential once he reached the cabin.

Halfway up the trail, snow became more of a problem. This was a section harboring more drifts than any other part of the route.

Although it would get higher in altitude all the way to the cabin, this area was shaded by a thick canopy of evergreens, part of a huge grove of firs on the side of the mountain that kept snowdrifts intact well into July. If a major drift blocked the trail, he might not be able to get through. Of all the adversities Energoes could handle, snow wasn't one of them. Give his bike a foot of water, or mud up to the axle, or an almost-sheer incline that looked too steep to even climb on-foot, and it would keep on truckin'. But give it a foot of snow, and he'd be stopped dead in his tracks.

And there was at least two feet of snow in some places. But it only lasted for short sections of the trail. So he engaged his lockers, and blasted on through.

Some of the corners were so steeply inclined that Shawn had to lean far to the outside of the curve while simultaneously pushing his thumb-throttle full against the stop. Mud would fly until it covered everything, including his helmet, and he had to find a level spot to stop and wipe the mud off his goggles so he could see well enough to continue.

This trail was built by Shawn and maintained by him as well. Part of the secret was to use it regularly, which he did during the summer and autumn, and let the Energoe clear the path. But small branches, especially from alders, intruded from the sides of the trail, as the forest constantly tried to reclaim its territory. So as he drove in these demanding conditions of mud and steep inclines and snow and roots sticking out to grab him, the passing branches whacked at his body. His face was protected by his helmet and goggles, except for the narrow breathing space between the bottom of his nose and his upper lip. The beating wasn't enough to produce blood, but it hurt sufficiently to remind him to wear a ski mask under his helmet the next time.

To put himself through such physical punishment over such a short stretch of trail meant the journey was important or the destination sacred. When he climbed the last fifty feet through one final stretch of rock and mud, he saw the cabin come into sight, and he knew the beating was worth it.

* * * * *

He parked near the front door, where a 3-step set of stairs led up to the narrow porch. The Snow Cabin was constructed almost entirely of yellow cedar logs, prime construction material found only in these higher elevations. Only 12-foot square, the cabin was nestled in a small clearing kept free of new growth by people like Shawn who ventured here, used the cabin for a few hours or a few days, and took care of it like it was their own. In recent years, as far as Shawn could tell, he was the only person who stayed overnight.

He was exhausted, and his muscles would ache for another day, mostly from the constant pressure on the handlebars. Although his Energoe had power-assisted steering, he rode it in the boost-disabled mode, which gave him more feel for the terrain on rough trails like this. It was simply safer that way, but it took its toll on his arm muscles.

For a few minutes, he simply sat on his bike, engine off, winding down from the journey, and taking a slow look around. Shawn loved this place, and came here often. Sometimes he would remain here for weeks during the summer. In fact, this is where he worked most productively. A modern shaman was a free spirit in every sense of the word. Your work could be done wherever you wanted, as long as satellites could be accessed. A place like this was perfect for Shawn. With satellite Internet and phone, he could stay here as long as necessary to get his work done, even taking his mini-laptop with him when he went out in the tin boat.

The boat had been quite a project. It was a typical small aluminum boat, leaky rivets and all. The 15-horse outboard was a bit of overkill on a 12-foot vessel, especially on a lake as small as Frog Pond. It was a 2005 model, a four-stroke that burned standard gasoline, which he had to haul in.

The name "Frog Pond" was Shawn's, since it wasn't labeled on any map he'd ever seen, but it was really much bigger than a pond. Nearly two miles in length, the oval-shaped lake was ringed by high mountains on all sides except at the outlet, where a creek ran down towards the Snow Cabin, about a half-mile away. The inlet on the opposite end was a majestic waterfall plunging down from the Sierras, fed by another lake so high up that Shawn had never climbed to it.

Getting the boat here was a major effort, towing it behind his Energoe on a homemade trailer. The first attempt resulted in a flat tire on the trailer (those pesky mudbank roots) only a mile from Mountain Main, so Shawn left it there, and came back the following day to fix it. Then, at a steep curve that seemed insurmountable towing a trailer, he abandoned the boat again, this time only a half-mile from the Snow Cabin. The next day he came back down from the cabin, and basically jammed the trailer through by using the Energoe's winch to haul it up the hill, bashing through the brush to blaze its own new trail.

The outboard motor came on another trip, and now the tin boat was here year-round, pulled up on shore when not in use. When hikers or other Energoe riders discovered it, they were free to use the boat, and they always left it in good shape. Complimentary gas was included as part of the deal, but visitors sometimes left him a few dollars as a polite expression of gratitude.

This was a life few 29-year-olds could afford to lead — a home in the outskirts of Kernville with an Edsel in the driveway, an airplane at the local airport (or a third of one), a cabin in the mountains, the latest model Energoe, and even a tin boat. But this is the way modern shamans lived, and for good reason.

* * * * *

"So that's the part of the offer I can make to you now," said the GC representative. "I'm not authorized to reveal anything further until you formally accept the job, which you can do by signing here."

Shawn and the representative had met for over an hour in his parents' home in Pomona. It was all a bit of a shock, yet it made a certain kind of wild sense. The government was starting a program to develop plans for the Heavenly Way's interaction with another galaxy, and the handful of new employees would work in a top-secret environment, each of them reporting only to selected individuals whose immediate supervisor was the President of the United States. The secret part wasn't the plans they would produce, for they would be public record as soon as the President signed off on them, one element at a time. What was secret was that individual "philososcience consultants" (already nicknamed "shamans") would be running the show, and their identity would be strictly protected. Over the years ahead, the public would assume the Galactic Collision Project was a government-run scientific think tank, with teams of scientists studying the matter and recommending action plans. In reality, only five individuals in the United States, working out of their homes, would comprise the decision-recommending force. Although their pay would be ordinary for the public sector, they would receive unusual benefits. Basically, if they needed something to conduct their shaman function, but couldn't afford it, the government would magically and immediately provide it. Need an Energoe to get out of town where you can think? – you got it. Need an airline ticket to Houston – put it on the government credit card. Need a woman to relax your brain so you can reprogram your software? – the government will be your pimp. (Well, no one ever mentioned the pimp part, but Shawn was convinced nothing was beyond a shaman's negotiable norm.)

Of course, the GC representative wasn't authorized to reveal these details to a shaman applicant who hadn't yet signed on the dotted line, but he was able to tell Shawn enough so he knew what he was getting into. As the representative told him: "We've researched the fine details of your personal life enough to know you're going to sign anyway, so there's little risk of a security breach at this point."

"So you never intended to hire any interns," said Shawn.

"No, they all went into the same hiring pool," replied the GC representative. "We needed a way to limit the applications. Making sure the jobs were low-paying, even the GS-12 positions, allowed us to look at only those who were applying for the right reasons. We're more interested in those who know how to properly pursue challenges than those with an outlandish IQ. If we have to teach you the self-assurance you'll need for this job, it's a lot harder than teaching you the science.

"So that explains why the interview was so weird," noted Shawn.

"I heard you were one hell of a wide receiver."

* * * * *

After his hiring in Pomona, the pace of things quickened. Shawn flew to Washington, DC, to meet his professional contacts, Kent Versace and Tom Suthers, who shared an office in the White House. Shawn immediately noticed both were young (Kent was 33, and Tom only 28), in keeping with the Galactic Collision Project goal of harnessing youth for some of the most grown-up jobs ever created.

Shawn and the nation's other four shamans would have an almost-direct route to the President of the United States. In fact, after meeting Kent and Tom, they walked him over to the President's office where he got to shake the hand of the nation's CEO. It was a quick meet-and-greet, with no mention of the GC Project. In keeping with the overall atmosphere, everything was kept low-key, in an attempt to assure protection of the privacy of shamans. They were intended to be nondescript individuals with direct access to the White House.

Kent explained he and Tom were members of an international task force that would meet regularly to consider the findings and recommendations of shamans around the world, sort of a Galactic Collision G-20. But there was considerable concern about the ability of some of the nations to guard the program's secrecy. Since the security restrictions extended only to the individual shamans, to allow them to accomplish their jobs without interference, the results of the international meetings could be made public. But the identity of the shamans would be protected. Shawn wouldn't be attending any of these important meetings.

"Already we've had problems in Brazil," said Tom. "Their philososcience consultant selection process has gone through two iterations, since those initially hired were leaked to the press. Fortunately, nothing about the international GC process was revealed, but now they're looking for replacement employees. They'll be running to catch up."

"But I'll be able to consult with other shamans?" asked Shawn.

"Sure," said Kent. "You'll be able to turn to anyone you feel might help your research – scientists, other shamans, anyone you desire. Of course, we'll be here to get you into any doors you might need opened, so never hesitate to ask."

"That might help my 'research,' as you call it, but I really don't know exactly what I'm supposed to be researching. Or maybe you're gonna' tell me that's not important."

"It's important all right," said Kent. "But that's the whole point. Nobody around here has ever been through a collision of two galaxies, so we decided to try some free-thinking young minds to figure out where to begin."

Chapter 5

Edsels and Telescopes

When Shawn returned from Washington, he knew he had to explain something to his parents, but it couldn't be the truth. Yet he was able to describe the GC Project from the standpoint of generalities, trying to explain that he'd be an independent consultant providing astrophysics research data. His application was so solid, for reasons proud parents could liberally interpret, that he would be employed in one of the GS-12 positions, rather than as a mere intern. All of which wasn't far from the truth. Except he really couldn't explain why he was moving to a remote location in the foothills of the Sierras, or how he could afford it while starting his first real job. And he didn't tell them right away he'd be buying a new Ford Edsel.

The Edsel was an unnecessary extravagance. Shawn couldn't think of a single realistic reason why he needed one as a modern shaman, but the purchase turned out to be ridiculously simple. He called Kent in Washington, told him he wanted to buy an Edsel for transportation (without any further explanation), and Kent explained exactly how to conduct the purchase at the Ford dealership. Shawn drove the fire-engine-red convertible home the next day.

The Edsel was one of the most coveted vehicles in the history of the American dream. The design was already fifty years old, but still popular with both middle-aged people and seniors. Younger people who had not grown up with the Edsel were less intense customers, but you'd occasionally see a twenty-something driver. Such was the case with Shawn, since he graduated from college at twenty-two, and bought the Edsel that same year. He remembered stories about the sporty Edsel his grandfather had driven, a 1958 Edsel Ranger with its unique front grill, upright oblong taillights, and push-button Teletouch transmission shifting system in the center of the steering wheel. His new 2008 model looked much the same, but the engine and transmission were completely different fifty years later. The Edsel still had the Teletouch buttons in the steering wheel, but they were now touch-pads. His natural gas convertible was the current rage. He loved to lower the top in the summer, and cruise down River Highway to town.

He remembered parking once in the only remaining angled pull-in spot in the old-fashioned downtown section of Kernville, with its two-story buildings with fake rustic wood siding. On his right side was another Edsel, a retro 1959 Ranger 4-door sedan, probably now worth more than his newer convertible. On his left was an original 1964 Mustang, probably worth only a few thousand dollars, even though it looked immaculate. The Mustang was Ford's albatross, what historians called "the wrong car at the wrong time." Following in the success of the Edsel, Ford tried to market a car that never gained popularity with contemporary car buyers, and sold poorly. The Mustang was a supreme example of corporate culture's failure to understand American consumers.

In the old downtown that day, Shaw remembered thinking what it would be like for someone walking down the street. There, side-by-side were two spiffy Edsels, one old and one new, and next to them the laughable old Mustang. What a contrast in public discrimination.

It would be over thirty more years before science cracked the historic code involving this seemingly-minor automotive irregularity. Proteus scholars, led by the research of shamans, would eventually ask the never-expected question: "Is the Edsel another Amelia Glitch, or just a blip in time affecting almost nothing?"

In any case, whose glitch was it? Those on Proteus would eventually learn their history flowed behind that of another planet in Zeus – a world currently unknown – by nearly 5 billion years. And Proteus historians would assume these glitches were their own planet's irregularities. Could time be so warped that the time distortion was located elsewhere? Maybe the Edsel was genuinely a better car than a Mustang or a Corvair, and Proteus historians might get it all wrong.

* * * * *

January 26, 1949

First light for the Hale 200-inch telescope was a momentous occasion. Under the direction of Edwin P. Hubble, the world's biggest telescope was pointed at OGC 2763, now referred to as Hubble's Nebula. With a primary mirror twice the diameter of its closest rival, the 100-inch Hooker Telescope on California's Mount Wilson, the new reflector was thrust into service every clear night. Had it been installed at the site originally planned, Mount Palomar in California, it might never have almost single-handedly revolutionized astronomy.

George Ellery Hale was a famous astronomer who had designed and supervised the construction of the Mount Wilson large telescopes, both the 60 and 100-inch models. He initially supervised the 200-inch planning and design. His chief optical designer from the 100-inch Hooker telescope had been George Ritchey, and Hale was determined to harness his talents again for the 200-inch reflector. Ritchey proposed a revolutionary design compared to the usual parabolic primary mirror used in all of the world's biggest telescopes. Although this optical model (called the Ritchey-Chretien design) would provide sharper images over a wider viewing area, and thus eliminate distortion, Hale opposed it. The project was running late and over budget, and the Rockefeller Foundation was balking regarding their proposed funding. Hale decided to proceed with the simpler parabolic mirror design, an attempt to get the project financially back on track. The complex hyperbolic optical curvatures proposed by Ritchey would have to wait for a future telescope, although it might delay potential progress in deep-sky astronomy by decades. The parabolic mirror of the 200-inch would work fine on the planets and provide impressive photographic results in the deep-sky, which was the payback Hale expected. An astronomer himself, Hale didn't want to impede progress, but he also understood the philanthropic power of mid-century media hype. But a few days before the expected resignation of George Ritchey from the

200-inch project (at least as documented in an interview of Ritchey by *Time* magazine in 1950), George Ellery Hale died in a car accident.

A replacement for Hale was needed, and fast. The Rockefeller Foundation appointed a temporary administrator for the project, who eventually became the permanent program director. This relatively unknown astronomer, Andrew P. Sawyer, had a strong business background in the private sector, and he proved to be just what it took to get the project moving again. He had worked with George Ritchey on previous programs, and he convinced him to stay. In return, Sawyer threw all of the available financial resources at solving the technological challenges posed by adopting the Ritchey-Chretien design to a telescope this large. The Corning Glass Works was contracted to construct the optics, and tackled the technology necessary to construct the hyperbolically-curved primary and secondary mirrors that were the key to Ritchey's optical design.

Hale had already selected an observatory location at Mount Palomar, north of San Diego. The previous telescopes on Mount Wilson were at a site increasingly light-polluted by its proximity to Los Angeles, and Hale thought Palomar would be a safe zone well into the distant future. He didn't know about the explosive urban growth that would plague the area in only a few decades. Sawyer saw things differently. He thought Mount Palomar would be adequate as a light pollution sanctuary, but he didn't like its elevation. To reduce the affects of the atmosphere, you needed to get above it as far as possible. Although the logistical challenges would be multiplied, he convinced the Rockefeller Foundation to pump in even more money – the 200-inch observatory would be placed atop Hawaii's Mauna Kea, elevation 14,000 feet.

One hundred years later, this irregularity in location would be referred to as the "third significant history glitch," and it became crucial in the pending revolution in astronomy. The clarity of the observing site on top of Mauna Kea, coupled with the superior resolution capabilities of the 200-inch Ritchey-Chretien optics, led to a frenzy of scientific project donations from individual millionaires and philanthropic organizations worldwide. The astronomical photos from the 200-inch reflector that appeared in newspapers and contemporary magazines were considered pivotal to the financial contributions that mushroomed, and provided a boom in telescope construction throughout the world. Everywhere, the race was on to build the most technologically advanced astronomical observing instruments ever conceived. The affect on the field of astronomy was phenomenal. In just a few years, astrophysics advanced farther than would otherwise have been possible over a period of decades.

Planet Earth

The Milky Way Galaxy

Chapter 6

Death of a Star

4,646,926,984 AD – Planet Earth

(2015 on Planet Proteus)

For society to have survived almost 5 billion years since the birth of Christ was a remarkable achievement, to say the very least. Planet Earth had changed a lot, but was surprisingly resilient. Its people even more so.

To simplify the calendar, humans were now designating their calendar years by simply using the last four digits. So the year was now 6984, when it was really almost 5 billion AD. Since lifespans were less than 250 years, it would be a long time until future generations would need to think about a new calendar. And by then, they'd need to consider a new way to measure years that weren't based on Earth's rotation around the sun, because there'd be no people left on the planet by then.

After life on Earth was finished, their galaxy would merge with Andromeda, which was a reminder of the immensity of astronomical time. In fact, the initial collision, known as "first contact" of the outer spiral arms, was already beginning, and it would continue for the next 200 million years, until finally Andromeda and the Milky Way were one.

But that wasn't a cosmic worry for Earth, since there was a much more pressing problem – the death of the sun. The planet, now incredibly hot at all latitudes, was still the best place to live in the galaxy, at least as far as humans knew. You could venture outside with moderate protective clothing, even briefly with no preparation at all, although it was almost suicidal, which explained why so many of Earth's youth took their own lives that way. Stay more than a few minutes, and you were cooked.

The atmosphere was still marginally breathable, which was more to say than for any other known planet in the Milky Way. Thus, a small population remained on Earth, mostly high-status scientists and government officials, along with a token of experimental families that represented a retrospective sample of life as it once was on Earth. People of Christ's era wouldn't recognize the Earth today, but it was still the most livable place in the known universe.

Since the Earth could sustain only so many people in it's decrepit state, the majority of the world's population lived on other planets within the solar system or in nearby stellar systems, wherever stable land and the necessary natural resources were present. Inhabitants of the inner planets and their moons actively mined nearby asteroids, and permanent colonies were even developed on the larger of these giant rocks. On Mars, terraforming provided the best alternative to Earth, but that planet would also expire soon because of runaway solar heating.

In nearby star systems, humans now lived under vastly modified conditions. On one planet slightly more than 90 light-years away, barely within the limits of human colonization, conditions were particularly hot and hostile. Two mini-cities on that remote planet were built on a movable foundation propelled over titanium rails by nuclear thrusters at a speed matching the small planet's rotation. These self-contained cities (called "trains") were located on the night side of the planet, just in advance of the terminator, rolling along in a location that wouldn't fry titanium or well-protected flesh. You could actually climb down off the planetary train, leave the city, and walk alongside. That required a spacesuit, of course, but it was possible to fall behind just enough to catch a glimpse of the planet's monstrous star as it broke the horizon at sunrise. If your glimpse was more than a sliver of the star, you'd be cooked immediately, but adventure companies excelled at organizing off-track tours, then catching a wheeled vehicle to catch up with the "train" again.

Why would man travel 90 light-years to such a formidable environment when there were plenty of other planets and moons nearer to the solar system, many of them farther from their stars and sized more like Earth? The answer lay in the general lack of a suitable atmosphere anywhere except Earth. If a small planet like this scorcher had a wisp of oxygen trapped in its rocks and some water tied up as ice in shadowy craters, it was better than what was found elsewhere. These critical resources could be fine-tuned to support life, though at a horrendous price in terms of time and innovation. The end result was still far short of a fully-breathable atmosphere, for there was no world other than Earth where you could walk outside without a ground suit. Thus, all colonies were domed communities. But it was the best that could be provided for a population needing room to sustain its own meager growth.

Technology had outwitted nature for billions of years, but at a huge cost in terms of human progress. Every time a new world was colonized, the energy that went into adapting to a new environment slowed the advancement of the species. Humans progressed by leaps and bounds for millions of years after first appearing on the savannahs of Africa, and knowledge of the universe grew at an enormous pace. Then, when colonization of new worlds became necessary, progress dwindled as mankind struggled just to stay alive. All of their energy went into space travel to distant locations, habitat design, construction, and massive unsuccessful attempts at terraforming new worlds.

Space travel did contribute to the technological advancement of the species, but most other aspects of colonization were dead ends. Efforts expended to establish colonies on hostile worlds slowed overall human progress, for nothing was left over for other pursuits. There was almost no time and mental energy for astronomy or philosophy. So the progress of the previous 5 billion years went almost unnoticed. What would solve this dilemma? Answer: a planet ready to inhabit – one with a breathable atmosphere, plentiful water, and the natural resources needed to promote life. But in billions of years of searching, never had anything similar to Earth been found.

Thus, in the year 6984, the only place where real scientific research flourished was the Earth. Astronomical observatories still existed, although Einstein wouldn't have recognized them. And outstanding minds still searched for answers. People looked and acted pretty much like they had for 5 billion years, and the people on Earth retained similar priorities in life. In all these years, intelligent alien life hadn't been detected on any other world, even after physically venturing out over 100 light-years and exploring with atmospheric sniffers all the way to the outer boundaries of the Milky Way. Other planets with an environment comparable to Earth were no longer considered a realistic possibility. Except maybe in Andromeda, which was now headed towards the Milky Way at 400,000 kilometers per hour. In fact, it had already started to arrive.

* * * * *

Earthlings were an elite breed. They remained on the planet only by invitation. The largest group was selected by a lottery designed to advance the species – family members in a controlled environment. They were often referred to as the "human zoo," even by the inhabitants themselves. They knew future generations would be on Earth for only a limited time, possibly measured in thousands of years, maybe less. The sun was getting that much hotter every day.

The fusion of hydrogen into helium at the core of the sun was slowing down, and that was the force that had kept the star's gravity in check. As hydrogen ran out, the core started to contract, and the sun's outer layers began to swell. The solar system's star would eventually expand outward to the orbit of Earth, destined to destroy the remaining human population by broiling it to death. That ultimate fate still remained a billion years in the future, but it was already getting unacceptably hot. The breakdown of the fusion process was pushing Earth's overall temperature upward. Solar output had increased by 10 percent from the days of pyramids and automobiles. Both polar ice caps were already gone, and much of the fertile land of the planet had been flooded. Eventually, as the temperature continued to rise, photodissociation of water vapor would take place, first in the upper atmosphere. Sunlight would break apart the water molecules, allowing the hydrogen atoms to escape into space. No more water, no more life. Unless you lived like those colonists light-years away, using all of their creative powers in order to merely exist. It was the Earth's fate to be broiled on its own orbital skewer.

And this was not the only cosmic problem Earth faced. The planet's tilt had grown significantly in the past billion years, magnifying the impact on the seasons everywhere on Earth. And Mars' orbit had become unstable, with the planet moving in closer to Earth. Although predictions of future collisions between the two planets stole headlines in recent millennia, they were repeatedly dashed by near misses with little direct impact on either planet except for an overall warming of Mars and further disruption of its own significant climatic variations.

Even with this bleak outlook, the individuals who still populated Earth took an optimistic approach, as many generations had done before them. They could live to be 250, and they still had time to find a habitable world for future generations. The lack of intelligent life anywhere in the known universe still vexed astrophilosophers and the public alike. But regardless of the "Great Silence," maybe they'd find an Earth-like planet spinning past them one day, as the galactic collision progressed. And they'd jump off this big blue dot, and hop on-board.

Chapter 7

Astrophilosopher

Among the accomplishments of the human race, few rivaled the knowledge explosion caused by astronomy, particularly in the ancient age of giant optical telescopes. In recent millennia, astrophilosophers were more valued than any other scientist in a long lineage seeking answers to the universe's questions.

Commensurate with the rise of astrophilosophy, the other sciences had suffered, caused in part by the extreme efforts expended in the development of new colonies on worlds that were basically uninhabitable. Terraforming was a failure, and living in pressurized domes was little better when it came to progress for the species.

Kane Suane, age 30, had watched the sky as a youth. He was selected by Earth's governing board, Miniverse Prime, to engage in the advancement of scientific values. As one of the chosen few, he had lived a carefree youth without concerns. The government took care of all his needs, as long as he didn't resist the regimented training they dictated. His education was a mix of elitist pampering and Miniverse Prime's attempts for interaction with the human zoo – within limits, of course. This educational philosophy was aimed at preparing Kane for life as an astrophilosopher, serving both the Earth's government and the general public. In fact, from the age of fourteen, he was groomed to fulfill the prestigious position of Astrophilosopher Laureate of the States of Earth by the time he reached thirty.

On a planet where just stepping outside was a major venture, he undertook the design of his own telescopic sniffer, a crude device by modern standards. His father helped him construct the elaborate apparatus in their back yard, encouraging his path towards astrophilosophy with the financial support of the Miniverse Prime.

Like good parents for eons, it was a matter of doing what's best for your child, while adapting to the determination of youth. In the meantime, father and son could share a slice of the sky.

Kane entered university training at age 27, in one of the most prestigious traditional institutes on Earth. Most of the school's students were younger, but Kane was on the Multiverse Prime track, where he spent his late teens and early twenties in extensive Astronet study programs to develop the extensive background he needed to be philosopher, astrophysicist, and social scientist. These days, most astrophilosophers were educated entirely on the Astronet, while growing up somewhere within the 100 light-year-radius Miniverse, the spherical-shaped zone of human life that surrounded Earth. The home planet now included less than one percent of the Miniverse's population, which meant Earth's population was fewer than 10 million. Experts universally agreed this was the maximum the planet could support, and the heating of the planet was making the situation rapidly worse.

The prestigious astrophysics program at the University of the Arctic was an ancient tradition, though it was now more of a catalog-filler for the College of Science than a complete curriculum. Most students at U of A (who didn't even understand the significance of the word "Arctic") took astrophysics classes as general education science requirements. These courses were commonly referred to as "primitive science." Astrophysics was a historic ritual rather than a modern discipline, replaced nearly universally by astrophilosophy. Still, it was the proper route for a student like Kane. If he was going to serve the public, he needed to interact with the human zoo in an educational setting. The Astronet would pick up the slack, providing the advanced academic training he needed. Throughout his 3-year residence at the university, he would pack extra Astronet homework into his studies.

Students in other disciplines seldom went outside the university's interconnected domes, but astrophysics majors were the exception. Their studies included on-the-job training at a real atmospheric sniffer, housed on a hill near the campus. They wore ground suits that allowed several hours of sun exposure without any hint of bodily harm, designed and monitored by other students from the university's environmental studies program. That's how Kane met Dyanne Chertneggen, and it's how he began his life of secretive companionship.

Once you entered Miniverse Prime's custody, rules of zero population growth applied, and even love affairs were banned. Too many individuals under the supervision of Prime had mixed with the human zoo, outside of matrimony, of course; a situation that Earth's relatively permissive society had few tools to deal with. Although population rules were solidly enforced, it was always difficult for the general public to deal with the cases, and it was the juries of the human zoo that held the power. The simplest solution was immediate eviction from Earth, a fate considered worse than death, considering the state of the Miniverse's colonies.

In his three years at the university, the attraction between Kane and Dyanne grew, regardless of their age difference, which was only a small part of the challenge. A man 10 years older than a woman was less important these days, when people routinely lived nearly 250 years. Similar relationships had developed early in life, becoming easier to justify as years progressed. As Dyanne said: "You seem wonderfully 'mature' to me now, but in a life together, we both have over 200 years to look forward to."

Except they really didn't. Laws on Earth prohibited marriage or even casual relationships between those in Prime's custody and members of the human zoo. Secret rendezvouses seemed to be the only temporary solution, sometimes outside the domes during excursions to the atmospheric sniffer. Dyanne would figure out how to schedule herself as the ground suit monitor, and Kane constructively wasted his sniffer time, yielding observing slots to other anxious students on his team. By the time he graduated, leaving Dyanne back in the Yukon, he knew two things: he would become a famous astrophilosopher; and he would find a way to be with Dyanne.

With his Astronet training program complete, coupled with a rare in-residence university degree, Kane was able to move up quickly within the world of science. However, if Dyanne was to join him, she faced a challenge equivalent to rising from the Outcast society of ancient India to the elite class at the top of government. Had it not been for Dyanne back in the Canadian States, Kane would be on his way to happiness and fortune, but it was not to be.

As it worked out in later years, Kane remained on Earth, where the best ground-based atmospheric sniffing was conducted. Space-based astroscopes were much simpler to program, since they required no electronic filtering of the Earth's atmosphere to prevent interference with incoming data. However, atmospheric sniffing required huge structures, not easily adapted to outer space or colonized planets; so Earth-based devices were where the most precise measurements were taken.

Like the heyday of observational telescopes, now a part of ancient history, the tops of the highest mountains were where the leading-edge work was accomplished. But on these tall peaks, with almost half of the Earth's atmosphere below, the impact of solar radiation on the body was most damaging, even protected by the best ground suit. The typical scenario for such situations was to heliotransport up to the observatory after sunset, when the sun's damaging radiation was gone. Observers still had to deal with the tremendous heat, even at night, but their bodies were better protected this way than during daytime observing, and it was technically just as efficient.

This was one of the few areas of science where remote-controlled observation could not be employed, an artifact of the need for moment-to-moment physical calibration of the sniffing apparatus as the observing session progressed. Most modern astrophilosophers left the calibration to appointed technicians, but Kane insisted on taking care of that detail when he was assigned observing time on a mountaintop sniffer. With his growing notoriety in the field, his request was always approved.

Atmospheric sniffing was the best way to retrieve detailed data regarding conditions on a world outside the solar system – an "extrasolar" planet. In historic times, gravitational influences were the first step in discovering new planets, even dating back to the discovery of the sun's outer planets. The wobble of an object in the sky, more precisely detected by spectrometry, became the next big step in finding the first extrasolar planets. Later, space-based observational telescopes made use of transits of stars by large planets, and still later the atmospheric sniffer came into vogue. It was the sniffer that allowed the detection of details of a small planet's real character, similar to measuring the molecular constituents of the air inside an enclosed room and determining what was on the invisible floor. Like similar techniques used routinely for crime fighting, the atmospheric sniffer opened new doors to planetary studies. At first, it would only work for nearby worlds, those objects within a few hundred light-years of Earth. Now the distance span extended nearly to the edge of the galaxy. Soon it would reach into the spiral arms of Andromeda.

Chapter 8

Time as a Tool

On the top of Mauna Kea in Hawaii, Kane stood next to the historic site, mostly old foundation and towering girders, along with a simple commemorative plaque. Of course, it wasn't the original cement or steel structure, which had worn away long ago, now replaced by synthetic look-alikes, but Mauna Kea Observatory remained the museum site of the great 8-meter telescope, a revolutionary giant of its time. Optical telescopes had disappeared completely less than two centuries after the great 8-meter telescope was commissioned, except for small instruments for recreational use and as novelty items for children. Still, this was the centerpiece of observational astronomy during its own pinnacle of astrophilosophical history.

So difficult to imagine, thought Kane, as he walked through the crumbling structure. People actually looked at images of stars and the wonders of the deep sky, photographed them, and used primitive spectroscopy to analyze the heavens. It must have been a beautiful time in history, when man could learn more from the eye than the computer.

Earlier this year, an archeophilosophy team had been on this mountain, studying lost history as best as they could with their modern equipment, and had uncovered an intriguing mystery. While examining below-ground soil samples near the site of the old 8-meter scope, they came upon evidence of an even older optical telescope, one that had never been on this peak – the 200-inch (5-meter) parabolic reflector installed on Mount Palomar. This historic instrument, even more famous in astrophilosophy than the 8-meter telescope, shouldn't have any remnants on this Hawaiian mountain, but the evidence seemed conclusive. When the discovery was reported in the Astronet's *Archeophilosophy Journal* a few months ago, the scientific conclusion was that soil from Mount Palomar in California had been transferred to this Hawaiian site without adequate historic documentation to carry forward 5 billion years. Why such an act would have occurred was unknown, but the research team concluded it might have been an ancient ceremony to preserve memories of observational astronomy in both California and Hawaii. Why history tablets had lost track of such a commemorative ceremony was anybody's guess.

But times had changed since then, and here was proof – the largest atmospheric sniffer on Earth, and Kane held the computer controls. After adjusting the nighttime settings of his ground suit (minimal radiation protection and slightly warmer airflow), he activated the touchpad that allowed him to select tonight's targets.

This would be the first detailed study of Andromeda P4531, a small planet orbiting a G-class star. The object was so far away it was barely within range of atmospheric sniffers, but the planet and its accompanying galaxy were rapidly closing with Earth. Within a few years – maybe even months, based on the current pace of sniffer technology – complete atmospheric data would be retrievable from objects this distant. For tonight, the best that could be expected would be verification of the presence of life, maybe even a hint whether it was intelligent. Ultimately, this sniffer or another like it would be able to determine nearly unimaginable detail about this small planet and any life occupying it.

As Kane focused the sniffer on Andromeda P4531, he didn't know his findings on Mauna Kea tonight would be eclipsed by the analysis of the mysterious dirt discovered by archeophilosphers on this same mountain. That ancient soil would become the cornerstone of a startling new branch of histophilosophy. Ground samples from around the world would be used to determine irregularities in history linked to the very same planet Kane was sniffing tonight. A primeval airplane called an Electra that crashed in the Pacific nearly 5 billion years ago, along with evidence from a mountain near San Diego would soon reveal irregularities in Earth's history as compared to P4531. Eventually, a motorcade in Dallas and an ugly ancient automobile called the Edsel would be frontline discoveries for a revolution in history. Two distant planets in two separate galaxies – soon to merge into one – would lie in the balance.

Planet Proteus

The Andromeda Galaxy

Chapter 9

Shamans as Philosophers

July 3, 2016

Shawn motored his tin boat towards the tiny island that sat near the inlet, a place where mist from the waterfall sprayed onto the water. When the drizzle became pronounced, he momentarily stopped, shifted into reverse, and backed away to a spot where he knew the mist wouldn't reach. He could sit here, engine off and drift all day, probably without getting wet.

From the little aluminum boat, he watched the majestic waterfall plunge downward to the lake. Shawn was in his element. Removed from society by what seemed like thousands of miles, he did his best work here. In the 8 years since accepting the GC job, he had come a long way. Now he was respected as one of the top shamans in the country, if not the entire world. And this spot in the universe was where his innovative mind hit peak performance.

After watching the waterfall and the ever-changing mist for a few minutes, he slid his mini-laptop out of its case, and powered it up. He clicked on "Satellite Connection," and both the Internet icon and the telephone symbol appeared in a few seconds.

First, he checked his Red Star messages, email originating from other shaman addresses. Finding no Red Stars, he clicked on the "Findings and Recommendations" link, which took him to a listing of recent reports by his fellow shamans, including those worldwide who reported to their own heads of state. He quickly scanned a report from India entitled "Zeus Planets within Ping Distance," a summary of what a shaman named Pandit Patel had concluded regarding the planets that might be worth further study as the galactic collision progressed. His study was extensive, but Shawn read only the summary page, setting the report aside for additional study later.

Now Shawn clicked on his address book and the name Fatius Lane. The satellite phone connection symbol popped up almost immediately, and dialed the number.

"Hey, Shawn, whatcha' doin'?" Fatius answered on the second ring.

"Same place, same thing. How 'bout you?"

"So you're on the lake. Must be nice. I'm on my balcony in Miami, watching the cumulonimbus rollin' on by."

"Sounds tough," replied Shawn. "Anything more on the visionary in Georgia?"

"I went up there over the weekend. About all I got was a speech I didn't need about the arrow of time. Typical nonsense about the reversibility of time, and his theory regarding precise predictions of the future, based on his supposed knowledge of the past."

"Nothing more specific? Did he offer any predictions to test his case."

"Just that USC is going to beat UCLA again this year," replied Fatius with a tone of seriousness.

"You're kiddin', right?"

"Sure I'm kidding," replied Fatius. "This guy isn't a rocket scientist, you know."

Shawn laughed, having been fooled by Fatius again. This fellow was his favorite shaman contact, and it had paid dividends many times as they independently researched their chosen topics. Bouncing ideas back and forth by telephone or email was a constant process, although they hadn't met in person since Shawn's interview in Pomona 8 years ago. Fatius had served on the interrogation team – the geeky guy with the pocket protector. As it turned out, he was a bigger football fan than Shawn would have guessed, and a diehard Bruin supporter. He held a doctorate in astronomy from UCLA, and still followed his team through web-streaming Sports TV.

"There's a report from the fellow in India who specializes in Zeus planets," remarked Shawn.

"Saw it this morning. He seems able to identify some of the candidates we'll pass closest to during the encounter. Not sure about that pinging technology though."

"India seems to have the best handle on it," replied Shawn. "We should encourage them to develop it, maybe by talking to Washington about some funding."

"You're right, Shawn. Let me take care of it."

"Gladly. And ask Kent or Tom about some other links on the subject. They may know about shamans elsewhere who are studying the same thing. I'd like to know more. What wavelength are they using?"

"For the pinging? Microwave, I think. Still secret, as far as the Indian government is concerned."

"We have our ways," kidded Shawn.

"You bet we do. Anything more about between-galaxy parallels?"

Fatius was referring to Shawn's chosen area of research, at least for the present, which focused on parallel universes on a smaller scale, galaxy to galaxy. As with much of the GC effort, shamans ran with any topic they found interesting, and it was amazing how often this divergence of research paid off. The Galactic Collision Project had discovered long ago that it's difficult to predict what technology will be pertinent in a merger of two galaxies, so shamans were encouraged to charge off in whatever direction inspired them. Already, some of these seemingly lame-brained topics had been put to good use in developing an overall collision scenario.

In this case, Shawn was studying what had been accomplished previously regarding multiverses – the concept that there were multiple universes beyond our own, raising the possibility a planet just like Proteus, including the same form of intelligent life, could exist somewhere else. Shawn's research was asking whether this notion could be applied on a smaller scale, within a galaxy or maybe between them. With Proteus' terrible record, so far, in finding intelligent life anywhere within its own Heavenly Way, it seemed improbable other galaxies would be any different. Then again, that was the whole idea of the Galactic Collision Project. Shamans weren't meant to be in-the-box thinkers.

"That's why I'm on the lake today," said Shawn. "Trying to work through this parallel worlds thing. Sometimes my tin boat does wonders."

"Or maybe it's the waterfall," replied Fatius.

"Hey, Fat, don't discount condos that look out over the Atlantic," kidded Shawn.

Go figure why a guy's parents would name their kid "Fatius." Didn't they just know what people would call him? In "Fat's" case, it worked out okay, because he was a skinny geek. Maybe naming him Fatius was what turned him into a geek in the first place.

"I'll want to see that report when you finish it," said Fatius.

"It'll be done before I leave here, but I'll need to wait until I'm home to transmit it. These satellites are great for guys who want to escape in their little boats, but too slow and not very secure."

"Get that report going," said Fatius, as they wrapped up their phone call. "I wanna' read all about myself on another planet."

* * * * *

Shawn's boat floated on Frog Pond for several more hours, just outside the mist zone of the waterfall. The sky was dark blue, a tone it took at this altitude on clear days when puffy cumulus clouds contrasted their brilliant whites and subdued grays against the background. His mini-laptop, connected to a small solar panel for constant recharging while he was aboard the boat, was the key to his success as a shaman. Shawn's knowledge of computer programming was minimal, but Washington took care of that requirement whenever he needed a new interface to guide his research. Currently, a new application was crunching numbers in the background, while he turned back to the report from India about extragalactic planets.

Once he got further into the lengthy article, he realized this was an area he should continue to follow, for it could be a key to the question the GC Project was attempting to answer above all other issues: If we find intelligent life in Zeus, what do we do next?

Pinging the approaching Zeus Galaxy was obviously on the right track. Optical-based astronomy was far too fragile when it came to matters of planetary resolution in other solar systems. Even in their own galaxy, the Heavenly Way, extrasolar planets still couldn't be seen up close and personal, and certainly not in enough detail to confirm intelligent life. Spectrometry, although a better indicator of life processes through atmospheric analysis, also wasn't adequate. Scientists hoped this route would open up when technology called "planetary environmental tracers" came off the shelf, but that would be years in the future. These proposed devices would be able to detect the details of planetary atmospheres far from the solar system, maybe with molecular detail that would allow the detection of intelligent life. The computer interface was already there, but the hardware would require metals and advanced composites still in engineers' dreams.

So that took Shawn back to atmospheric pinging, a technique only India seemed to be attempting. According to the report, the technology was straightforward, using mostly off-the-shelf hardware, although at a tremendous financial cost in terms of site preparation and construction. The biggest problem was the time lag – send a signal and wait years, decades, centuries, or even longer for a reply. Which is where Shawn came in. His focus of research (although it changed almost weekly) was parallel worlds. In theory, a planet in the incoming galaxy of Zeus could be inhabited by beings nearly the same as (or a duplicate of) the people on Proteus. If such a planet existed, there was hope for communication. And if the speed-of-light problem could be solved, mission accomplished. Just crank up the phone, and ask for the information you need.

Extraterrestrial life had always been one of the focal points of the GC Project, since the world's governments thought it could provide a solution for the what-do-we-do question. At least it could be used as a focus for spinoffs in other technological directions. If there were intelligent beings out there, maybe they could help Proteus solve its problems. And if the aliens were more advanced than Proteus, and hadn't yet blown themselves up, problem solved. Unless, of course, they were hostile, in which case they would best be avoided altogether.

It was an improbable set of circumstances, but that's what the GC Project was all about. And once Shawn had beaten the topic of parallel worlds to death, he could head off in a different direction. For GC shamans, there was no norm for success that could be used for comparisons.

To find a self-contained separate species coexisting with one's own world would require tools not yet invented. The Indian pinging project was a prospective instrument that needed, among other things, less time lag in their signals. An easy solution would be a universe with no relativistic limitations and no speed limits imposed by the velocity of light. That wasn't totally unrealistic, but not when two galaxies in the same universe were involved. Although there was no direct evidence these same limits existed in other galaxies, the indirect proof was everywhere. Astronomy had grown by leaps and bounds in the past hundred years. The 200-inch Mauna Kea telescope had set off a revolution that couldn't be slowed, and science history books already pointed back to that important time in history as a watershed moment for astronomy. Galactic research was a direct recipient of the explosion of knowledge, and everything seemed to work the same in the Zeus Galaxy as at home in the Heavenly Way. And that included the speed of light.

Science historians concluded that, if it had not been for the catalyst of the Mauna Kea 200-inch telescope, Proteus would be in a difficult position as the collision with Zeus approached. Maybe now there was a chance to break the Great Silence, because of the monumental advances in astronomy. Like the amazing conditions for life found on Proteus in the first place, it was often questioned why the 200-inch had come along when it did. A single event seemed to have ordained astrophysics history.

Understanding parallel universes might allow comprehension of similar worlds in the same universe. If this field of study progressed at all, the question would arise: Will the worlds be exactly alike or divergent? In the first case, large differences between two cultures could still lead to strong similarities. Individuals in one world could have a counterpart in the other, with the same ancestry, appearance, and even personality. In the second case, divergent worlds, the two planets could share the same history up to a point of separation, after which histories become more different as time elapses. Similar worlds and divergent worlds – either required a considerable stretch of the imagination. But cosmologists had been imagining multiverses and parallel worlds for decades. Shawn was merely seeking results on a smaller and more restrictive scale, limiting himself to two galaxies in the same universe.

Applying quantum mechanics to the problem, Shawn had concluded his conjecture was on the right track. If he could handle a few more mathematical equations, he might even be able to prove it. For the computational part of his research, he had handed the problem back to Kent Versace in Washington, who in turn assigned the analysis to a shaman in Germany. The results weren't in yet.

The quantum effect predicted (at least holistically) that the future is only potential and not actual. Any future outcome was possible, all based on probabilities and Schrodinger curves, and that's where the math came in. The immediate conclusion was that more than one future might exist simultaneously. If it did, it might exist on another habitable planet. Unfortunately, that other planet was likely in another universe.

Shawn used the remaining daylight on Frog Pond, after storing his mini-laptop in its case, to ponder the avenues he had pursuing for the last several weeks. Sometimes, without a bunch of crunched data in front of him, he could see the big picture better.

Shawn slipped off his T-shirt, lifted his feet with their zippered low-cut boots and high wool socks up onto the gunnel, and leaned back in the boat's padded plastic seat. He pulled his baseball cap down over his eyes. The early-June sun beat down with sunburn force, and he let his strong chest absorb it. Ultraviolet radiation shining down, worries of the world tumbling out.

Such was the life of a modern shaman on Frog Pond. He kicked back and thought intensely about four factors that might be related to each other – dark matter, dark energy, gravitons, and Zeus.

Chapter 10

Turning Thirty

Farley raised his glass of beer in a salute: "To the birthday boy! Never trust anyone over thirty."

"Still just a kid," said Cherokee, the waitress who had stopped by to wish Shawn well.

Shawn hadn't wanted a celebration to mark his 30th birthday, but Farley had insisted. And you never won an argument with Farley.

The obvious place for a party was Cheyenne's, a steak house and dive just north of town on River Highway. Farley and Shawn met there regularly, occasionally with some other friends. Cheyenne's served the best steaks in town, and the atmosphere was pure Kernville – Old West and proud of it. Even when he came here alone, Shawn usually saw Cherokee, a foxy lady who also worked at the airport café. Around here, it sometimes took two jobs to make ends meet. Not because you needed a lot of money, but because wages couldn't keep up with the not-so-wild West. Cherokee was a single mom with two kids to support at home, as well as her own mother who served as baby-sitter. Shawn felt for her, leaving some of the biggest tips of the night.

Cherokee was her chosen waitress name, since all of Cheyenne's employees had Wild West names, like "Kitty" and "Slim." She was such a fixture here that she'd taken on "Cherokee" as her nickname wherever she went in town. Shawn suspected Cheyennes and Cherokees hadn't gotten along very well in the real Wild West.

"Can't say I'm thrilled at turning thirty," said Shawn. "But I do appreciate you all harassing me about it."

"Never feel sorry for a man who owns an airplane," said Jimmy, a river rafting guide from the local adventure tour company.

"Only one-third of an airplane, Jimmy. And I never seem to find time to fly it."

"All that hard work you do, I suppose," said Farley. "Must be tough writing those electronic books. And think about all the expenses – electricity and such. I don't know how you have time for anything."

Shawn laughed, because this was the topic of conversation with Farley so many times before. Others must wonder, too, but Farley took it on as his personal vendetta. It was only in jest, and a good issue when all else failed. Shawn was always prepared to lay it on thick.

"Well my fingers have been getting awfully tired on that keyboard," he quipped.

Cherokee was across the room now, over by the bar, ringing up someone's bill. Farley sat next to Shawn at the rustic picnic table, empty peanut shells covering the floor. Jimmy and his friend, Jane, sat across from them. At the center of the table sat a cardboard six-pack container filled with salt-and-pepper shakers and various bottles of steak sauce. On the wall next to them was a poster with a poor caricature of Jesse James with his six-shooter pointed at the table, and "Wanted: Dead or Alive" in giant letters.

"What kind of books do you write?" asked Jane.

"Mostly just articles for magazines," replied Shawn. "They pay better than books. Electronic magazines are the bomb these days."

"And you really own an airplane?" added Jane.

"I share a Cessna with two other pilots, both women. It's the only way you can afford it these days."

Female pilots were more plentiful than men, a trend that began with Amelia Earhart and continued well into the next century. She was one of the all-time great promoters of equal rights, focused tightly on the aviation industry. Except for military pilots, which remained almost exclusively males, women piloted most of the world's airliners. It made sense – air carriers wanted pilots with attention to detail. Women were generally more meticulous when it came to checklists and aircraft operational procedures than most men.

"A big Cessna, or a little one?" asked Jane.

"A little bug-smasher," replied Shawn. "Maybe you'd call it medium-sized, but it's just a single-engine. It's called a 182RG, which is an old model built in the 1980's. The RG stands for 'retractable gear.'"

"His wheelies go up and down," joked Farley.

"That they do," said Shawn. "She cruises at about 150 miles per hour, and runs on a diesel engine."

Diesels became popular for small airplanes when low-lead avgas disappeared right after the turn of the century. Leaded fuel for airplanes was a holdout from the earlier days of automobiles, and environmentalists wouldn't put up with it. Some smaller aircraft engines were converted to lead-free gasoline used in cars, but that wouldn't work for bigger motors like the one in the Cessna 182RG. So the previous owners of the airplane converted to a diesel in 2002. With Shawn logging only about 100 hours per year, and his two partners using the airplane even less, they were slowly coming up on the diesel's TBO, time between overhaul. That would mean they'd need to overhaul or replace the engine, an expensive cost that could mean they'd need to sell the airplane. Shawn's flying days might be limited.

Private flying, in general, had become so expensive that fewer and fewer small airplanes were seen at airports around the country. And the little airports that supported them were disappearing. Maybe Kern Valley Airport would be gone in a few years. A complex and expensive web of landing fees, luxury taxes, and other government charges was killing the bug-smashers. Even air traffic control was pay-as-you-go these days, which meant a lot more little airplanes trying to fly without ATC. Scud-running was killing pilots and simultaneously killing the general aviation industry.

But flying was Shawn's passion. He might not do it very often, but when he did, it was pure immersion. When he was at the controls of the Cessna, he seldom thought about anything other than flying, which was both a good thing and a safe thing. Similarly, he could become absorbed in riding his Energoe, which distracted him from his real occupation as shaman. But he had another hobby, too – backyard astronomy – which didn't pull him away from his real occupation very far.

* * * * *

Driving up the River Highway from Cheyenne's, a regular routine on nights like this, he kicked back in the Edsel's comfortable seat and considered his 30-year-old situation. He had no financial worries, since everything he needed was supplied by his GC salary or indirectly (and secretly) by the government. He was strong and healthy, getting plenty of exercise during his travels into the forest on the Energoe. In some cases, he'd spend more time pushing his bike out of mud-holes than riding, and there were always lots of physical challenges when he got to the cabin – firewood to cut, swimming in the lake, hiking here and there. His mildly-aging body was still athletic looking, with healthy biceps and leg muscles. And there was certainly no lack of mental challenges, considering his shaman activities, flying, and amateur astronomy from his backyard.

"Whoa! That was way too close!" yelled Shawn to himself, as a beat-up old car came around a blind curve and caught him by surprise.

The car was sticking out into Shawn's lane, and now swerved recklessly in his rear view mirror. Shawn should have been looking for the lights. Then again, this vehicle was coming down the highway, whereas Shawn was driving up the winding road from Cheyenne's where most people had a few beers. Maybe it was just a July tourist, gawking at things. Or maybe there was one too many beers on his side of the double yellow line.

Consciously coming off the Edsel's gas pedal, Shawn slowed to 50 on the next straightaway, even slower on the following curve. By the time he arrived at the Mountain 99 turnoff, he was again thinking about the stars.

* * * * *

Shawn's amateur telescope was an 8-inch diameter Schmidt-Cassegrain, stored in his tool shed. His professional telescope was an 8-meter giant on the top of Mauna Kea, or wherever else he desired to inquire. If he needed the biggest telescope in the world, he could usually manage it through Kent or Tom in Washington. The results would be transmitted to him immediately after the observing session. Yet, even with the world's biggest astronomical instruments at his disposal, he couldn't resist a look through his amateur telescope every now and then. There was something very special about "live" observing that could never be matched by the biggest of the biggest, which no longer utilized a human eyeball at an old-fashioned eyepiece.

His Schmidt-Cassegrain was purchased with his own hard-earned money – hard earned by thinking in a tin boat on Frog Pond – and it was money spent with a great sense of satisfaction. As a child he had owned smaller and less-sophisticated telescopes, a 3-inch refractor, and then a 6-inch Newtonian reflector. This 8-inch model was only slightly bigger (and even shorter) than the Newtonian, but light-years ahead when it came to optics and computer technology. It was similar to the historic Mauna Kea 200-inch Ritchey-Chretien design, downsized and not as sophisticated on the optics end, but even more ample when it came to Go-To technology. In the almost 70 years since first light on the 200-inch, computers had revolutionized astronomy, and his 8-inch Schmidt-Cassegrain's point-and-track technology exceeded anything dreamed of in 1949.

In his living room, Shawn dressed for the observing session, while his small telescope acclimated itself to ambient temperature in the back yard. He sat on the old yellow couch with the tan flowers, and pulled on a gray turtleneck shirt, long-sleeved with a zipper at the top; then knickers over his baggy shorts, even though it was July. Every inch of his body would be protected from a curse worse than sweating – Sierra mosquitoes. At night around here, the bugs were vicious, chewing on any extremity they could find. He slid his black low-cut hiking boots back on (removed only so he could slip into his knickers), with his standard knee-high wool socks sticking out above them. Then he donned a blue baseball cap with *Dodgers* logo, and pulled on some cloth fingerless gloves. He'd need to use his fingers for the Astro-Controller of his LX90 amateur telescope, so the mosquitoes would have something to attack tonight, including his face. He thought about putting on a ski mask, but it was stored in the box on the back of his Energoe, and it might push the sweat thermometer beyond uncomfortable. A liberal amount of "bug juice" would have to do.

Backyard astronomy in the foothills of the Sierras during July was meant only for the stout of heart. Besides the constant war against mosquitoes and the self-imposed sweat under layers of clothing, there was the lack of darkness until almost 11 o'clock, and by 3 am morning twilight was already pushing deep-sky objects back into oblivion. Winter observing was so much easier – dress in thick layers, with no mosquitoes or any sweat, and be at the eyepiece by 7 o'clock in the evening.

When Shawn stepped outside, he immediately remembered one of the reasons he loved this place so much. Compared to the light-polluted skies of Pomona, this was pure heaven. Bright stars blazed down from all directions. Nearly directly overhead, the flow of the Heavenly Way wound down to the southern horizon. Intersecting the disk of his own galaxy, and now nearly as bright, was Zeus, a giant whirlpool cutting across the plane of the Heavenly Way. The Double Stream.

To say the collision would begin in the year 2050, as the Galactic Collision Project now reminded everyone, was even less defined than saying you begin to die precisely at the age of 30. There was more to it than that, especially for this galactic merger, which would take 200 million years from time of "first touch," leaving most stars and their planets in a different location within the new galaxy but otherwise unscathed. The GC Project's computer simulations had already determined that Proteus would be one of the many escapees. Even the concept of "first touch," that supposedly critical moment in 2050, would be merely a gravitational interaction rather than physical contact, a process going on with increasing intensity right now. Spiral arms would initially intertwine without a single star being blasted into oblivion.

Yet when you looked up on nights like this, the naked eye told the truth. Something mighty important was happening overhead – a giant spiral of stars was crashing into the Heavenly Way.

* * * * *

The next morning Shawn arose to the sound of the alarm clock, after a night of sleep delayed until 2 am by naked-eye Zeus and the highly magnified Pinwheel Galaxy, another giant member of the local galactic group. It took lots of magnification to make the Pinwheel look like more than just a smudge. He dressed quickly, pulling on gray knickers, a T-shirt with a *NetSearch* logo, and his zippered hiking boots.

He headed down the River Highway. Passing Cheyenne's and then the River Kern General Store, he drove another 3 miles south to the airport. Pulling off the highway into the dirt parking area, he watched an old Piper Apache pull up in front of the café and shut its engines down. The faded red-and-white twin-engine airplane was still used for flight training these days, and that was a miracle in itself. The powerplants were diesels now, but the old twin still couldn't stay airborne very easily on one engine. As one of the sayings about the aircraft went: "If you lose an engine in an Apache, find a place to land real quick, because you're going down."

Two young women stepped out of the cockpit, down off the low wing, and headed to the café. Shawn recognized the older woman, probably in her late twenties, as Corinne, a flight instructor from Bakersfield who often brought her students here for cross-country practice. She loved the little airport with its comfortable café and hearty breakfasts, plus it was a nice change of pace from Bakersfield. You could fly here, even scud-run if you were careful, without talking to air traffic control. And, believe it or not, Kern Valley Airport still didn't have a landing fee.

"Hey, Cory!" yelled Shawn, as he made his way towards the café from the Edsel.

Corinne waved, and then continued up the cafe stairs to take a seat at one of the tables on the big porch, where pilots usually engaged in hangar flying over breakfast every morning during the summer. The airport sat in a wide valley next to the Kern River, where it entered Lake Isabella, and its north-south runway made for an easy approach and departure. But this was high desert, so it was best to fly during the summer only in the morning or evenings when temperatures were acceptable. Afternoon takeoffs from Kern Valley in the hot, thin air of July could be way too exciting in any airplane.

Shawn sat down at the table next to Corinne and her student, not wanting to interrupt whatever they might need to discuss about flying during their breakfast. But he consciously angled his chair so he could talk to Corinne, if the opportunity arose. He didn't know her very well, but he would like to.

Cherokee came over promptly and took their orders, first their table, and then his. Pigs-in-a-blanket was the special today, so he ordered it, knowing there was no way to go wrong at this place.

"The pigs are still squealing," said Cherokee, matter-of-factly.

"That's okay, I'll need the extra protein for a visit to my parents," replied Shawn.

"You should try the biscuits and gravy," said Corinne over her shoulder. "They'll give you extra strength if you need to muscle that Cessna around."

"Unlike a Piper with two engines," countered Shawn. "Does it take two pilots to fly that thing?"

"Now, children, be good," said Cherokee, as she walked away with a smile on her face.

Corinne wore her short blond hair in a pony-tail tucked through the hole in the back of her black baseball cap. Her skin was light, as if she hadn't been out in the sun in a long time, and she wore an olive-drab flight suit with the yellow *BFL* logo of her flight school on both shoulders. She had a Velcro nametag stuck to her chest pocket, a bit crooked and emblazed with her radio call sign: *Sky Queen*. If Shawn had to guess, he'd surmise she was a lesbian, but he often guessed wrong. He did know she didn't have a boyfriend, or at least that's what Cherokee had told him.

Living alone when he first arrived here, Shawn was content to himself. He'd dated a few girls from Kernville, but he never dated any of them twice. Cherokee was a close pal – always had been since they met 8 years ago. Sometimes he felt a connection with her that was more than just a friend, but nothing serious had developed over the years. Still, he found himself here at the café and at Cheyenne's at times when he could easily eat at home.

Now, firmly established as a government shaman (which he couldn't share with anyone), he felt a certain loneliness that had crept into his life the last few years. Another birthday certainly didn't help. Which came back to the premise that you began to die when you hit thirty.

But this morning, sitting near Corinne and bantering with Cherokee, he felt he had plenty in life to keep his male hormones occupied. But he wasn't so sure he had enough challenges for his soul. It would be nice to find a woman he could be with for more than a café moment. Over 30 years remained until the GC Project even entered the "first touch" phase, and he might still be a shaman. By then he'd be in his 60's, which seemed impossible. He might be retired without ever really knowing a woman.

Cherokee brought their plates of food, and the two women discussed Apache engine-out procedures and reviewed emergency checklists as they ate. They were nearly finished with their meals before Shawn found a lull in their conversation, and finally took advantage of it.

"Dead reckoning cross-country?" asked Shawn.

"Not really," replied Corinne. "It's more of a multi-engine lesson. Of course, the only way to get here from Bakersfield is by dead reckoning. Denise is working on her multi-engine commercial ticket, so we're practicing some simulated emergency procedures."

"I heard you never need to simulate emergencies in an Apache," quipped Shawn.

"Very funny, Mister Cessna Man," replied Corinne.

"First lesson in an Apache?" Shawn asked, speaking towards Denise.

"No, second. Cory pulled the left engine on me when we took off from Bakersfield today."

"That must have been a bit of a scramble," said Shawn. "You know what they say about losing an engine in an Apache?"

Corinne gave him a direct stare, as if saying: *Don't you dare!*

Denise shook her head: "No, what do they say?"

"When you lose an engine in an Apache, the only value of the other engine is to speed you to the scene of the accident."

Denise laughed, and Corinne scrunched her thin blond eyebrows at him, possibly in true disgust.

"Thanks, Shawn," said Corinne. "A student needs advice like that."

"You never know when you might need some useful information," replied Shawn in a deadpan tone.

"Apaches are oldies but goodies," said Corinne. "Like you. I see you're still wearing those knickers."

Crushing! Shawn turned red, and couldn't believe what he was hearing. He didn't know Cory very well, but he didn't think she was outright mean. And right after his thirtieth birthday.

"So maybe I'd look better in those conservative cargo pants the old guys wear," mocked Shawn, trying to smile and act like it was no big deal.

"Either would be better than these flight suits," countered Corinne, maybe trying to quell the embarrassment she might not have expected in Shawn.

He thought of a retort, but held it back. Shawn felt a little better now, realizing Corinne was also making fun of her own outfit, and she must be approaching thirty herself. Besides, his response would have been way too bold, because the only thing he could think of was: *You fill out a flight suit mighty fine!* Just thinking about it made him turn red again.

"Flight suits are okay, and so are cargo pants," said Shawn. "But you're right – my knickers gotta' go."

"I guess you shouldn't pick on old Apaches," said Corinne. "Some of us oversensitive flight instructors can't take it. Okay, we gotta' get out of here. What about you?"

"I'm heading to Brackett Airport, so I should get going, too."

"Race you!" taunted Denise, looking very girlish.

"Well, if you use both of your engines, it'd be a tie," replied Shawn. "If you use only one, guess who wins?"

He slipped a cautious glance at Corinne. She was smiling, and it looked genuine.

* * * * *

"Transponder, set – twelve hundred, standby," said Shawn out loud as he ran the last item on his pre-takeoff checklist.

Talking to yourself might be considered a sign of insanity, but Shawn felt it was an extra safety precaution when he flew alone. And he flew alone most of the time. There were several instances where it had seemed to work to his advantage, when he caught things at the last minute that could have otherwise been missed. Say it aloud, and you might pay closer attention.

He dropped his feet from the top of the rudder pedals to the bottom, releasing the brakes, and simultaneously applied a little power. The Cessna 182RG pulled out of the run-up area, and a little pressure from his right foot angled the airplane toward the departure end of Runway 17. He looked carefully at the final approach zone, where inbound airplanes could easily blend into the muted background of the high desert's rocky landscape. Without stopping, he pulled out onto the runway, while pressing the push-to-talk button.

"Kern Valley Traffic, Cessna four-one-two-seven-tango, departing Runway One-Seven, straight out departure, Kern Valley."

Shawn had been taught to always say the airport name at both the beginning and end of each transmission on a UNICOM frequency.

It was a bit of overkill that not all pilots adhered to, but it worked for him. And it showed his attention to safety in the cockpit. If his transmission got cut off in the beginning by another aircraft, other pilots would still know where he was.

As the Cessna pulled into position on the runway, just before pushing the throttle forward, Shawn moved the transponder knob to the "ALT" position and noted the time: 10:39 am.

Then he pushed the throttle all the way forward, glancing at the CHT and EGT gauges to verify the engine power looked good. At 60 knots, he eased back on the wheel, and he was airborne.

"Positive rate. Gear up," he said aloud, verifying he had obtained adequate vertical speed.

He raised the landing gear handle, and as the wheels retracted, Shawn could feel the aerodynamic change, and then the solid *Clunk!* as the landing gear plopped into the wheelwells. He was up and gone.

* * * * *

Shawn's flight to Brackett Airport near Pomona, an inland suburb of Los Angeles, went well. After only 90 minutes under mostly tailwind conditions at altitude, he was maneuvering the Cessna into right traffic for Runway 26 Right, an efficient trip, except it wasn't the most convenient runway for a quick exit to transient parking.

"Two-seven tango, the left runway is available, if you prefer," offered Bracket Tower, as if they read his mind.

"Roger, two-seven-tango is going to transient parking," replied Shawn.

"Two-seven-tango, Expect Runway Two-Six Left. Report turning right base."

The landing was picture-perfect under almost calm conditions, and he was parked on the transient ramp a few minutes later.

Shawn's parents picked him up, and drove him past the fairgrounds to their nearby home. When they walked through the door, their old dog, StickTail, greeted him by racing around in circles to show Shawn he missed him. It was a good start to a visit that sometimes didn't go very smoothly.

Shawn and his parents had suffered some rocky times because of his GC job. Although his mother and father were proud of his accomplishments, they carried a continual suspicion about his lifestyle, related to his inability to tell them the whole truth.

But he could share some of his work with them, although it was in the context of what was routinely revealed in the news, including the microwave pinging program the U.S. government had just announced. He stopped short of explaining his involvement in that program, simply explaining he handled some of the computer programming, which made sense for a low-level technician who worked from home. It explained some of the Cessna flights he conducted to Arizona and research institutions in the Pacific Northwest (for consultation with other computer programmers, of course). Since his parents had visited him in his home north of Kernville, it even explained the big antennas on his roof.

Still, Shawn was simply lying to his parents, even though he tried to convince himself it was only little white lies. And it didn't make him at all comfortable. And somehow his parents knew he was lying, as any mother or father might see through the bluff. So there was a continual sense of unease when they were together. Which is why he visited Pomona so seldom.

Shamans were a secretive profession, and Shawn couldn't violate that in any way. But that meant his parents had to guess where his financial success came from, and their questions often related to whether he was in any sort of trouble. Did he know about California's new drug amnesty program? Had he seen the article about importation of firearms from Mexico, and how the recent crackdowns had resulted in severe penalties? But over time, as his life near Kernville settled down, they noticed his possessions leveled off rather than increasing. Maybe they thought he had stopped doing those terrible things. In any case, they stopped questioning him so much, and seemed to feel more at ease with his situation in the foothills of the Sierras. They even came to visit on (finally) a non-hostile basis, without questioning everything around him. After a trip back up River Highway after a night of surf and turf at Cheyenne's, his mom said: "You know, Shawn, we're awfully proud of you. But that Farley fellow looks like trouble, so maybe you should be careful."

Shawn was convinced it had been a wise decision by the government to keep shaman activities in the shadows, since it provided tremendous latitude when fame would otherwise interfere. He maintained complete privacy at home, during his extensive stays at the cabin, and anywhere he went. Without that privacy, a shaman's job – described by Fatius as thinking and then thinking some more – could easily be compromised. This was true for all five of the nation's shamans, and probably similar situations were evident in other countries as well.

None of the nations involved (currently there were 11) had disclosed the identity of their shamans (34 worldwide), but there were occasional discussions in the news media about unusually overpaid government scientists. In Russia, a radical New Communist group had suggested there were individuals being paid by the government to secretly study the upcoming galactic collision, but no individuals were specifically identified. In China, a shaman blew his own cover while trying to personally profit from a media promise of even greater riches. But in both instances, the public paid little attention. Everyone knew the world's governments were openly collaborating on action plans relative to the pending collision, and no one called for full disclosure of the prime researchers involved. It was simply not of interest compared to the bigger issues of prolonged financial recession and military friction between India and China. So shamans continued to do their jobs (thinking and then more thinking) with the privacy they required to make progress. And progress was beginning to show.

India had asked their three shamans to concentrate on remote pinging, which was similar to old-fashioned radar or sonar. Send out a signal, and wait for a reply, which was almost instantaneous anywhere on Earth. For 70 years, radar and its derivatives had successfully mapped details of the objects it hit. It was even applied to the planets of the solar system, with considerable surface detail. Apply it to an object 4 light-years away (the distance to the nearest star), and you raised four main problems. First, the distance is so great that any signal requires enormous strength to reach its target. Second, aiming the signal accurately becomes tremendously problematic, and mapping anything requires even more precision. Third, charting doesn't solve the prerequisites, for we have detailed maps of many objects within our own solar system, and the surface tells you almost nothing about environmental conditions or alien life. But even these major challenges were overshadowed by the obvious – round-trip transmission to the nearest star would require 8 years, almost unimaginably longer for objects in another galaxy.

U.S. and Indian shamans were concentrating on the transmission delay problem first. If they couldn't solve that challenge, the rest of the problems were mute points. All that was needed was a way to travel faster than the speed of light, preferably instantaneously.

Chapter 11

Kitt Peak

After visiting his parents, Shawn cranked up the Cessna 182RG, and headed for Tucson, where he had a meeting scheduled with Dr. Trevor Cantrelli, an astrophysicist at the University of Arizona. Like most U of A astronomers, he had access to nearby Kitt Peak's big telescopes. In Dr. Cantrelli's case, he could go to the front of the pecking order on the observing schedule when he needed to, based on his notoriety in galactic structure. Usually, instrument time had to be scheduled months or even years in advance at the biggest observatories, but Dr. Cantrelli could bump someone with lower seniority on extremely short notice. He tried not to take advantage of that fact except when absolutely necessary, such as when the GC Project requested it.

At Tucson, Shawn stayed in the University Marriott, in the heart of the tiny Tucson suburb adjoining U of A. He'd been here many times before, spending time with astronomers of outrageous esteem, his introduction paved by Kent in Washington. The biggest surprise was how folksy these great astronomers were, many of them starting as backyard amateurs, just like Shawn. Dr. Cantrelli had spent his undergraduate days at Cal Tech, transferring to Arizona for his doctorate. While working on his PhD dissertation, he had three main hangouts – in the funky village where the Marriott sat, Kitt Peak where he worked on dissertation research behind a spectroscope, and in the desert outskirts south of Tucson where a bed-and-breakfast combined with a semi-professional observatory catered to astro-freaks like Shawn.

The bed-and-breakfast hired U of A graduate students to provide one-on-one telescope training sessions to any of their guests willing to pay $20 per hour. Trevor Cantrelli and other doctoral candidates would drive out the winding road south of town when they got the short-notice phone call, sometimes interrupting a pizza and beer session at the pub. Then they'd meet a couple at the bed-and-breakfast who were looking for a unique evening while touring Arizona. Trevor would crank up one of the small ETX telescopes in the sliding roof observatory, which served as an open deck for several families to observe the desert sky at the same time. The ETX was still popular as an easy but efficient way to explore the heavens, the first amateur instrument to incorporate a computerized database and a Go-To button to access the faintest of deep-sky wonders. After taking a bed-and-breakfast couple through a tour of the night's most spectacular objects, Trevor would wait for his buddies to finish up, and they'd all drive back to the university together to finish up the late night with one more round of beers.

"Man, that was an interesting place," recalled Dr. Cantrelli.

"I was there once," said Shawn. "When I first started in the GC Project, I met here on campus with Dr. Stromberg. I think he's at Colorado State now."

"Yes, he's still studying links between solar flares and atmospheric science. You might want to pursue that yourself."

"I can see how it might fit in," replied Shawn. "Anyway, back then there was a receptionist named Cassie who worked there. Do you remember her?"

"Cassiopeia? Sure, sure. She was pretty much a fixture there when I used to help them out. It was usually Cassie who called me when they needed a mini-astronomer to give some tourists a sky tour."

"Well, the only time I was there, Cassiopeia really got me going," continued Shawn. "When I checked in, a little nervous about being in a bed-and-breakfast as a single guy, she gave me the grand tour. I perceived right away that she was knowledgeable in astronomy. In fact, I thought she might be a semi-pro astronomer, regardless of her silly ancient-Egyptian costume, better suited to a Cleopatra than a Cassiopeia. Her little welcoming speech was a bit stilted, obviously rehearsed, and interspersed with astronomical factoids that seemed accurate to me. When we walked down one hallway, she stopped and pointed out a photo of the Heavenly Way with Zeus intersecting it, just like you see with the naked eye when you look up on a dark night. She said: "That's Zeus, of course, very large and still a long way from Proteus – over a million miles."

"A million <u>miles</u>?" laughed Dr. Cantrelli. "Miles, not light-years?"

"That's what I heard. So I asked her to repeat what she'd said: "How far did you say?"

"Over a million miles," she said.

"Well I've heard the figure 10,000 light-years," noted Dr. Cantrelli. "It's a conservative number used in news releases, based on measurements from Proteus to the edge of Zeus. So that puts Cassie pretty close to accurate, if you leave out a factor of… let's see… maybe ten-to-the-tenth power or so. Heck, I'd need a calculator."

"I soon realize Cassiopeia had learned some basic astronomical facts and could apply them to her job as hostess," related Shawn. "Later that night, I heard her talking to some astro-tourists in the sliding-roof observatory, while I was with my university 'rental' astronomer – heck, wouldn't it be funny if it had been you? Anyway, Cassie was using one the those ETX scopes to show some people the center of the Zeus galaxy, and I overheard her explain it was over a million miles away."

"Mighty funny," quipped Dr. Cantrelli. "Not much left down there, as I understand it. A guy from Phoenix bought the place, and still operates it as a bed-and-breakfast. But he turned that great sliding-roof area into a barbecue patio. It'll never be the same."

Shawn and Trevor Cantrelli got along famously, and they both had a hard time settling down to the topic at hand. But eventually they immersed themselves in a discussion of alternatives for remote pinging – other frequencies that might work better, and how to exceed the speed of light.

"If we're looking for habitable planets like Proteus, we may be trying it the hard way," suggested Dr. Cantrelli. "If we were more technologically advanced, we could probably solve the problem in a heartbeat using instruments we can't even imagine today. So what we need is to find someone advanced enough to tell us how to do it."

"We look for little green men inhabiting another Proteus, and they tell us how it's done," reiterated Shawn.

"Right. But that, of course, sounds impossible. Maybe, however, finding advanced alien intelligence would progress quicker if we had another galaxy to use as a laboratory. Like Zeus."

"But communicating with aliens anywhere outside our solar system faces the same problem," said Shawn. "You can't do it in our lifetime, even in a galaxy as near as Zeus, if you can't exceed the speed of light."

"Very true, my young friend. Unless, of course, they find us first. Then they just tell us how it's done."

* * * * *

Back in the Marriott the next morning, Shawn's cell phone rang him awake. The blackout curtains were drawn tight, so it felt like the middle of the night.

"Shawn Russell," he answered in his most professional tone, acting like he was awake.

"Hey, Shawn. It's Trevor Cantrelli. About time to wake up, isn't it?"

Shawn glanced at the big red numerals on the hotel alarm clock: *7:08 AM.*

"Sure. I'm awake. Sort of."

"I wouldn't have called so early, if I didn't think you'd want to know. We've got a slot tonight on the 8-meter, and we'll need to go over our observing plan this morning, and then drive out to Kitt Peak in the afternoon. Can't miss the steak house at the base of the mountain that I'm dying to take you to, so we'll have to hit there before 5 o'clock, if we're going to make it to the top before sunset."

"You bet!" said Shawn, now wide-awake.

There's something great about a renowned astronomer who plans his schedule around a steak house in the desert.

"Can we meet at Molly's for breakfast?" asked Dr. Cantrelli.

Food, food. It's only 7 am.

* * * * *

Later that morning, after breakfast at Molly's Cafe, they went back to Dr. Cantrelli's office and talked about an observing profile for the night's session at Kitt Peak. The observing slot would be short, but only an hour of telescope time would be needed for what they hoped to achieve. The bumped astronomer from the University of Michigan would have plenty of time for his previously scheduled telescope run immediately afterwards, which made Dr. Cantrelli feel better about displacing another astronomer.

They talked at length about the idea Dr. Cantrelli had proposed to Shawn the day before, trying to decide what celestial object would be best for the test. The concept involved spectroscopic analysis of a stellar system with a known planet fairly close to Proteus. Then, by comparison to older spectral data from the same star system by previous observers, Dr. Cantrelli wanted to see if any differences could be detected in the spectrums. Since capturing spectral data from an extrasolar planet was beyond the resolution limit of any of Proteus' current telescopes, the idea was to apply the results to the entire stellar system. If changes could be detected, it might be possible to isolate them to changes within the planets orbiting the star rather than the star itself.

"It's stretching the limits of spectroscopy, even for the 8-meter telescope," explained Dr. Cantrelli. "But it's a starting point for a research project that might get us closer to the goal of using environmental tracers to detect planetary molecular details. If nothing else, it'll allow us to look at the problem from a different viewpoint."

Which was a perfect example of how both an astrophysicist and a shaman did their jobs. There was no way Shawn could out-think the world's top astronomers. But he could enlist their help in getting projects rolling. Then, with the financial backing of the GC Project, which Shawn could influence in an instant, new ideas could head in various directions, and pretty soon things could begin to snowball. In this case, Dr. Cantrelli was about to launch into new territory that might prove valuable for the GC Project, drawing the attention of other astronomers along the way. In reality, Shawn didn't understand the details of this spectroscopic comparison, or how it could give any valuable information, but he really didn't need to know. A shaman didn't need to know how to juggle; he just needed to get the balls in the air. Scientists had a wonderful habit of attending to details, whereas a shaman was more of a generalist. His job was to get things started, and then keep feeding the fire.

"So, for example, what do you think might cause a change in spectrum?" asked Shawn.

"Well, suppose there's several planets like Proteus orbiting this star. Unlikely, of course, but just suppose. So all of these planets go through seasons, and that means production of chlorophyll and oxygen, and absorption of carbon dioxide, and who-know-what else, especially if it's an environment we've never encountered before. All of these things combine to change planetary atmospheres over time, maybe enough to change the stellar spectrum."

"But aren't all of these planets in conflicting seasons while they orbit this star, effectively cancelling out the results?"

"Sure, that's to be expected, but let me show you a few equations," said Dr. Cantrelli, reaching for a whiteboard marker.

"No, no, please," said Shawn. "No math right now. I'll leave the equations to you."

"Okay, I didn't mean to get carried away. Besides, right now we have a higher priority if we're going to crank up that telescope tonight. We'll need to select a stable star, which will be less likely to taint things with spectral changes, and we'll want a system with multiple planets. The planets need to be ones discovered as long ago as possible, so comparison of tonight's spectrum to the original strip will have a better chance of detecting a change over time. Proteus-sized would be nice, but we've been finding those only recently. And it might be nice if the stellar system is above the horizon tonight."

"Yes, that would be nice," laughed Shawn. "So would clear skies."

* * * * *

They got their clear skies, crystal clear, in fact, which made the drive to Kitt Peak through the desert a lot of fun for them both. It had taken all afternoon to settle on the target stellar system, but finally they found one that would be adequate, although not meeting all of their preferences. The star was 55 Dantri, nicely positioned between the prominent constellations of Keto and Deanna. Dantrus was a minor constellation riding fairly low in the south as viewed from Kitt Peak tonight. With five known planets, discovered between 1997 and 2007, this star provided plenty of ammunition. The stellar system, 40.3

light-years away, had already received some previous notoriety when a METI message was sent to 55 Dantri on July 6, 2003. Using Eurasia's 70-meter Eupatoria Planetary Radar, the attempted extraterrestrial contact was named Cosmic Call 2. It would arrive at 55 Dantri in May 2044.

After a delicious T-bone steak at the base of Kitt Peak, they started up the winding road to the observatory. It was a good thing they didn't try this after dark. By now, Shawn was comfortable calling Dr. Cantrelli by his first name, and even comfortable calling out a few instances of "Watch Out, Trevor!" on some of the more interesting curves. Astronomers aren't known for their superior driving skills.

Just after sunset, in the parking lot at Kitt Peak National Observatory, Dr. Cantrelli packed up a briefcase full of paperwork, mostly computer printouts, while Shawn slid a brown pair of cargo pants on over his shorts. One thing he liked about these pants (purchased during his visit with his parents in Pomona) was that he could pull them right over his zippered hiking boots. Now that he thought about it, he liked cargo pants. They felt comfortable and athletic, and went well with his tall and lanky frame.

The temperature had already gone from scorching hot to comfortably warm, and the clear skies should cool things down rapidly at this altitude, so he also grabbed a sweatshirt from his bag in the back seat of the car. The shirt's chest boasted *Astro-Nut*, which seemed appropriate for the situation.

Both Trevor and Shawn were in their element here – Trevor because he loved observational astronomy more than anything else, and Shawn because he enjoyed learning from famous scientists and he loved the great outdoors. Here on this mountaintop, both men were preparing to enjoy the self-imposed show.

They walked along a paved scenic path leading towards the 8-meter observatory dome. The largest of the jutting rocks along the side of the paved trail were so tall they dwarfed pedestrians. Looking past the boulders, they could see the desert far below, now glittering with the first lights of evening. The establishments of humanity were never out of sight from this majestic viewing perspective, at least on clear nights like tonight. The view of the desert below from this perch on the edge of the mountain was spectacular, but the astronomers and their assistants who worked here weren't normally impressed. Instead, they were totally focused and mentally preparing themselves for the first images from the stars.

As they weaved down the path to the 8-meter telescope, the sky was almost completely dark to the east, the western glow behind them was nearly gone, and there wasn't a hint of wind. The metal structure of the observatory retained some of the heat of the Arizona sun, but was cooling rapidly, and so were the mirrors and lenses that needed to reach ambient temperature before accurate resolution was possible.

Just before they reached the dome, it began rotating towards the south, responding to the right ascension and declination coordinates Dr. Cantrelli had submitted earlier in the day. The telescope operator was already at work, preparing the 8-meter instrument for their observing session, and it would be the first of three that night. Which was both good and bad, since it would be nice to get down the mountain early. In fact, Shawn and Dr. Cantrelli had planned to drive all the way back to Tucson tonight, although it would take them nearly to sunrise. Neither of them was normally so brutal on their bodies, but they both had appointments the next day they really shouldn't miss.

The bad part of this early observing session was the lack of complete darkness and the premature stabilization of temperature within the dome and the telescope. Both were normally essential, but a spectrographic session would be minimally affected. Besides, the fact of the matter was this was more of a motivational session than a scientific absolute, a kickoff to a project that might develop wings. Or, like many similar projects, it might not. You had to start somewhere, so this would be a good way to begin. If the analysis of spectrums of extrasolar planetary systems proved valuable, it would continue. If not, it would be dropped like a hot potato, so energy could be quickly focused in a different direction. Science was like that – thousands of ideas, many of them dead ends. But for every thousand bad ideas, a good one emerged. You had to try and try again to achieve meaningful results.

Both Dr. Cantrelli and Shawn knew their presence wasn't even necessary tonight. The telescope operator and his computer could transmit all of the signals necessary to guide the telescope, and the astronomers directing the observing session often stayed back in their university offices, watching the results on their computer screens. But there was still something very special about being in the observatory dome as the results came in, just like the good old days of observational astronomy.

By now the telescope operator had installed the spectroscope, and was guiding the 8-meter instrument to its target 40.3 light-years away in the constellation of Dantrus. The spectrographic strips would be available for viewing almost instantly, but the analysis of them would take several days. So when Shawn and Dr. Cantrelli finally drove back down the mountain in the dark of night – "Watch out, Trevor!" yelled Shawn, twice at critical curves – they knew nothing of where tonight's observing session would eventually lead.

* * * * *

On the way back to Tucson, they took turns driving, planning to catch catnaps to allow them to make it through the next day. But they got along all too well, and the car was seldom quiet. They spoke about a topic that dominated the GC Project, although it had almost nothing to do with tonight's observations.

"Why couldn't light, in certain forms, be an instantaneous thing?" questioned Dr. Cantrelli.

It was the kind of question that would be more expected from a shaman than an astrophysics expert like Trevor Cantrelli. So Shawn quickly kept the conversation going, since it had started in the right direction.

"As Einstein said, to paraphrase a bit: 'It's a wave; no, it's a particle!' Something that can simultaneously be both could have lots of hidden secrets, it seems to me," said Shawn.

"Faster-than-light isn't a ridiculous concept," replied Dr. Cantrelli. "Einstein's special relativity doesn't forbid it, and CERN's tachyon experiments have drawn blood, I'd say. So why shouldn't we consider it as a method of observation, if not communication, when it comes to the planetary systems we'll be seeing soon in Zeus?"

"That's taking a pretty big leap," said Shawn, playing devil's advocate. "The CERN results are still debated, as least for those of us who get our scientific knowledge from *Newsweek*. And there's a big difference between detailed observation of planets hundreds of light-years away and communicating with them."

"I hate to break the bad news to you, my astro-nut friend," said Dr. Cantrelli. "Proteus is still <u>thousands</u> of light-years from the closest outer spiral arm of Zeus. Regardless of all that 2050 'first touch' crap, we'll need to see planets farther away than we've ever deemed possible, so we'd better look into a simpler way to solve the problem."

"You don't think the spectrographic comparison method holds promise?"

"Even if it does, how are we going to push it up a notch to 10,000 light-years? My suggestion is to spend our energy learning how to communicate rather than how to observe. In fact, it's a simpler problem, since we stand a better chance of solving the speed limit problem if we don't use light."

"Good point, Trevor. So are you talking about using gravitons or what?"

"Actually, gravitons are worth considering, even though gravity seems to adhere to the speed-of-light limit in astronomical settings. But it's deduced information, not laboratory confirmed data, since we don't have the technology yet for measuring the speed of gravity in our labs. Sometimes a small shortcoming can prove to be a big break, if you don't get too established with what you think you see."

"General relativity – not to get too focused on dear ol' Einstein – says gravity propagates at the speed of light," countered Shawn, maintaining his contentious role in the discussion.

"Yes, but ol' Einstein could be right in some settings, and wrong in others. If light can be both a particle and a wave simultaneously, then why can't relativity be applicable over here, but not over there? Quantum entanglement is the perfect example. It's definitely not dependent upon the speed of light, but information is being exchanged."

"Now wait a minute, Trevor. I'm sure you've heard the arguments about that. Quantum entanglement works instantaneously – agreed. But it's not really information that's being transmitted."

"So now we're down to arguing over a definition of 'information.' What are you? – Some kind of shaman or something?"

Shawn couldn't help laugh out loud. In his contacts with Dr. Cantrelli, he hadn't once hinted at the word "shaman." But it was general knowledge in the scientific community that the GC Project relied on "philososcience consultants," commonly referred to as "shamans." And when Dr. Cantrelli got his phone call from Washington asking him to drop everything, he knew he was meeting with a shaman.

"Well, Trevor, if I were a shaman, I'd say you're onto something."

With that, they both laughed, and then drove on into the night.

* * * * *

At 5 am that morning at the hotel, Shawn was still trying to fall asleep, hoping to catch up on a few hours of physical renewal before facing a meeting with a U of A astrobiologist at 9 o'clock. The meeting had originally been planned without knowing he would be driving back from Kitt Peak in the middle of the night. And without knowing all of this talk about solving the speed-of-light problem would keep him wide-awake.

On the ride back to Tucson, he and Dr. Cantrelli discussed astronomical situations where the speed of light might be exceeded. There actually were a few documented examples, since faster-than-light travel was technically possible outside of a single frame of reference. Even Einstein would have accepted the observed results, but he would have argued this really wasn't an exception to the laws of relativity, merely another way of looking at the speed limit of light.

Distorted regions of space-time could allow instances where the speed of light might be exceeded, but these seemed to have little practical application for a project involving either observing over long distances or trying to communicate. The graviton route also seemed headed in the wrong direction for their needs. But Cornell University had been experimenting with a device they called a "polarization synchrotron," and it held some hope for the route Shawn was trying to navigate.

The synchrotron combined radio waves with rapidly spinning magnetic fields in a 2-meter long curving arc. The biggest area of promise lie in the small size of the device compared to other theoretical concepts requiring huge structures. Even though the Cornell scientists thought this apparatus couldn't carry information, transmitting anything at a speed greater than light was an important parameter to use as a starting point. From there, maybe information flow could be added.

As Shawn pondered these concepts, he finally managed to fall asleep, only to be awakened by the telephone only a few minutes later, or so it seemed. But as he glanced at the clock, leaning out of bed to grab his cell phone, he noticed it was a few minutes after 8 o'clock, so he had actually slept several hours.

"I'm calling from Master Aviation at the airport," the voice said. "We've got your Cessna 182 here, and I need to talk to you about what we found."

What we found, thought Shawn. How could they have found anything, since he didn't ask them to do anything except change the oil and check the spark plugs? When he or one of his co-owners stopped overnight at a large airport, they'd coordinate scheduled maintenance actions such as oil changes. With no maintenance shop at Kern Valley, they found this was the best way to get things done without constantly ferrying the aircraft to Bakersfield for minor maintenance items. Since Shawn put the most hours on the airplane, and stayed overnight more often, he had taken on the role to the extent that he seldom even coordinated with the other two pilots. He simply kept track of the maintenance schedule, and let them know what was done when he got home, and requested reimbursement from their joint fund. Shared ownership wasn't as simple as Shawn had hoped, but it worked when the participants were as easy-going as the three of them.

"So what did you find?" asked Shawn, still waking up and running his long fingers through his curly blond hair as if to straighten it, which was impossible.

"Well, when we checked your spark plugs, we found a crack in cylinder number three, right at the plug hole. It's only a hairline, but it's grounding, I'm afraid. So you'll have to decide what you want us to do about a replacement cylinder. There aren't any jugs for this model engine here in Tucson."

What good news on a morning when time was tight. There was an appointment with an astrobiologist, and then the flight back to Kern Valley, which obviously wasn't going to happen in the Cessna.

"Let me think about it, and I'll call you back in a few minutes," said Shawn. Which really meant he needed to get busy real quick – calling his partners to decide on a course of action; cancelling his appointment with the astrobiologist; booking a series of airline flights to get him back to Bakersfield before dark; and reserving a rental car to get him to the middle of nowhere before midnight.

What Shawn didn't know was that it would be an even more unusual day than expected. And it would affect everything about him for decades to come, maybe even more than his part as a shaman in the Galactic Collision Project.

Chapter 12

Backyard Astronomy

Shawn sat in the Phoenix Airport, waiting for his next connecting flight. It was an airline change from Tucson here, and another one to a commuter carrier in Los Angeles. Then Diamond Car rental at Bakersfield Airport, and a round-trip drive to Kernville, which was the only choice. So he'd need to figure out how to get the car back to Bakersfield before the daily charges cost the government an arm and a leg. He wouldn't even bother submitting any "Remarks" when he mailed the credit card receipt to Washington, since he'd learned long ago that anything goes, so why bother?

Despite the fact it was all time rather than real money, it was already wearing him out. After he finally got settled in at home, he'd need to figure out how to reverse course and get the Cessna 182RG back from Tucson once the cylinder replacement was complete. Since he instigated the problem, though it was just one of those things, it was only fair he be the one to retrieve the airplane.

His flight to LAX was, if nothing else, fast – just an hour, mostly up and down, and then a shuttle bus to the Commuter Terminal, where he waited as patiently as he could for the Brasilia turboprop to Bakersfield. There were two flights a day, spaced at 12-hour intervals, and he had three more hours to wait.

In the meantime, he did a little catching up on his self-imposed shaman homework, finding one Red Star message waiting for him on his mini-laptop. A shaman in Australia was asking for a copy of his full report from Kitt Peak. Since the extrasolar planet spectral analysis wasn't complete yet, he replied accordingly, promising to forward the report as soon as it became available. Then he phoned Fatius in Miami to bounce a few ideas off him.

"Hi, Shawn. Glad you called. What's up?"

"Actually, I'm a bit down. To be exact, down on the ground at LAX, waiting for a connecting flight to Bakersfield."

Shawn went on to tell his horror story regarding the Cessna 182's cracked cylinder and his convoluted flight itinerary. When shamans got together, they spent a lot of time just bullshitting, but they usually earned their GS-12 salary when they finally got down to business.

"Imagine what they'll do in Washington when they see your travel charges on the credit card," said Fatius.

"Just what will they do?" countered Shawn.

"They'll do what they always do. A few keystrokes on a GC administrator's smart phone, and it's paid. You should have charged the cylinder change, too."

"Right. That would have been fair."

"Hey, you're Mr. Shaman, west coast version. Me, I'm Miami Priceless."

"Look, Fat, I know you're just as careful of your expenses as I am – well maybe not – but it's been agonizing. By the time I get home, it will have taken all day. At least I've had plenty of time on this trip to think about polarization synchrotrons."

"So you finally get around to something interesting," said Fatius. "I suppose you think I know something about them, don't you?"

"I suppose I do. So do you?"

"Do I who? Who do you do?"

"Fat, knock it off. I'm really not in the mood. Maybe I should call tomorrow when I'm sober."

"Ah, Shawn, my boy, you're really not cut out to be a shaman. Too serious. And now over thirty."

"I suppose you're going to tell me to stop wearing knickers."

"What do knickers have to do with it? And yes, I know a bit about polarization synchrotrons."

"Did you hear about the work at Cornell?" asked Shawn.

"Not all hocus-pocus. Just enough for a shaman. The only thing that really travels faster than light in their studies is a radio wave."

"But that's exactly what we need. Now the big question is how do you get the wave to carry information, and then how do you make it powerful enough to travel over 10 thousand light-years?"

"Which puts it into the outskirts of Zeus, of course," said Fatius.

"Exactly the point. What do you really think, Fat?"

"What do I really think? I think you'd better get an airline ticket to Cornell. The route to Ithaca probably will be even more complex than that fine journey you're taking today."

* * * * *

When the turboprop taxied to the terminal at Bakersfield, it was almost 6 o'clock. By the time he rented the car, it was well after most businesses on the airport had closed, including the airport café. But remembering Corinne's flight school was somewhere on the field, Shawn took a chance and drove to the first big hangar he saw. It sported a "BFL" logo on its entry door, just like the one on Corinne's flight suit.

When he walked in, Corinne was in the combined office-lounge, sitting on a brown leather couch next to a curly-haired fellow who looked barely 20 years old. Their backs were to Shawn, but he could see a sectional chart on the coffee table in front of them. Corinne was finishing up her instructions: "So go ahead and file our flight plan through DUATS, making sure you check the NOTAM's, especially anything for Bakersfield or Fresno."

"Hey, Cory!" said Shawn, as nonchalantly as possible, as soon as she was finished with her sentence.

Corinne swiveled around to see him behind her, looking totally surprised, and maybe just a little bit thrilled.

"Shawn! What are you doin' here?"

"Just came to visit you."

"You're kidding, right?" Her eyes were bright now, and focused clearly on Shawn. Maybe she was actually excited to see him.

"Well, I did want to look you up, since I happened to be at the airport. I didn't expect to find you working so late."

"So you came in your Cessna 182. Nice flight from Kern Valley?"

"No, actually I arrived on a Brasilia from LAX."

"Huh?" Her puckered lips showed her confusion.

"Long story, Cory. But I just wanted to say hello before I drive back to Kernville."

"You're driving your Edsel?"

"Wrong again. A rental car. I had a problem with the one-eighty-two in Tucson, and I've been on the road ever since. Terrible airline connections."

Suddenly, he felt out of place here. Corinne in her wrinkle-free flight suit, her student in a button-down collar shirt and silky-looking knickers, and Shawn in severely crumpled pants and shirt from a hard day of travel. But at least they were cargo pants.

"What's wrong with the Cessna?" she asked.

"Cracked cylinder? You got any lying around here?"

"Bummer. No, Jack doesn't stock anything that doesn't come with the arm of a student pilot attached. But there's no way you're taking a rental car to Kernville. How are you going to bring it back?"

"That's an extra complication, but I'll work it out. Maybe you can fly me."

"Sure, it's exactly what I was thinking," replied Corinne, with a wide smile on her face. "Tom, change your flight plan from Fresno to Kern Valley, airport designator L05. It's practically the same place."

"No, no, I was just kidding, Cory. You can't do that."

"Too bad. I just did."

* * * * *

The aircraft was a single-engine Piper Arrow, one of Shawn's favorite airplanes. The performance factors were similar to his 182RG, both airplanes with retractable landing gear and similar engines. He'd received his instrument rating in an Arrow at Kern Valley, and had rented one for several years after that for cross-country trips until buying into the 182 partnership.

Corinne's student was a commercial license applicant, polishing off his skills for his flight test. Today's flight was a combined cross-country navigation exercise, night flight (on the return leg), and some airwork along the way. The good news is Shawn knew the restrictions on the Arrow, and it wasn't certified for spins, which also meant no aerodynamic stalls today, since a passenger in the back seat pushed the center of gravity too far aft. A good flight instructor considered every practice stall with a student to be a potential spin. And he was sure Corinne was a level-headed instructor. Which was particularly heartening, since he hated riding in the back seat, and he didn't like fancy airwork. When he received his private license, it had been for one purpose – to get places fast and comfortably. A 182RG or an Arrow were perfect machines for that purpose.

After takeoff, Tom maneuvered out of Bakersfield's traffic pattern, and climbed to 7500 feet, an altitude commensurate with their visual route of flight to Kern Valley. The early evening air was smooth, a blessing when entering the heat bowl of the high desert during the summer. Most of the thermal convection activity had died down this late in the day, and they should be on the ground shortly after sunset. That would give Corinne and Tom plenty of time to get airborne before it got dark in the valley; yet late enough to count as a night flight back to Bakersfield.

"Tom, give me a steep turn to the right, one complete three-sixty," said Corinne into her headset microphone, after they'd leveled off at 7500 feet and taken up their en route heading towards Kern Valley. "Shawn, you don't mind, do you?"

Mind? Why would Shawn mind? After all, he was an accomplished pilot. Just one who didn't particularly like airwork. He knew the private pilot standards called for a 45-degree bank to fulfill the requirement for a steep turn, and it was probably the same for a commercial license. It would visually be somewhat disconcerting, along with a bit of g-force. Shawn never liked practicing steep turns when he was at the controls in the front seat. From the rear, it seemed like it would be a lot more taxing on his body, or maybe only on his mind.

"No, I don't mind," replied Shawn into his headset mike, trying to sound totally relaxed, which he wasn't.

Tom made a clearing turn to the right, and then to the left. Then he entered the steep turn. Shawn had selected the left seat in the rear of the airplane, since he wanted to be able to see Corinne more clearly. As a flight instructor, she sat in the right front seat, and Tom in the left. So when the aircraft rolled into the turn, he had to look over Tom's shoulder to watch the attitude indicator. The instrument rolled right past the 45-degree mark, and settled solidly on 60-degrees. It suddenly seemed like they were upside down. The g-force felt like they were in an Apollo capsule at liftoff.

"Oh!" yelled Shawn in surprise (and a bit of fright).

Corinne glanced back at him, saw his shocked face, and transmitted an *Oh, I'm sincerely sorry* facial expression directly at him. Shawn felt nearly the same as he did when Corinne had criticized his knickers, but he was too scared to turn red.

"Good work, Tom," said Corinne calmly, while still staring caringly at Shawn. "Hold it right there at 60 degrees."

The tender look on Corinne's light-skinned face soothed Shawn in a way he didn't know he could be soothed. But his stomach was still knotted up in a ball.

As they approached rollout from the turn, Shawn waited for exactly what he knew was coming, a gentle bump as they hit their own wake turbulence, the sign of a 360-degree turn that holds perfect altitude.

Bump! It came and was gone quickly. But Tom failed to ease the backpressure he was holding on the control wheel during the turn. The backwards force on the yoke was necessary during the maneuver, but a flight examiner would deduct a few points for failing to release it upon rollout, since the airplane would then climb another hundred feet or so.

As the airplane hit the little bump, and Tom rolled out of the turn (without easing the backpressure), Corinne continued with her fixed stare on Shawn. She was now talking to her student through his headset, but with her focus on her passenger in the back seat.

"Nice job, Tom. Good bank control all the way, and nice backpressure during the turn."

Shawn added: "But ease off the backpressure when you roll out, so you don't gain altitude." He now had a smile on his face, mockingly squinting at Corinne. She continued to stare at Shawn, now reaching for her yellow-tinted sunglasses and lowering them so she could glance over the top of the rims. Her eyes were penetrating, and her stare unwavering. Then a puckered smile and a slow nod of her head: "Yes, that's right, Tom" she said. "You've got to reduce the backpressure to maintain your altitude."

"Okay, got it," said Tom. "One to the left now?"

"No," said Corinne, finally turning her head back towards her student. "That's enough for today. Just take us to Kern Valley, straight and level all the way. And do me a favor, if you don't mind."

"Whatever you say, boss!"

"How about taking your headset off, so I can talk to Shawn in private for a few minutes. I'll listen on frequency for traffic, and you can just concentrate on getting us there smoothly like a good commercial pilot. Act like you're hauling a crate of eggs, and you can't afford to break a single one."

"Sure. My ears are off," replied Tom as he removed his headset and set it on top of the dashboard, the cord dangling down in front of the flight instruments.

"Just wanted to talk to you for a few minutes," said Corinne. "Tom is ready for his flight test, so tonight is pretty much academic."

"Sorry about back there," said Shawn. "I guess I expected a 45-degree bank."

"It's 60 degrees for the commercial license, but you're right about the backpressure. And I shouldn't have done it with someone in the back seat. If it was me, I would have totally puked."

Shawn felt like a bumbling idiot, being held in the continued gaze of this gorgeous flight instructor. One hint of praise thrown his way, and he felt like a little child. And she had graced him by having her student take off his headset to allow them to talk in private. But it was more than that. He somehow knew she had never done this before, temporarily ignoring her job to talk to Shawn for reasons he couldn't comprehend.

"I doubt you would have puked," replied Shawn. "But I almost did."

When Corinne laughed, her lips scrunched up into a cute twist she bashfully seemed to be fighting back. She shook her head gently, seeming to say: *I really like you.*

That's the way Shawn interpreted it, mainly because it was the way he wanted it to be. If he was bold enough, he would tell her so.

"This day started out dreadful," he said. "But it sure has ended nice. I really like you."

She blushed, turning her face away, but only after making sure he had seen her grin. When she turned back to him, she was still smiling.

"Maybe I should tell Tom to just keep flying," she said. "We can head back up to Fresno, then over to Oakland, and then keep looping south until we start to run out of gas. Then we probably should land."

"Fine by me. I could stay with you for a while."

"Maybe we'll do that someday soon. I hope," said Corinne.

Shawn hoped that too.

* * * * *

Tom began the descent about 20 miles west of Kern Valley Airport, a nice smooth glide that wouldn't break any eggs. As they passed through 6000 feet, Corinne yelled over the loud drone of the Arrow's engine: "Time to get back to reality!" while gesturing towards Tom's headset on the dash.

With all three of them back on headset, Corinne asked Tom to set up for a right-hand traffic pattern for Runway 17, landing to the south. She worked the radio while he ran the pre-landing checklist.

"Kern Valley Traffic, Arrow four-one-eight-seven-romeo is inbound from the dam, right traffic Runway one-seven. Will report downwind, Kern Valley."

Shawn noticed Corinne's radio technique, with the airport name at the front and rear of her transmission.

Tom entered downwind, and Corinne made the radio call. Then he lowered the landing gear, and ran through the GUMPS checklist out loud as the three green lights appeared: "Gas – left tank, fullest; Undercarriage – three green; Mixture – full rich, with the pump; Prop – full forward; Seatbelts – secure." Tom looked over at Corinne, confirming her shoulder harness was engaged, and then asked: "Shawn, how's your belt?"

"Secured for landing," replied Shawn.

Tom was going to make a fine commercial pilot.

* * * * *

Once they were on the ground, Tom made the first turnoff to the left, which took them down the lengthy taxiway to the café area, where the Edsel was parked. The sun was far enough below the horizon that they used the landing light to guide the Arrow into a spot on the end, where there was plenty of space to maneuver. Getting a rear passenger out of an Arrow is like removing a sardine from a packed can, so Tom shut down the engine and ran the postflight checklist, as Corinne unlatched the door on her side, which was the only exit.

"We're here!" yelled Corinne to a nearly dark ramp, with no one in sight and the café locked up tight. "Tom, I'm going to walk Shawn to his car. I'll be right back, if you don't mind waiting here."

"Sure, boss," Tom replied, with the headset incident still clearly in his memory, and probably wondering where she and Shawn were sneaking off to now.

"Nice flight," Shawn said to Tom, offering him his hand as he exited the plane. They hardly knew each other, but Shawn would put his life in Tom's hands any day.

"Nice meeting you. Hope your Cessna gets well soon."

Shawn and Corinne walked past the dark café to the red Edsel with the black cloth top, parked up against the wooden fence.

There was a moment of awkwardness as they navigated slowly in the dwindling twilight, neither of them knowing this airport at night.

"Thanks again for the ride. It was great, and also a lot of fun being with you."

"Fun for me, too. Could you tell?"

"I think so. Maybe I should call you later tonight to make sure you get back to Bakersfield okay. Should I call you at the flight school or home?"

"Well, if you want to know the truth, I'll probably make it home fine. This aviation is no kid's game, you know, but I sorta' know what I'm doing."

"I noticed," said Shawn with a grin wide enough to be seen in the dark.

She handed him a business card: "Use my home number. I'll be there by 11 o'clock, so call anytime after that. I'll be waiting."

He liked the way it sounded: she'd be waiting.

Then, without any forethought, which was a good thing considering how clumsy Shawn was with things like this, he looked Corinne straight in the eye, and bent his head down the few inches necessary to lower himself to her lips, and he kissed her. She definitely kissed back.

* * * * *

After he watched the Arrow taxi out and takeoff on Runway 17, he lowered the top on the Edsel, and headed up River Highway. He climbed the grade and rounded the curves, passing Cheyenne's without stopping. At Mountain 99 Road, he turned right and drove until the pavement turned to gravel and then to dirt. He parked his car in his driveway next to the shed.

It was shortly after 10 o'clock when Shawn hauled the LX90 out of the shed. The 8-inch Schmidt-Cassegrain telescope was simple to setup and align, best done with two bright stars on opposite ends of the sky. Tonight, he selected Bentreus and Ganapellis, since they were easy to identify in their respective constellations, and far enough apart to provide good alignment for the telescope.

In the Astro-Controller, he selected "Guided Tour," and then "Tonight's Best." The first object that scrolled up was the Whirlpool Galaxy in the constellation of Telephanae. Shawn pushed the "Go-To" button, and the LX90 slewed towards the spiral galaxy. Live and up close, the Whirlpool popped out of the black sky in 3-D, an open-faced spiral interacting with its smaller companion galaxy. It was this 3-dimensional here-and-now that always enticed Shawn when he looked through a small telescope. It was nothing like the giant professional telescopes on the high mountains, but this was 100 percent live.

Shawn spent the next few minutes jumping from one object to another on the Astro-Controller's list of "Tonight's Best," including his favorite planetary nebula and two giant globular clusters. He might be only an amateur astronomer, but Shawn thoroughly enjoyed looking live at the deep-sky wonders of the night sky from his personal observatory, an 8-inch computer-driven telescope in his back yard.

By the time Shawn was ready to go back inside, the Pinwheel Galaxy was rising high enough in the northeast to clear the trees, and the big spiral rested in the notch of the mountains, so the view in that direction was open. The Pinwheel was the third big sister of the Heavenly Way and Zeus, another giant spiral galaxy of the local group. A punch of the "Go-To" button, and the LX90 crept towards the big spiral positioned low in the northeast, but slowly rising. The drive motors slowed further, as the telescope inched its way for the last minute of targeting. Then a gentle "beep" said: *I'm there*. In the 17-millimeter eyepiece, the Pinwheel Galaxy floated against a stark black background, slightly off-center. Shawn adjusted the drive buttons, bringing the object into the center of the eyepiece.

Whenever observing conditions permitted, Shawn turned to the Pinwheel Galaxy to remind him of what was about to happen. Here in the small field of his telescope was a spiral galaxy much like the Heavenly Way and Zeus. In the LX90, it was only a faint smudge, sometimes with hints of spiral arms when he viewed it under perfect atmospheric conditions. There were no longer three independent spiral galaxies in the local group, for only one individual now remained. Zeus and the Heavenly Way were already merging into a new and bigger giant elliptical galaxy, minus the spiral arms. Observing the Pinwheel live was an important reminder to Shawn that the galaxy his species had long called home was dramatically changing. *We used to be like this – now we're like that.*

Tonight, nearly directly overhead, sat the most amazing set of objects in the nighttime sky. Draping down from above, headed towards the southern horizon, Zeus crossed the Heavenly Way like a sword plunging inward, its giant spiral arms already penetrating into the outer reaches of Proteus' galaxy, the Double Stream.

At 11:15, Shawn stopped his tour of the night sky, and went inside to call Corinne. She answered on the first ring.

Planet Earth

The Milky Way Galaxy

Chapter 13

Life on Earth

4,646,926,985 AD – Planet Earth

(2016 on Planet Proteus)

The great minds of society had discussed the concepts of multiple universes and parallel worlds for nearly 5 billion years. After all that time, little was known about duplicate heavenly bodies within our own universe, and never had anything been verified. Until now.

The mysterious soil analyzed by archeophilosphers on Mauna Kea led to a revolution that swept the field of histophilosophy. That dirt provided the people of Earth (and their extended Miniverse) with proof of irregularities in history linked to Andromeda's P4531, the object Dr. Kane Suane was comprehensively investigating. The planet soon became a Miniverse-wide observational target that appeared to be exactly the same as Earth, probably right down to the individuals occupying it. So far, three irregularities in P4531's history had been confirmed, and two of these seemed to have had noticeable impact on the planet. Histophilosophers, working hand in hand with astrophilosophers and arch-rival archeophilosophers were able to observe sufficient planetary detail to determine this was a world almost exactly like the Earth, but out of sync in its timeline by almost 5 billion years. What was now happening on P4531 was nearly an exact copy of what had occurred on Earth in the almost-forgotten past.

P4531 had survived major alterations in its historical path, as compared to Earth. The Mount Palomar 200-inch telescope had been built on Mauna Kea in Hawaii, which indirectly set astronomy ahead several decades. The assassination of President Kennedy had significantly changed the course of history in the sociopolitical arena, in a different way than on Earth. A less-significant change regarding the survival of Amelia Earhart during her round-the-world flight seemed to have little impact on the course of history. There were other differences that had likely eluded histophilosophers, but overall P4531 and Earth seemed to follow each other in parallel, except their timelines were almost 5 billion years apart.

Arguments among histophilosophers included the unanswerable question of where these irregularities in history had actually occurred, on Earth or its distant sister. Since Earth was so far advanced in terms of the planet's timeline, the nod usually went to P4531 as the source of historic malfunction. After all, Earth had experienced their history first. On the other hand, as the argument went, people on Earth always thought they were the center of the universe, an assumption that was repeatedly shown to be wrong on larger and larger scales over time.

Meanwhile, as histophilosophers worried about the timelines, astrophilosophers like Kane Suane focused on the planetary details in the here-and-now. Techniques for faster-than-light communication had been established nearly a million years ago, and atmospheric sniffing was extremely advanced. Combined together, these technologies allowed the gathering of intricate information about P4531, with "images" (meaning extrapolated data portrayed on computer screens) down to a resolution of a mere 10-meters. Thus, scenes on this distant planet could be studied on the scale of small buildings, even specific rooms within structures. The simulated optical output was an ingenious technology combining atmospheric sniffing with waves of the type that could exceed the speed of light, like linking old-fashioned spectrometry with modern quantum computers. The result was a detailed visual "picture" derived from nearly a billion years of advancement in astrophilosophy.

Critics argued this technology painted pictures not even based on light waves, but the proof of its adequacy rested in the laboratory. Tests on Earth showed that the images created by these advanced technologies accurately approximated reality. As Kane often explained at his public lectures on the topic: "It might not be real, but the correlation with reality can't be argued. We've found a method of 'seeing' without eyes or even optics, and we've been doing this since a primitive device called radar was discovered in ancient times. Today we simply do it over distances of thousands of light-years, and we do it instantaneously."

Thus, Earth's astrophilosophers, in conjunction with their co-workers throughout the Miniverse, expended almost all of their research budgets on P4531, collecting an increasing volume of information about the planet. They knew nearly everything about this world, right down to the routine actions of its humanoid equivalents. Astrophilosophers admitted that the human element was extrapolated from the data, since 10-meter resolution didn't directly allow it. Although new observing techniques were still being developed, astrophilosophers were working with histophilosophers to successfully predict future actions of these beings based on known historic anomalies on P4531 and the Earth's own historic records – admittedly sketchy after the passage of almost 5 billion years. What Miniverse Prime hadn't yet decided was how or when to break the news to the people of P4531 – We are here, and we're ready to talk.

* * * * *

Dr. Kane Suane possessed a work ethic that was unequalled by others in his field. He loved his job, and he had no regrets, except when he thought of Dyanne Chertneggen. She was graduating from the University of the Arctic this year, and then would begin her family-oriented career, relegated to Earth's sub-science culture. She would maintain her designated place in the human zoo. It wouldn't be a bad life, just a basic one, not allowing contact with those like Kane who grew up in the real sciences.

Now that they'd both completed their student life, Kane would be unable to have physical contact with Dyanne, but communication through the Astronet was technically possible. Of course, it wasn't strictly legal, but many lovers in similar circumstances transgressed carefully on the Astronet, and took advantage of the government turning a blind eye as long as nothing further developed. After all, the Earth was still a tolerant place. Direct contact, however, was an entirely different matter.

Kane had recently come up with an idea that occupied his dreams, although he knew it had no direct application. In recent months, he had been studying an old science called genealogy, long abandoned as an area of interest in the Miniverse. With human beings so widely dispersed, there simply wasn't a lot of interest in studying distant family bonds now cultivated only in Earth's human zoo. Genealogy fell into the outskirts of scientific study, along with obsolete sciences like astrology and alchemy.

But Kane decided to study Dyanne's genealogy, as well as his own. Since they both grew up with roots on Earth, he could trace where Dyanne had come from, and that knowledge gave him hope. If he knew how he and Dyanne weren't directly linked in genealogical history (except as all humans were distantly linked), maybe it somehow could be changed. Exactly how wasn't clear to Kane, but at least his personal research on the subject allowed him to indirectly feel the presence of a woman he could never see again. So he spent hours on the Astronet researching their mutually exclusive genealogy.

Most of his time, of course, was devoted to his part in the discovery of the millennium, P4531. As the lead scientist on this project, he was now able to call the shots on his travel itinerary. World travel was quick and efficient, with rocketplanes flying suborbital arcs on their way to most destinations. The continents were rearranged now into Amasia, plate tectonics having changed the landscape like it did in prehistoric times when Pangaea huddled as a massive single continent. All the old continents were now clustered near the North Pole, where a historic Canadian territory (still called Yukon Region) was now nestled against Siberia. South America had slid up alongside North America's east coast. Within North America itself, the continental geography was similar to the era before Amasia began to assemble itself.

Living in the region called Mexican California, near the ancient site of the once-great city of Los Angeles, Kane would sometimes catch a rocketplane to Hawaii, a few hundred miles west, and then rent a heliotransport. Personal rental of a combined surface-air vehicle wasn't unusual these days, and the simplicity of the automated design allowed it to be an unlicensed activity. A helio on the road was completely computerized, following the glowing green stripe in the pavement right to your destination without operator intervention. In the air, navigation was point-to-point by EGPS, the flight controls operated by built-in computers. Most astrophilosophers couldn't afford such a luxury. Kane, however, was blessed with the financial backing of Miniverse Prime, which demonstrated how high up the scientific rank his stature had risen.

Heliotransports and roctketplanes were examples of the seeds of technology that had advanced so remarkably in recent millennia. In fact, the biggest leaps in society were related to the field of transportation and its computer interface. Within the sciences, astrophysics led the way as it transitioned to astrophilosophy over the past million years. Similarly, computer science allowed the harnessing of robots for most mundane tasks of life, with one exception being the human zoo on Earth. The zoo was retained more out of nostalgia than a real desire to see where the human experiment would lead.

The expansion of the species to other planets, with its exotic accomplishments in transportation and communication technology, far outpaced progress in other fields. In fact, the most surprising outcome in the advancement of the human race was how little had changed over billions of years. Colonies on other worlds were common, but the people lived and acted like their predecessors dating back to the beginning of the age of computers. Some of the lack of progress was due to the tremendous effort needed to propagate the species to other worlds. The endless time and energy put into colonization caused humans to take a hundred steps forward, only to be faced with ninety-nine steps back. New colonies were essential in keeping humans alive during Earth's period of dwindling resources and intense solar heating, but the process of colonization was civilization's own worst enemy. Except for modest advancements in space travel, the sciences and the humanities slipped backwards, and so did progress for the people of Earth.

Society had tumbled along the way. Once a population that seemed to be exploding out of sight, the Miniverse was now smaller in total Homo sapiens than ever before in modern history. The species was no longer dying, nor was it growing, except in the extent of real estate conquered. Earth had been dwindling in population for over a billion years, now that the sun was heating the surface past the balancing point for survival. Those few fortunate souls authorized to remain on Earth wore ground suits outdoors most of the time, yet it was still far better than anywhere else in the Miniverse. Living one's life almost entirely inside a dome or even inside a modern home on Earth led to stagnant development of the species.

Kane was one of the few who traveled freely, although he still spent most of his life inside a ground suit when he wasn't within a pressurized vessel or habitat. He considered himself privileged for his lifestyle, although it was always without Dyanne. He thought of her every day.

Chapter 14

Collision Committee

"Doctor Suane, please tell this committee what you've learned about the historic peculiarities detected regarding the object known as P4531, with emphasis on the importance of these irregularities, as you view them." The Chairwoman of the Milky Way Merger Committee, Senator Deleana Graham spoke into the microphone with a clarity that reflected her time in the Senate.

The Merger Committee, as they called themselves, represented the Senate of the States of Earth, which served as the legislative branch of Miniverse Prime, although many would argue that other worlds had little interest in the processes of government. Miniverse Prime ultimately called the shots on major policy decisions, but what the States of Earth recommended was usually enacted.

Each world had it's own informal government that made the important decisions regarding survival on distant planets, paying little attention to Earth, and Miniverse Prime seldom intervened. Even with nearly instantaneous communication, most worlds were still so far away that almost nothing decided in the Senate of the States of Earth directly affected them. These remote worlds were basically independent, but the senators went through the motions as if they were governing the entire Miniverse.

Most people called the Milky Way Merger Committee the "Collision Committee," in defiance of the long-standing government position that there was nothing to fear. With another galaxy hurtling at your home at roughly 400,000 kilometers per hour (and increasing), it's difficult not to be skeptical. Much of the public's bickering about the approach of Andromeda, including dissent by planets light-years away, was directed at the government scapegoat, the Collision Committee.

"We're still accumulating data," replied Kane. "It will be several more months before we can claim conclusively we know there are differences in the history of P4531 compared to Earth. Before proceeding, I'd like to make sure you know my statements today are based on preliminary data."

"Of course, Doctor," said Senator Graham, with an undisguised tone of frustration in her voice. She was a woman of action, not known among her colleagues as the "Senate Queen" for her patience. "We understand it's all preliminary, but you expect your results to be confirmed, don't you? So let's get on with it, so we can get things moving one way or another. If we don't make our decisions soon, we'll never get started in the right direction. We stand ready to deviate as the facts change."

Kane felt humbled and even insulted by the "Queen." He knew what he was talking about, so it was wasteful of everyone's time to start out with excuses. At age 31, he was still young and energetic, and could look forward to at least a century ahead of him as Earth's Astrophilosopher Laureate, if he didn't crumble to the government's pressure on days like today. What was needed was a simple summary of the truth, as he perceived it, not groveling in the face of authority. He knew his work, and he needed to place his confidence in himself.

"You're right Senator," said Kane. "I'm prepared to outline all of the details, and I'm confident they will be confirmed in due time. First, let me emphasize we've only discovered a few specific historic anomalies, and there are undoubtedly others, but most such irregularities provide minimum impact on the society established on P4531. These people are so similar to us you could call them exact duplicates of persons on Earth. Of course, none of us in this room have parallels on P4531, since its people are billions of years behind Earth in the cycle of time."

"Let me interrupt you for just a moment," intervened Senator Graham. "Let's make sure we're perfectly clear that you have evidence these beings actually exist. There must be a possibility your sniffing equipment is returning erroneous results."

"The sniffing equipment isn't our primary source of feedback, although it's helpful as a tool to verify our results. We're using a technology called wave pattern differentiation for most of our research, but atmospheric sniffing is a proven resource we rely on to confirm specific findings. Together, these two programs correlate nearly 100 percent, which is why I'm so certain of the results. For example, whenever we've turned to our sniffing data for verification of the existence of specific individuals, it matches the wave pattern differentiator every single time. The history irregularities are particularly important, since they allow us to verify that we're not seeing an exact mirror image of the Earth, somehow displayed back to us from an earlier epoch. That is, these irregularities are a valuable proof of the validity of our data." Kane paused for effect, and to give the senators a chance to ask questions, which he expected would be abundant today.

"The Chair recognizes Senator Terrax of Eurasia," stated Chairwoman Graham.

"Thank you, Senator Graham," replied the senator from Eurasia, who Kane knew as a friendly force from Terrax's previous visits to sniffer facilities. "Doctor Suane, please give us a perspective on how many specific individuals you've identified, and how they can be correlated with people on Earth when almost everything about the era of P4531 is long lost in Earth's historic records?"

"First, Senator Terrax, let me give you some specific numbers. We've clearly identified 148 individuals. Unfortunately, most of them are lost in history. However, we've been able to find a few specifically identified individuals from our historical records of this era. Contrary to what you might expect, there are a number of people who are still in Earth's records dating back nearly 5 billion years who are alive and well on P4531. They may be minor figures, but our records are quite good in some areas. For example, a few famous sports figures and some leaders of major countries are documented in our own historic records. So far, we've found seven individuals in these categories, and we've confirmed they're exact duplicates of Earth's historic figures, at least as much as we still know about them today.

"For each of these seven people, the correlation between what we've found and what we have in Earth's historic records is flawless. That complete lack of contradiction causes me to believe we're on the right track. These were blind tests, by the way, meaning we gathered the information based on names alone, and then checked what we found only after gathering data from P4531. The match was perfect every time. We even tried looking at traits very difficult to measure, such as personality types and sexual orientation, and even there we found good correlation.

"Let me give you one more example regarding parallels with Earth's records. Some of the differences in P4531's timeline when compared with Earth have had a minor impact on conditions on that planet, but they're valuable evidence our histophilosophers are on the right track. As you know, our heliotransport technology grew out of ancient machinery, automobiles and helicopters. In the case of automobiles, there's a lot of documentation in Earth's records about ancient wheeled transportation, so we can compare what we 'see' on P4531 to our own historic records. P4531 currently occupies the year 2016 AD, and we expected to find specific models of automobiles on their roads. What we've found, instead, are vehicles approximating the designs we had on Earth in 2016, but not exactly the same. Which says something changed in the automobile industry on P4531 – not significant to the overall situation, but such changes offer proof we're not looking at ourselves in the past. If' we had found 'images' that were exactly the same, we'd be suspicious of our techniques of wave pattern differentiation and atmospheric sniffing. In other words, a minor difference in the two planets is further confirmation of the accuracy of our research."

Again, Kane paused, knowing he had to give these politicians their moments in the spotlight. If they were going to accept what he was saying, he needed to allow them time to shine in the public mediavision being beamed to all parts of the Miniverse.

"So this topic of personal transport vehicles is a specific area you're continuing to investigate?" asked Senator Terrax, giving his best public relations smile for the mediavision transmitter.

Kane composed his thoughts before replying. He didn't want to lose an important ally like Senator Terrax, but he also didn't feel further details regarding automotive design were a valuable direction for his testimony.

"As a matter of fact, we've decided to abandon that particular avenue of research – meaning automobile design variations – since it's probably ingrained in historic details that would take time away from other more- important areas we're pursuing. I give it as an example only because it validates our research methods. And it also provides this committee, hopefully, with a feeling of the kinds of details we're capable of investigating."

"The Chair recognizes Senator Hao Zhi Lan of Sino Republics."

"Thank you. I'd like to ask you, Doctor Suane, do these 'pictures' of this planet show you things in video format regarding specific individuals, including facial details and that sort of thing?"

"Let me clarify about the images we see, Senator. The smallest detail we're able to discern involves objects approximately 10-meters in breadth, so that obviously rules out facial features or even being able to directly image individuals our size. However, I remind you that what we're 'seeing' isn't a real image but a conjured rendition based on inputs from our wave pattern differentiator and computerized outputs. Quantum computers are very efficient at this task, and we thus 'see' objects that are both interpolated and extrapolated to produce an image we're familiar with in everyday life. I apologize for getting technical here, but it's a very involved process that provides realistic views of what's going on at a very small scale. So, to summarize, we do 'see' details as fine as facial features, and they are in moving video format, but we always need to keep in mind it's a rendering of what we would see if we were actually in the same room with these people. I think it can be considered quite accurate, however, and we hope our technology will advance quickly to the point where we'll be able to bring the overall resolution down a lot further. Then facial details, for example, can be confirmed."

"We rely on your profound experience in this area, Doctor,' replied Senator Lan. "I assume, in the case of the seven sports heroes and political leaders that you're able to confirm personal features as well as names and compare them to what we know from our own historic records."

"That's correct, Senator. In each case, the correlation was exact."

"And this was all conducted in real time," replied the senator from the Sino Republics. "There was no time lag between what you're looking at and the present day."

"A slight lag, of only a few seconds, due to computer processing time. Otherwise, it can be considered real time with no delay."

"Thank you, Doctor Suane. No further questions."

"Senators, we're running short on time due to the upcoming vote on Miniverse health reform in the Senate chamber," said Chairwoman Deleana Graham. "I'll accept one more question from…" She looked around and found three hands in the air. "The Chair recognizes Senator Damond Kerill of Mars."

Mars was the only planet other than Earth that provided Senate representatives to the States of Earth, which said a lot about who supported the government that ran the Miniverse. Damond Kerill seldom threw his weight behind most bills affecting Miniverse worlds, because he found most of the proposals were counterproductive to the needs of Mars and the other colonies. His attitude favored a hands-off government in all matters involving colonies, and he took it upon himself to speak for all the planets beyond Earth. Which was a bit contradictory, considering the fact that Mars tried so hard to emulate Earth's lifestyles.

Kane knew Damond Kerill would be a stumbling block today. If Chairwoman Graham was progressive, Senator Damond Kerill could be considered regressive.

"Thank you for testifying today, Doctor Suane. I'd like to ask how you recommend we handle the forthcoming problem of the transition onto P4531 for the people of Earth and those Miniverse planets that wish to participate. That is, to start with, how would it be best to contact the beings of P4531, and when should we do it."

Kane expected this. If it hadn't come up from the questions of one of the senators, he'd planned to address it in his closing remarks. So he wasn't caught off guard, but he still wasn't sure how he should express his recommendations on this issue. In preparing for the committee meeting, he had finally decided to let his conscience guide him when the time came. And now was the time.

"Senator Kerill, I appreciate this committee's concern with the issue of initial contact with these beings and all of the discussion that's gone on previously about the proposed 'Jump-Off' scenario. First, let me remind you that the opportunity to exercise such a plan, if you do decide to progress in that direction, won't be available for at very long time. Let me put it into perspective.

"If we make some very liberal assumptions regarding the collision of our galaxy with Andromeda, and include our best-case projections about the development of our space travel technology in the future, it will be at least several million years before Earth is close enough to P4531 to allow the movement of our people to that planet. Presently, we can operate only 100 light-years away from Earth, which is a drop in the bucket compared to the distance to P4531, which is currently about 15,000 light-years from Earth. Orbits of both planets will be deflected by the collision, but not enough to significantly influence these figures."

"We prefer to call it a merger, rather than a collision," interrupted Senator Kerill. He was half-joking, but it made for a good media moment.

"My apologies, Senator. You're right, it's really more of a merger than a collision, but it's still a long way in the future. So that makes you wonder whether it's best contact this alien intelligence now. After all, a lot can happen in even a thousand years, so why upset a functioning society on P4531 for something that may never come to pass."

Kane had barely paused when Senator Kerill interrupted: "But we need to prepare ourselves and this other planet, if we intend to accomplish a Jump-Off scenario," he said, looking more at the mediavision transmitter than Kane. "It's not a minor undertaking to prepare two planet-wide populations for an exchange of humanity like this. To say nothing of our outlying Miniverse planets that will be involved, too. And we must not forget that we don't have a million years – Earth will be heated to oblivion by then. So our space technology will just have to be developed much faster, which all of us seem to agree upon. This committee is working closely with the Appropriations Committee in that regard."

"But even the scale of preparation needed for Jump-Off won't take us millions or even thousands of years," countered Kane. "I reiterate – a lot can happen in that period of time."

"Give us some examples," challenged the Senator.

"Well, for one thing, they could blow themselves up long before then. Or, even more likely, something might happen that no one in this room could possibly predict. In fact, considering the pace of things in astrophilosophy, I'd be willing to bet on it."

◊ ◊ ◊ ◊ ◊ ◊

Planet Proteus

The Andromeda Galaxy

Chapter 15

Feeding the Flames

September 14, 2017

Shawn's tin boat bobbed in the Frog Pond breeze, gently swaying as he shifted back in his seat and dialed the satellite connection on his mini-laptop. It was a warm day for September, and Shawn's blond curls were damp under his ball cap. He wore a too-warm long sleeve T-shirt with *Global Warming – It's Hot!* on the front. His chest and armpits were sweating, but the shirt helped keep the bugs away, as did his thick cargo pants. Wool socks extending above his low-cut hiking boots also helped, but there was really no true reprieve during bug season.

"Hey, Shaman!" said Fatius when he picked up the phone.

This satellite line was only semi-secure, but neither of the two friends gave it any concern. Proteus was still a planet not focused on the galactic collision or the people who were studying it. Fatius had sometimes called Shawn on his totally unsecured cell phone, and they'd openly talked about advances in the pinging technology being pursued by the shaman in India.

"Hey, Fat! Whas'-up?"

"Just sitting here my friend, watching the breakers roll in and waiting for your call. At the lake today?"

"Beauty of a day here, but a little smoky. There's a fire to the north, and the winds aloft are bringing me an ugly cloud. So far, the surface wind is from the south, so there's no real danger. Anyway, that stuff at CERN yesterday sure got my attention. What do you make of it?"

"Not my area of expertise, buddy, but we've known the Higgs boson exists since 2012, although now those European fellows are getting fancier about it. CERN's energy output keeps going up, and the technology improves at the same time, so that puts them in the sweet spot. If the 'God Particle' really gives other particles mass, I'd say it's worth our investigation, but how do you really know?"

"That's exactly the point, Fat. If it's more of a field than a particle, which sounds logical to me, then we can ask some mighty big questions. Like: 'What if the Higgs Field messed up occasionally, and failed to give a particle mass?' Wouldn't that mean we'd have a candidate for faster-than-light travel? By the way, I hate when the press calls it the 'God Particle.'"

"Sounds intriguing, Shawn, but what's the chances of the Higgs Field failing now and then. That's not any different from saying gravity fails here and there, but there's certainly no evidence over eons of study. But if something went suddenly massless, it would be an invitation for us to toss it somewhere faster than light. Einstein would probably say the speed limit would go away completely. In other words, instantaneous."

"Which is exactly what we're looking for, Fat. If we could harness it, we've solved the communication time warp. Now, if we could only find someone to communicate with."

"Lots of open questions," said Fatius. "But let's tackle them together, my Bruin friend. And while we're at it, let's see if we can tie this into the latest from Leiden University involving extrasolar planet atmospheres."

"Okay, I'll get started in that direction here at Frog Pond, when I'm not busy gawking at the scenery or swatting bugs."

Astronomers at Leiden University in the Netherlands had just announced an enhanced capability for detecting atmospheric gases from extrasolar planets. Using the Very Large Telescope in Chile, they were studying hot planets, close enough to their suns to allow astronomers to extract a spectrum in the infrared. It only worked, so far, for the gas-giant planets so close to their sun that the atmosphere was heated to tremendous temperatures, but the technology was rapidly improving. Leiden scientists had used the VLT to detect carbon monoxide in the atmosphere of several "hot giants." They selected carbon monoxide for their early studies since it generates a strong spectroscopic footprint in the near infrared. Now they were moving on to methane and water vapor. If the technology could be improved to include Proteus-sized objects farther from their suns, it could be a major step past India's research into pinging technology. Of course, seeing planetary details didn't give the whole picture. There was still the time-delay problem.

"Okay, Shawn, I'll look into it from my end. Let's compare notes in a few days. Thank God for the God Particle."

* * * * *

That night, as Shawn settled into his sleeping bag in the Snow Cabin, the wind shifted. It was part of a normal mountain breeze, caused by the high desert of Kern Valley cooling slower than the mountaintops near Frog Pond. The resulting local low pressure that developed in the valley, drew air down from the mountains. This routine summer effect, called a mountain breeze, grew more substantial than normal this night, probably related to the late summer temperature extremes in the Sierra Nevada. Air poured violently down past Frog Pong, headed for Kernville. The door of the cabin rattled, awakening Shawn, and drawing in smoke from the nearby forest fire. Now, here on the surface, wind was blowing the giant fire closer to the cabin, and much faster than Shawn would have guessed. When he awoke in the morning, the air was filled with smoke in all directions, and he thought he saw an orange glow to the north.

He packed up quickly, loaded his Energoe, and started down the trail. From here in the mountains, it was almost direct line of sight to Kernville, and he was able to listen to the local AM radio station through the mini-speakers in his helmet. The station was transmitting live from the quickly-formed fire base at Kern Valley Airport, reporting on the recently arrived firefighting aircraft. Civilian tankers and helicopters would work from here, but the runway allowed only smaller aircraft. The bigger planes would be based at Bakersfield, with the biggest of the big flying out of Point Mugu, 150 miles to the southwest. At Mugu, Air National Guard C-130's equipped with MAFFS equipment would be the biggest aerial asset, carrying a mixture of 3000 gallons of water and fire retardant on each drop. The Modular Airborne Fire Fighting

System had been around for over 30 years, and the current MAFFS equipment was a step up with more efficient water bombardments using sophisticated C-130's, the high-tech J-Model.

Military C-130's weren't normally used on a fire until "surge capacity" was reached. At that point, when civilian tankers are exhausted, the four-engine C-130 Hercules turboprops left Point Mugu. However, in this case, with the fire developing so rapidly and already threatening Kernville and maybe even Bakersfield, government officials declared surge capacity while tanker bases were still being established. The fire was that big, having grown from a nonthreatening blaze in the high mountains yesterday to an enormous fire encroaching on population centers this morning. Overnight, everything had changed.

Shawn rode down the wilderness trail connecting the cabin to Mountain Main. The overhanging trees gave him no opportunity to stop and use his satellite phone to check on conditions in Kernville. As good as satellite technology had become, it was still line-of-sight, and trees got in the way. But he rode with his helmet speakers connected to his portable radio, listening to firefighting progress reports. Airplanes and helicopters were already taking off from Kern Valley Airport, and he might see them overhead soon. They would try to cut off the fire as it raged down the mountain towards Kernville. The path of the fire, gleaned from aerial photos, indicated it would rush past Frog Pond, and Shawn held little hope the Snow Cabin would be spared.

Similarly, the radio reports indicated his home near River Highway was in danger, the fire rushing nearly headlong in that exact direction. Firemen on the ground might be able to make a stand there, but their resources would need to be concentrated at the population center of Kernville, so fire trucks on Mountain 99 Road would be severely limited. The only good news was that fires like this burned so fast they sometimes skipped over one house only to devastate the homes next to it. It had happened elsewhere, but nothing said it would happen here.

Overhead, Shawn spotted a firefighting aircraft, an old civilian tanker, maybe a converted military airplane. Then he saw a big helicopter with a low-slung bucket. Fighting forest fires with buckets seemed a futile cause, but it was a reasonable way to attack small hot spots that could change the course of the blaze.

Shortly after 10 o'clock, after nearly beating himself to death on the rough trail at speeds he couldn't normally muster, he came to the intersection with Mountain Main. This was the first and only time he'd ever navigated down from the Snow Cabin without stopping at least for a breather or two. Today, there was no time for such luxuries.

He turned right at the intersection, now heading west towards his house near the junction with River Highway. Behind him to the east and north was the glow of bright orange flames cresting the ridges. Surely he could outrun this fire on his bike, especially on a wide forest road like this, but then again the fire seemed ominously closer than it had been before he left the cabin.

He could increase his speed now, and he felt his safety wasn't in doubt. His home, on the other hand, was threatened in a very real way. Hopefully, he'd have time to gather some of his most cherished possessions, load them into the Edsel, and drive down River Highway before the fire outpaced him. But smoke could easily surround him, severely limiting visibility on the road, and it undoubtedly was nearly the same all the way down to Kernville. It would be slow going, maybe more so in the Edsel than on his Energoe.

As he came within a mile of his house, just before the spot where the dirt road widened, but well before it turned into gravel, he saw it in the western sky ahead. A big C-130 Hercules was dropping dangerously low, flying north along the Kern River, going upstream as if looking for a place to turn around. Shawn knew there were no such places north of here, so the airplane would need to climb higher to turn or go all the way to the intersection leading to Sherman Pass before reversing course. Even then, it would be an extreme maneuver for an airplane, especially one as big as a Herk.

The low-flying C-130 disappeared behind a cloud of smoke just as it passed the area where Shawn knew his house stood. He heard the roar reverberate off the mountain slopes on the other side of the river, sounding closer than it was. The path of the aircraft was taking it farther from the fire, so Shawn assumed it would turn around and head south for a fire retardant drop or continue up the river and then up and over the mountains near Sherman Pass. From there, it could fly back down to the fire from the north, but he could see no sense in that. Maybe it would somehow turn around and drop near his house on its trip back down the river.

Normally, small spotter planes led the water tankers, but Shawn saw no such aircraft. Today might be different – available resources could be so overloaded that the C-130 was surveying its target on the trip up the river, then planning to execute the water drop after somehow turning around. An interesting scenario, but Shawn knew little about firefighting. He only knew the Snow Cabin was probably already burned to the ground, and his house was severely threatened.

Shawn pulled into his driveway just as he heard the C-130 rushing back again from the north. It approached rapidly, now down even lower, 200 feet above the ground at the most. And it was headed directly towards him. Maybe this was his lucky day, and the big Herk was planning its fire retardant drop at the biggest little outpost of human activity in this area north of Kernville, a few houses in a clearing on Mountain 99 Road. He hoped and hoped, and looked up praying to see the water pour downward. In just a few more seconds the C-130 roared directly overhead and a huge cloud of red mist suddenly bellowed from the rear of the aircraft. For a full ten seconds, the brilliant cloud surged out of the airplane, and started slowly downward, a mixture of water and red Phos-Chek, used as a fire retardant. It was a somewhat dangerous cloud, not to be breathed, but it was also his savior. As the cloud floated towards the ground, Shawn wisely took shelter inside his shed, waiting for the ground to become covered. When he stepped outside again, everything within sight was covered with mucky red Phos-Chek – the trees, the grass, the dirt road, and his house. The C-130, based on what Shawn surmised to be a direct hit on its target, had saved his home and those of his nearby neighbors.

While rushing around inside his house gathering some possessions to take with him, Shawn suddenly wondered how much of a coincidence this was. When it came to modern shamans, Washington could react quickly when necessary. Was his house saved because of specific intervention, or was it merely a coincidence. He didn't want to think a load of fire retardant was used specifically to save his home, and he wished it was just one of those things. But whatever the case, he was grateful to the skill of the C-130 pilots. And he was sure glad they'd found a place to turn around.

Chapter 16

Home is Where a Shaman Lives

A second C-130 came a half hour after the first, as Shawn was slowly making his way through the smoke, down River Highway in his red Edsel. The top was rolled up, with the air conditioner cycled off and then back on in a battle to find breathable air that wasn't stifling. He saw the Herk headed north up the Kern River, and it then somehow turned around and came back down River Highway a few minutes later, passing the Edsel, now safely climbing after its drop. A second load of soggy red fire retardant would cover every house in his block. Shawn's home would survive the flames, along with all the houses on Mountain 99 Road.

The forest fire hit the intersection almost dead center right after the second C-130 drop, then veered south to follow the river canyon to Kernville, where it met a two-pronged defense, firefighters on the ground and a concentrated aerial assault from the fire base at Kern Valley Airport.

Getting tankers in and out of the airport for their supply of water and fire retardant became a serious problem after the heavy smoke engulfed the valley, bringing visibility to nearly zero. But the C-130's from Point Mugu and civilian tankers from Bakersfield continued without letup until the flames were finally subdued on the banks of Lake Isabella the next morning, although the fire would continue to burn under semblance of control for the next three days. Ground units managed to hold the line around the town of Kernville, and only three structures were lost in flames that jumped over the barrier of fire trucks. Two outlying homes were also burned, and one death was attributed to the fire. A man fleeing from the approaching flames near his home adjacent to Cheyenne's went off the highway and down the embankment to the Kern River below. All in all, the Forest Service after-action report declared the firefighting effort a major success against tremendous odds.

When Shawn couldn't reach Corinne on her cell, he became concerned. She'd been airborne on and off out of Fresno Airport, where she'd taken one of her students in a company Cessna 172 the day the out-of-control fireball rolled down River Highway. When the news of the fire broke on TV, she was safe and sound in the Fresno corporate terminal, where news media were huddled. They conjectured that the fire might jump the ridge to Bakersfield, so she elected to stay in Fresno with the Cessna and her student, continuing to operate in high visibility skies while watching the ominous cloud to the southeast. She stayed another day, with more flight training from Fresno the next morning.

Corinne knew Shawn was at Frog Pond, and worried endlessly, but her cell phone coverage went down with a host of other local telecoms when the fire destroyed towers in several remote areas. Telephone circuits across the network were quickly destroyed by a combination of increased call volumes during the crisis coupled with the reduced number of relay towers. The problem was so acute that it indirectly affected an estimated 5000 square miles, a good chunk of south and central California.

Shawn did manage to get through to Corinne's flight school in Bakersfield, only to be told she'd headed north, with her current location unknown. He knew her independent nature, and figured it would see her through without threat to her safety. But it would be nice to know where she was.

"What a relief," he said, when he finally reached her in Fresno, using his satellite phone. "You okay?"

"Well, Terrance, my infamous student, tried to kill me yesterday, but it happens all the time. Other than that, all is well. But I've been worrying about you. Where are you?"

"Back home now. All the houses here were saved by C-130's. Quite an airplane."

"Probably women pilots, I'd guess. What about Frog Pond."

"Don't know. But I'm going back up there on Friday to find out. Worse case scenario – the cabin is burned to the ground. But it can be replaced. Getting the tin boat up there was just a test to prepare me for this. If I need to, I can haul building materials on a trailer behind my Energoe, and use the logs already there, if there are any unburned ones left."

"You'll have a hard time manufacturing glass windows out of cedar logs. Just imagine how much you'll have to bring in."

"You know, the government might agree to help. After all, the old Snow Cabin was pretty historic, as well as a shelter for hikers. Maybe they'll helicopter some things in for me. At the very least, they may allow me to cut some trees to rebuild it. I can't imagine hauling lumber all that way."

"I can get Friday off, so I'm available, in case you're wondering."

"Oh," replied Shawn.

No, he hadn't wondered, since he didn't think Corinne would want to make the trip. She'd been to the Snow Cabin once, and really enjoyed herself, but riding double on an Energoe wasn't easy on the rough trail up from the intersection with Mountain Main. He hadn't considered inviting her under conditions like this.

"So can I go?" asked Corinne. "I promise not to be a back-seat driver."

"Sure, that'd be great," replied Shawn. "But you'll have to hold on tight, because I drive like a maniac."

"Which is exactly how I like to hold on. In fact, my theory is you drive like a maniac when I'm on the back so I have to hold on tight."

"Well, it's true," joked Shawn. "I do that a lot these days," said Shawn. "Why stop now?"

* * * * *

Shawn picked her up at Kern Valley Airport on Thursday afternoon in his Edsel, and they drove to town for an ice cream cone to-go, a familiar pattern they both liked. Then, with the top down on the red classic, they headed up River Highway, stopping at Cheyenne's for an early dinner.

"Nothing like dessert before our main meal," said Corinne, finishing her ice cream as they pulled into Cheyenne's dirt parking lot.

Shawn had finished his cone a mile back, but Corinne liked to enjoy things slowly. It was one of their minor differences. Over the past year, they'd discovered that the little things they could argue about in jest were far exceeded by how much alike they were on the big things. They got along extremely well, and these days they enjoyed their relationship with an increasing sense of what was ahead. Ever since their first kiss at the airport, they'd been nearly inseparable, regardless of jobs that took them in different directions. They both knew this was turning serious. But for now, they were enjoying things as two single people sharing important slices of their own worlds, Corinne as a flight instructor and Shawn as whatever-it-is he does.

Corinne had already guessed that Shawn was a government shaman. Their intimacy provided her access to a lot of secrets Shawn wouldn't share with anyone else, not even his parents. But Shawn kept to the official doctrine of keeping his job as much of a secret as he could, under the circumstances, and Corinne never pried, although she knew enough to put two and two together.

"Do we need to take anything extra this time?" asked Corinne between swigs of her beer at Cheyenne's. "If the cabin burned down, we'll need a tent, I suppose."

"The weather's still warm, even at night," said Shawn. "But there are wolves in the area, so it's best to be under cover. I've got a tent on my packing list, since I always carry it in case I get stranded on the trail. Its pretty much business as usual, but I'm taking some heavy duty tools, in case we need to move things around."

Shawn always carried his chainsaw on the Energoe, since he might need it for a fallen tree on the trail, and he always had his sleeping bag and air mattress, even when sleeping inside the cabin. Corinne had her own sleeping bag and ground pad, and those plus the extra tools would pretty much max out the Energoe. It could haul almost unlimited weight, but there was only so much cargo space, especially with Corinne on the back. The rack would be loaded high in front.

"Maybe I'll leave my mini-laptop home," added Shawn. "With you there, I won't spend a lot of time working."

"And remind me," said Corinne, looking him straight in the eye. "What exactly is your line of work?"

Shawn laughed, and Corinne joined in. Cherokee broke loose from the table she was serving, and came over to see what was going on.

"Hey, kids, what's happening here? Too many beers tonight?"

"Not enough," replied Corinne, still laughing. "Mr. Does-It-All has to drink root beer tonight, since he's taking his favorite woman up River Highway, but I'll take another."

"One more beer, coming up," replied Cherokee. "How does he do it, Cory? I mean what about the lucky break that saved his house. Now that was something."

"Something indeed," replied Shawn. "A bit of luck, and lot of box canyon talent for those C-130 guys."

"Gals," corrected Corinne. "Just like how he found me. Another lucky break, but who's complaining?"

"There was no luck involved," said Shawn. "You won me over with your sexy flight suit."

"Oh, you mean my flying pajamas. They're cool looking, aren't they? Or maybe the government intervened again to give you what they thought you wanted, a flight instructor who is a terror on wings."

"The government?" said Shawn, giving Corinne a be-careful look. Sometimes with best friends like Cherokee, they kidded together, but he should be more careful. The government had kept their side of the bargain, and he needed to keep his.

"You know what I mean," said Corinne with a lilt in her voice. "Surely you know the government contacted me years ago, and said to seduce you, because it's what you needed. Just me and you, your little government whore."

Shawn was shocked by what Corinne said, even if she had one beer too many (meaning one). It wasn't particularly funny, since he thought the government might take such action if a shaman requested it. The government as pimps was almost as disgusting as thinking of Corinne as a whore. But there was little his GC Project status wouldn't allow, if he asked for it.

"Mr. Shaman-on-a-Pond," said Cherokee. "How did the cabin do through all this, anyway?"

Corinne, Farley, and Cherokee were the only ones who kidded like this, and Shawn would never give them confirmation of his shaman status, but between them it was pretty much understood. Tonight was going way too far, particularly in a place as public as Cheyenne's. Cherokee had given him a way out, and he immediately pounced on it.

"Not sure," replied Shawn. "Cory and I are going up to Frog Pond tomorrow. I'm expecting that the cabin is gone, and the whole area charred and ugly, at least for now. It'll recover though, and I might be able to rebuild the cabin. At least it'll be worth a try."

"Let me make a prediction," said Cherokee. "When you get there, the fire has devastated everything. But the cabin has been spared. Somehow the government made the fire jump right over it."

* * * * *

When Shawn and Cory arrived at Frog Pond the next afternoon, it was immediately obvious that Cherokee's prediction was wrong. The cabin was gone.

The fire was so hot that the only remaining evidence of the building was its four corner cement posts, sticking up out of the ground a few inches, and a few pieces of twisted metal. The tin boat was in such bad shape it would need to be replaced, aluminum contorted by the fierce heat that ravaged the area. The outboard motor was nothing more than a chunk of melted metal, the engine's leg lying on the ground behind the wreckage of the boat, with the charred metal propeller dug into the ground.

The pond was, of course, entirely unscathed, yet bigger looking now that all of the trees were burned to the ground. It would be years before nature returned the small lake to its original condition, but that would come in time. While the environment did its work, Shawn planned to do his. It would take two full years of hard work to restore the cabin, but he'd do it. As a shaman, it could even be considered therapeutic, as a reminder of the power of nature in both its good and bad moods. On a cosmic scale, the collision of two galaxies was somewhat similar.

* * * * *

Shawn was at home when he phoned Fatius, using the computer in his living room as a videophone. When the call connected, Shawn noticed on the display that Fatius was sitting at his kitchen table in his condo, the fuselage of a model airplane and some unassembled parts off to the side.

"Hey, shaman. You rang?" said Fatius.

"Hi Fat. Building another supersonic fighter?"

"I'm working on a faster-than-light drone that will serve as the prototype for the real thing," he replied.

"That'll be helpful. Say, before I was interrupted by a forest fire, I came up with some stuff that might interest you."

"What a terrible loss," replied Fatius over the videophone link. He looked sincerely saddened by the fire, knowing how much the cabin at Frog Pond meant to Shawn.

"Everything will grow again, even the cabin and the tin boat, if I have anything to say about it."

"You need the boat, man! That's how we did our best work. You in that little boat and me on the balcony sipping a martini."

"I didn't know you were a drinker," said Shawn.

"I'm not. But if I was, I'd definitely drink dry martinis."

"Anyway, both the Netherlands' work on extrasolar planets and the Higgs particle are topics I consider hot. The Higgs field in particular seems like a direct course to instantaneous communications. Even if failures of the field don't occur in nature, we might be able to coerce them. With high enough energies, CERN or any of the other supercolliders should be able to turn off the Higgs field momentarily, at least long enough to get a signal out to planets in Zeus. Maybe a blanket approach, like the early attempts to find ET, sending data blind and hoping someone intercepts it."

"And what if they do?" said Fatius, playing the part he knew was best tonight.

They often did this, bouncing ideas off each other, with one playing the aggressive role like a salesman, and the other keeping the flow going with a series of questions, like a reluctant customer. Sometimes what worked best was a negative approach by the customer, hitting the concept with any ammunition he could muster. Then the salesman would have to strike back with his most fine-tuned sales pitch, an action that often pushed things up a notch.

"If someone does intercept the signal, since it's instantaneous both ways, we get a dialogue going," said Shawn. "And who knows what we might learn from that."

"But how do we know they already have the technology to communicate instantaneously? If they haven't progressed that far, they hear what we say, but can't reply. End of story."

"Not so, Fat, because we send the technology to them as part of the initial message: 'Here we are. Now here's how you answer us.'"

"Of course, to come down off my negative soapbox for a moment, that's not even a worry, is it?" said Fatius, smiling into the camera, as if he could solve the dilemma right here and now.

"What do you mean?" asked Shawn.

"Well, you know the statistic. What are the chances we'll make contact with a civilization less advanced than us. Not a snowball's chance in hell, considering how many years lie ahead in technological advancement compared to what a short distance we've come so far. It's only been a few hundred years for us since the machine age. Check back in a million years, or maybe a billion, and what do you expect to find?"

"Well, you're right, Fat. They'll undoubtedly be more advanced than us, if they haven't already blown themselves up."

"And if they have, my dear shaman, we transmit, and they never even receive. So we move on to the next planet."

"You know, this all goes back to the big picture, doesn't it?" said Shawn.

"You mean that videophone picture of you on my screen, looking like you're up way too late on the west coast. What the heck time do you think it is here?"

"Oh, I guess it's past 2 am there. How do you put up with me?"

"I love you for your mind, not your body."

"Seriously, we've gotta' ask the right questions – that's the big picture. What do we really hope to accomplish for the GC Project by communicating with other planets? What does this have to do with the collision?"

"It has a lot to do with the collision," replied Fatius, looking wide-awake at 2 am. "For one thing, if we can make contact, we can add tremendously to our technology, probably even immediately extend our lifespans, all while passing near an advanced civilization in another galaxy. We start the dialogue, which gets easier to do the closer we get to Zeus, and continue it right on through."

"You're right, of course," said Shawn. "Global warming is the example I always think about. Solved in an instant – what an advancement for all of the people of Proteus, just because we found an intelligence near enough to us to talk."

"Of course, there's the other side of the coin, too," noted Fatius. "If they're so damned advanced, maybe that means they've expended almost all of their own natural resources. Or if they have all that advanced technology, it probably means their planet and their sun are getting old. So they'll be looking for a place to hop off when we pass. I say, using my best negative attitude, let's just keep our mouths shut. Broadcasting to another galaxy may be like looking for a girlfriend, only to discover she's a deadly monster."

"Even that might give us a way out," suggested Shawn.

"Such as?" asked Fatius, now kicked back in his chair, looking proud of himself.

"Well, if we beam our signal to everybody, maybe we'll find more than one suitor. Then, if we meet the monster you imagine, we play matchmaker. If we don't want them to jump aboard, maybe we can find them another planet that looks even better."

Chapter 17

The President in Dallas

November 22, 1963

President Kennedy was at his prime. Everybody in the country felt close to him, either loving or hating him. There was little middle ground. The early sixties were an exciting time in Proteus history, and John F. Kennedy was right in the middle of it all. Today, as his motorcade entered Dealey Plaza, he rode with his wife, Jackie, and Texas Governor John Connally and his wife, Nellie. They sat propped high in back of the limousine convertible, waving to the crowd as the motorcade meandered slowly from Dallas Love Field to the Trade Mart, a route selected to provide maximum exposure to the city's crowds. The President was positioned farthest to the rear on the right side, just above the rear fender, riding with a comfortable smile, his arm resting on the sill of the rolled-down window. The crowds cheered and the President waved with wide sweeps of his thin arms.

Nellie Connally turned to President Kennedy, who was sitting behind her and on the opposite side of the vehicle, and commented: "Mr. President, you can't say Dallas doesn't love you."

The President grinned and shook his head. He was obviously enjoying the enthusiastic crowd.

Passing the Texas School Book Depository and continuing down Elm Street, three gunshots rang out over a brief period. Most witnesses on the scene, at first, thought it was firecrackers or a vehicle backfiring. Jackie on the left side of the limousine, next to her husband, turned her head instantly to the right, where she saw John F. Kennedy holding his elbows and clenched fists in front of his face. She leaned across the rear seat to try to help him.

The Governor also turned his head to the right towards the sound of the first shot, and then quickly turned forward again, a reflex reaction. That's when he was hit by a bullet in the right side of his upper back. In his pain, John Connally shouted: "Oh, no, no, no! My God! They're going to kill us all!"

A second shot, and then a third right behind it! The limousine's rear interior was now covered with skull fragments, brain matter, and blood. The President was dead, and Governor Connally seriously injured.

Jackie wasn't acting rationally, as she began to climb out of the limousine onto the trunk, maybe trying to gather her husband's brain matter. As she climbed back into the back seat, she yelled: "They've killed my husband! I have his brains in my hand."

A secret service agent from the car following behind them jumped off the running board, and ran forward to the President's car, leaping onto the trunk. The limousine sped off towards Parkland Memorial Hospital.

* * * * *

Meanwhile, in another limousine farther back, Lyndon B. Johnson rode in a disgruntled mood. Beside him, his wife "Lady Bird" was trying to enjoy herself, waving at the passionate crowd. Of course, their passion was for the president, not LBJ, which is why his limousine was positioned so far behind.

Up until now, Johnson's political career had been a two-stage act, with a very successful showing in the U.S. Senate, followed by a lackluster stint as Vice President of the United States. Before being elected VP in 1960 (which means drawn in on the coattails of John F. Kennedy), he was one of the most powerful men in the nation. Twelve impressive years in the Senate, followed by the second act – the official representative of the President at official ceremonies, mostly funerals.

He was close to depression, for there seemed no exit from where this was heading. He couldn't go back to the Senate, even if he decided to do so, for the voting public would never reelect him after his uninspired showing as Vice President. Then again, the real job of this political position was to serve as the President's footman, riding far in the back seat. Today he was doing exactly that, mumbling to himself in the back seat of a limousine, a long way behind his boss, the President.

When shots rang out in front of him, he too thought it was a firecracker. Then a second, and then a third. He leaned forward, now thinking something serious was happening. In the vehicle in front of him, he saw secret service agents jump out, running in the street. The driver of his own vehicle seemed confused. It was time for Lyndon Baines Johnson to take control. He yelled forward to his driver: "Speed ahead! Speed ahead!"

Just then another gunshot rang out, this time closer, nearly directly to the right. In a single shot, the Vice President of the United States was dead.

* * * * *

After that tragic day in Dallas, the political landscape in the nation changed suddenly. All of the Democratic programs John F. Kennedy had initiated were suddenly overwhelmed by the change of command. Succession went to the Speaker of the House, John W. McCormack, a Democrat who filled out the remaining presidential term with almost nothing accomplished. Few of President Kennedy's dreams were fulfilled.

The following year, in a normal-cycle election, Barry M. Goldwater, a Republican Senator from Arizona, was elected President of the United States. Democrats warned that Goldwater, known as "Mr. Conservative," was a dangerous right-wing fanatic. He didn't accomplish a great deal in his four-year term, but neither was there noticeable damage to the country's status quo. Presidents come and go, and usually it's difficult to tell what's changed. Looking back, it seems times simply march on regardless of presidential leadership, and it's difficult to identify specific policies that help or hinder a nation's growth. The same goes for political parties. Both Democrats and Republicans have their good and bad moments in history, and it's difficult to determine what precipitates change and prosperity.

Yet there's no doubt the constant cycling of Democrat and Republican presidents into the White House has had an effect on history. In this case, who knows what would have happened if John F. Kennedy hadn't been killed that day? Or what might have been different, looking back in history, if a disgruntled Lyndon Baines Johnson had survived the tragedy in Dallas and gone on to be elected as president in 1964?

Planet Earth

The Milky Way Galaxy

Chapter 18

Absence Brings Fondness

4,646,926,986 AD – Planet Earth

(2017 on Planet Proteus)

"Where do you stand officially on the jumping-off debate?" asked Kane's best friend and fellow astrophilosopher, Kermin, age 98, who sat across from him at the energy shop. "I mean, as far as the government is concerned."

The shop's outside patio provided a great setting at the base of the mountains, although it wasn't really outdoors. The seamless "full-view" glass made you feel like you were outside, even to include a wavering flow of air simulating the original outdoor breeze millions of years ago. The temperature, too, felt cool and comfortable, like long ago. Neither Kane nor Kermin remembered those days, of course, but it was certainly the climate of many modern cyberbooks and mediavision dramas.

"I stand publically the same as I stand with you," replied Kane. "In other words, I can't make up my mind."

"That's a heck of a thing to say. To think the second greatest astrophilosopher on Earth can't make up his mind."

"And I wonder who's the first?" replied Kane. "Well, I don't mean to brag, but I really don't see you testifying before any government committees. I'd almost think you've never been asked."

"Not enough time for things like that when you're my age. Of course, I'm not exactly the Astrophilosopher Laureate, am I?"

Kane laughed, and took a sip of his steaming energee, still a bit too hot for his taste. Kermin wasn't nearly as well known as Kane, but he relied on Kermin to bounce ideas around. Even at 98, he was one of the most ingenious astrophilosophers in the Miniverse.

"You know, Kermin, I've been thinking about what's right and what's wrong more than I should lately. But there's more to it than that. For one thing, Earth was never a jump-off point for another civilization, and our history is linked with P4531, so how do we resolve that dilemma?"

"Meaning... If we didn't experience it, neither should they?"

"Yes," replied Kane. "Even though there's nothing that says our histories have to stay in synch forever. In fact, there's already plenty of proof that things have strayed here and there. That major irregularity during the presidential assassination in Dallas, for example."

"But that's a minor event, when you compare it to a planet full of people hopping off onto another world," noted Kermin. "Swashbuckling pirates, git out of my way! I'm comin' aboard."

"Not so funny, if you ask me?" responded Kane. "Especially because it's pretty close to how I imagine it."

"I feel like the old guy with the peg leg – Captain Hook – ready to pounce."

"You've already got a peg leg, Kermin. It's just that yours is a bit more technologically advanced than his."

"And you're like Peter Pan, trying to act forever young, flittering around, trying to save the world."

"Thirty-two is plenty young these days. We'll both be long gone before we get close enough to a planet in Andromeda to jump ship. But the good news is we might be able to influence that decision, because they really do listen to us."

"I know who "they" are, Kane, but what do you mean by 'us?'"

"Okay, they listen to me. But you're my trusty sidekick, and you know it. I rely on you for ideas, although they give me all the credit. Someday, history will set the record straight."

"Hi Ho, Silver!" yelled Kermin, causing some of the patrons to glance at their table. Kane had no idea what he was talking about, but Kermin considered Hollywood nostalgia his favorite hobby. He knew about things long forgotten by most. Which caused Kane to change the topic.

"So, Kermin, what do you know about genealogy?"

* * * * *

A love affair on Earth was challenging, even under the best of conditions. For Kane and Dyanne, it was simply impossible. Unless, of course, you considered love from afar an acceptable alternative.

Although they had not seen each other for two years – since their college days at the University of the Arctic – they kept in close contact on the Astronet. Technically, this was prohibited, since Kane was under Miniverse Prime's custody and Dyanne a member of the human zoo, but the permissiveness of Earth shined through. Or made things worse.

The Astronet was deceivingly appealing for lovers, with its almost-intimate interface capabilities, including advanced mediaphone and holographic interactions. But it wasn't direct contact, and that's what both Kane and Dyanne craved. For two years, the Astronet allowed them to test the challenges of their age difference, and they both survived the test. For it wasn't the years separating them, but their predetermined circumstances instead. If they were found together for even a few minutes, their fate would be even worse than their unfulfilled love, for they would be deported to separate colonies. Miniature SkyBots were nearly everywhere in the human zoo, with the exception of the few places zoo members were allowed to interact with those individuals supervised by Miniverse Prime. The university had been that way – a meager attempt by Prime to assess mixed social interactions in a controlled environment, an experiment going nowhere.

Deportation from Earth was the most severe punitive tool of its time, for the privilege of living on Earth was becoming increasingly cherished. Even with its overheating and dwindling natural resources, their planet was still the garden spot of the Miniverse, and few would give it up voluntarily. Even the human zoo wasn't a bad place to live, considering the stark realities of colonial worlds. In cases of "hybrid" love affairs, Miniverse Prime had learned that banishment from Earth served the situation best when both individuals were deported, to separate planets many light-years apart. Not only would their romantic entanglement be defeated, Kane and Dyanne would each lose everything else they held dear. Kane would lose his astrophilosophy credentials and Dyanne would lose her entire family.

Thus, there really was no solution, except to give up their relationship or continue on the Astronet in secrecy. Love at a distance was sometimes worse than no love at all.

"I could never give it up," said Dyanne one day on the mediaphone. "Nor can I live this way forever. I love you dearly, Kane, but how do we ever resolve this?"

"I think of you every day, Dyanne," replied Kane. "But that's the present, which can't be changed. Nor can we control the future, where these Earthly rules will undoubtedly be upheld well beyond our lifetime. But there might be one way to change the present for the best."

He paused, and Dyanne was afraid of what he might say next.

"And that is?..." she asked.

"Well, if we could somehow change the past, certainly that would affect things."

Chapter 19

Into the Planetary Void

This was Kane's second deposition in front of the Milky Way Merger Committee, his first being a year ago, and most members of the committee still held their seats. The chairwoman remained Senator Deleana Graham, and that was a plus. During his first session of testimony, she had protected him from some of the more aggressive committee members, and kept the questions on track.

Now, however, a lot had changed. In the course of merely a year, government priorities had intensified, and research scientists had responded by gathering together related technologies to make enormous strides, particularly in the area of computer simulations that allowed anyone who had the proper clearance to "see" day-to-day activities on P4531. All members of the Merger Committee possessed that level of security, and they had met several times since Kane's previous deposition to discuss a course of action, if there was to be any. What they had discussed was considered privileged information, and even the Astrophilosopher Laureate didn't have access to it. But today he expected to learn a lot from the committee members, maybe more than he'd be able to provide to them, and it was this committee that would eventually make the big decisions, with or without the concurrence of Dr. Kane Suane or anyone else.

In the time between his visits to the Senate, Kane had spent a lot of time with his colleagues, including Kermin Kuwine, exploring scenarios within the current level of technology or involving breakthroughs expected soon. You never could predict what would happen in science, but it was sometimes possible to make a good guess about where technology would be in another few years or centuries, based on trends in specific fields.

Health Sciences were a good example. Synthetic replacements were now available for nearly every component of the body, except a few involving neurological systems. That explained the advancements in human lifespans, although they had plateaued several thousand years ago. Few people lived longer than 250 years, even with most body parts replaceable, and anyone over 200 would certainly be fully retired, since the brain wore out early in life. Most components of the forebrain could be replaced, but eventually the core cells of the hypothalamus died, and no replacement procedure had yet been devised. So the brain wasn't yet fully replaceable, except for synthetic models that did nothing to extend the quality of living, along with subcomponents that were routinely transplanted to temporarily prolong life.

The military and certain dangerous professions used artificial brains constructively, but an organic brain was what distinguished man's success from other animals. Health scientists were getting close to growing a complete brain in the laboratory, and most experts in the field predicted new organic versions would be commonplace within less than a century, if the government allowed it, which they probably would. So in such an instance, experts could rather confidently predict another technological success story, but the exact timing was impossible to forecast.

Where this fit in with the Merger Committee was in the area of old-fashioned astrophysics. Using techniques that had failed in previous eras when the appropriate scientific tools weren't yet available, astrophysics was making a comeback. Big radio telescopes, long ago abandoned for financial reasons when nothing of further value seemed to come from them, had been reactivated. In most cases, these huge arrays were brought up to date using modern quantum computer techniques, and the search was on for new challenges in the cosmos. There's nothing like a galactic collision to get uno-dollars flowing again. Atmospheric sniffing, once considered a dead end, was prospering again, bringing in new talent from the universities. Scientists were once again well respected, after the numerous tragedies they were blamed for during the Third (and hopefully last) Millennium War.

There was even talk about tapping the talent of the human zoo, when it came to an increased need for university-educated scientists.

Kane wasn't holding his breath, for he knew any such change in government policy wouldn't happen overnight, but it did give him hope for his relationship with Dyanne. There must be a way for them to be together, and this seemed like the only viable hope. He would probably live another 200 years, and so would she. If they could spend even half of their lifetimes together, Kane would be ecstatic. Realistically, however, he knew organic brains and spaceships to Andromeda would be fully functioning well before that ever occurred.

* * * * *

"**D**octor Suane, thank you for appearing again before this committee," said Senator Deleana Graham. "Since your testimony last year regarding Andromeda P4531, we've received regular updates from you regarding your study of this extrasolar planet, just as this committee requested. We thank you for that, and I can assure you we've reviewed all of this material thoroughly. It has been very helpful in our committee's continuing discussion of what decisions need to be made prior to the galactic merger. Some of our members have additional areas they'd like to explore with you today, based on the data you've provided.

"Now, before we begin, I need to remind you the discussions conducted by this committee, including your visit today, are officially designated 'Highly Sensitive.' You'll notice there's no mediavision equipment in the room today. It's not our intent to keep this information from the public, but we do reserve the right to release it at a time and under the circumstances we feel is best for the Miniverse. Do you have any questions, or anything further you'd like clarified in this regard?"

"No, Senator Graham. I have no problem with any of that."

"Thank you, sir. So with that behind us, let's proceed. The Chair recognizes Senator Terrax from Eurasia."

"Thank you, Senator Graham. Doctor Suane, I'd like to revisit a topic we talked about when you last appeared before this committee. At that time, you discussed the technique called atmospheric sniffing, combined with quantum computer analysis and instantaneous wave communication, which allowed you to provide the 'pictures' we've all been gawking at around here for the past year. Could you give this committee an overview of how these technologies have progressed since your last testimony in this room, with emphasis on what this now allows us to 'see' that we couldn't a year ago?"

Kane exhaled a long slow breath. Senator Terrax was the kind of committee member every astrophilosopher needed in life. His general questioning gave Kane a lot of latitude to start things off in the direction he thought was best today. He didn't know how he could ever thank him, but he'd certainly try.

"Senator Terrax, one of the things that's changed in the past year has been a much finer scale of resolution. For example, we can now discern objects down to slightly less than a millimeter, whereas initially it was about 10 meters. That's a 10,000-fold improvement in what we can see. In fact, although we expect the resolution to increase even more over time, there's really no reason to need such capability. To put it into perspective, we can now make out facial features as detailed as anyone with average vision would be able to see when standing at normal talking distance. So, as you can see, we now have all the visual cues we need to make any kind of decision about this planet and it's beings.

"Another change involves our ability to select scenes that prove most valuable to us. At first we could only look at areas on the planet that the quantum computer fed to us randomly. Sometimes these scenes would be extremely revealing, and just the kind of data we needed to progress further, but more often we were wasting time on routine locations with no activity that contributed to our bank of knowledge. Now we can specify where we want to go, and get there immediately. We refer to it as 'dropping in.' So now we can 'drop in' at a specific government office, for example, and extract data about someone we think may be important to our future decisions. In this way we've accumulated a lengthy list of individuals who might be our key first contacts, if there is to be a contact, that is."

"Dr. Suane, I respect what you're doing in this regard, but I must admit it seems a little creepy, listening in to others like this, and whatever else you might be able to do in violation of their privacy."

Maybe Senator Terrax shouldn't be on his Christmas list after all. Yes, Kane had considered this privacy issue many times, but how could he best express it to this committee?

"Senator, I appreciate your concerns. I've tried to make sure the technicians who work with me on this project – and as you know, it's a very small and select group – take every measure possible to protect the privacy of these individuals. However, I remind you that this involves a tradeoff. We need this data for the good of our entire Miniverse, and there's really no alternative to using surveillance methods beyond the knowledge of the individuals we're looking at. I can assure you that we work under a strict code regarding what we allow ourselves to look at and what we don't. I know it's a small consolation, but I consider it my duty to enforce privacy procedures as best I can. The good news is my technicians are some of the finest individuals you'll ever meet, and you'll remember this committee looked closely at each and every one of them before they were allowed to take part in this project."

"Thank you, Doctor Suane. I recognize we have to give you the authority commensurate with what we've asked you to do. I'm very proud of your handling of this whole thing, but I'm concerned how we'll deal with this when we go public. There are lots of groups that will ask questions regarding any perceived violations of personal privacy, so we'll need to be prepared. No further questions."

He's back on the Christmas list.

"The Chair recognizes Senator Kerill from Mars."

The good, the bad, and the ugly. Senator Kerill was always a lot to handle.

"Doctor Suane, let's get right to the Jump-Off discussion that's been the topic of heated debate by this committee. When you were here last year, you seemed unsure of your position on this issue. Have you resolved how you feel about a Jump-Off scenario, because our committee recognizes that you, more than any one else in this room, has the best perspective on the whole issue. Quite frankly, I don't fully understand half the things you say, but I respect you for trying to explain these technical details to us."

"You ask tough questions, Senator."

The chuckles cascaded down the row of senators. The few approved visitors, mostly powerful politicians not in the Senate, also began to laugh.

"Hey, this isn't all just gawking at aliens that look like us," joked Chairwoman Graham. "Besides, Mars pays Senator Kerill big uno-bucks to harass those of us living on Earth."

Snickering broke out again, but immediately settled down. Kane started speaking.

"I'm still divided regarding the Jump-Off scenario. If you think we might be violating personal privacy issues by watching the citizens of P4531, imagine the implications of taking over their whole planet."

More laughter. This time, Senator Graham banged her gavel on the table: "Order. There will be order," she stated, but Kane thought he saw a hint of a smile on her face. Things quieted immediately, and Kane continued.

"I'm quite serious about this, since it's a major issue. The question is whether we have the moral authority to take over another world. Yes, Earth is doomed to even hotter days ahead, and our atmosphere now barely supports humans without ground suits, even under the best of conditions. But does that mean we have the right to take over another planet? If there were no intelligent beings there, and the planet could support us in its ecosystem, that would be a different matter. But P4531 is almost an exact copy of Earth in the beginning of its second millennium, using a calendar based on the birth of Christ. We've been there, and we know serious problems were developing back then regarding global warming and diminishing natural resources. P4531 has no better capabilities than we had at the time to solve these problems, considering their existing technology. They'll have to work their way through it, and they can. After all, we did."

Kane paused, but kept his head lifted high, so no one in the room doubted he had more to say about this issue. He looked down the row of senators, and then continued talking.

"But the beings of P4531 now have an even bigger problem – us. They don't know about us yet, but there's no doubt we'll overload their resources if we simply 'jump off.' Even if we give them adequate preparation time, the scenarios aren't good. Maybe they'd feel it necessary to declare a war against us, which would decimate their population and probably kill and injure many of our own people.

Fighting would be futile for them, of course, but other storylines aren't any better. If we allow them to stay on their planet, and we merely join them, we immediately compound their problems. Even with our help with planetary cooling technology, there's still the decimation of natural resources and all the problems associated with a sudden population explosion. And let's not kid ourselves – if we have access to a hospitable planet, we all know that we'll immediately proliferate, no matter what laws might be developed to try to prevent it.

"So what do we do? Banish them to... where? To Earth, which is already dying? To nearby extrasolar planets, like our feeble colonies? Even with our help, they'd be no better off than we are now. So, yes, I'm still undecided, because the other side of the scenario is to leave them alone, with eventual death for our own planet's people, with only our frail colonies surviving. Now I know this all sounds like doom and gloom, and it's perfectly correct to interpret it that way. But there's one more possibility this committee might consider."

Kane paused. He knew he had the attention of everyone in the room.

"What if we pour even more money into this project? What have we spent so far? How many trillions? We've been looking for alien life for billions of years, and we've found only one place other than Earth, P4531. But suppose we don't give up the search? We know we've thoroughly sought life in our own galaxy, and haven't found anything more complex than basic plants and maybe, depending on how you interpret the data, some very primitive animal life. But now there's a whole new galaxy that's just beginning to fall into the range of our atmospheric sniffers and wave pattern differentiators. Admittedly, we were lucky with P4531, partly because it's located in an outer spiral arm that's first to collide with the Milky Way. But with a few more trillions here and there devoted to extrasolar planet research in Andromeda, maybe we'll find something else, especially if we push up the bar in what tools we buy and how we use them. Just maybe – like the old days when we pumped funds into scientific research until we were blue in the face – we can find an adequate place we can go that isn't occupied. Now that's a place to jump off! Breathable air, big oceans, and land already covered by forests, but no people. And maybe then we could finally find time for attention to the sciences and the humanities, and our Multiverse would make progress once again. Humans could thrive rather than merely wasting time in inept attempts at colonizing planets that are far from livable."

Kane was obviously finished for now, but no one spoke. Finally, Chairwoman Graham took advantage of the silence.

"I suppose you've worked out a complete budgetary plan for this. Would you share it with this committee?"

"Of course, Senator Graham. I'll transmit it to all members of the committee immediately after this session. I'll warn you though – it's a whopper. Do you remember the famous Apollo project that took man to the moon for the first time? This is on the same scale, corrected for inflation, of course. But with enough funding, including a big increase in university science programs, we'll have the tools we need to search far into Andromeda. Maybe what we'll find is still too far away to be realistic to reach in our spacecraft, but we can work on that, too. What are we doing in space travel after all this time? Answer – floundering around on planets only 100 light-years away. Give me a break!"

There was more laughter now, but also a scattering of applause from the senators themselves.

"Further questions?" asked Senator Graham, and then she paused. A hand went up at the far end of the row.

"The Chair recognizes Senator Christina Duante of the Canadian States."

This was a new member of the committee, someone Kane had never seen before today, but he'd heard she was an aggressive supporter of the Jump-Off scenario.

"Doctor Suane, I'm new to this committee, but I've tried to bring myself up to date in a very short time. One of the things that has impressed me is your extensive work on historic beings now living on P4531. I and the other members of this committee appreciate the reports you've sent us regarding these individuals. Is it your opinion that one or more of them should be our first contact? – if there is a contact, of course."

"Senator Duante, we've studied these individuals primarily because they provide verification of our technical methodology. We have information about some of them in our old historic records, so we can correlate what we find on P4531 for calibration of our own surveillance methods. But you're right – if your committee decides to engage in two-way communications, these would be prospective individuals for first contact, since they hold considerable decision-making power on their planet. Unfortunately, like Earth in the same era, there's no world government to speak of on P4531, so contacting a specific country might aggravate our communication problems further. Another possibility to consider is finding a scientific leader who could more easily understand our initial messages without upsetting the world political structure. P4531 has talented individuals called 'shamans' who serve roles similar to our astrophilosophers, and they might be a good point of contact. They report to their own governments, so they aren't worldwide representatives. But they would be more likely to understand the nature of our initial communications. We never had shamans like these on Earth, since we didn't face a galactic collision during our early history, so we've been studying them with specific interest."

"You mean galactic 'merger' rather than 'collision,' don't you?" interjected Deleana Graham. "Don't forget, this is the Merger Committee."

At this point, with the mornings questioning about to conclude, everyone laughed, including Kane.

"They call it the Galactic Collision Project on P4531," noted Kane. "But what do those pesky aliens know about protocol?"

Planet Proteus

The Andromeda Galaxy

Chapter 20

Shamans as Philosophers

August 5, 2049

Corinne came downstairs to find Shawn asleep at his micro-laptop, the screensaver showing the Pinwheel Galaxy in all its glory. The small device was still cradled in his hand, draped from a lifeless arm resting on his lap. He looked peaceful, and she knew he was – a senior shaman, now over 40 years into one of the most unusual career paths on Proteus.

At age 63, Shawn still looked strong, and there was no doubt he was healthy. In some ways, he felt better than he ever did before, except maybe during those days of intense physical fitness as a third-string wide receiver at UCLA. His heart-to-heart conversation with Corinne last night had explained a lot. After 30 years of marriage, Shawn had finally revealed his real profession, which had been of no surprise to Corinne.

In the first years of his marriage, even with a wife he loved dearly, Shawn kept his secret. But over the years, it became less and less practical. His contract provisions regarding secrecy were clear, but his shaman activities became more obvious to Corinne with no words needed. How could such a loyal husband spend long periods at a remote cabin in the mountains, always alone there, and on an obvious mission? The concept of modern shamans had hit the news media several times in recent decades, once when a Galactic Collision employee – a high-placed administrator – decided to bring the shaman program to the attention of the TV networks. Whether it was financial greed or a mere slip of the tongue, shamans and project managers worldwide sometimes surfaced to talk about their jobs. Yet the public turned its head on the stories, since more interesting wars raged in remote places, and Hollywood personalities generated bigger headlines. In the 4 decades of the GC Project, not one U.S. shaman name had been revealed, a tribute to the strength of the program. Worldwide, three names had come forward, and then slipped quickly into oblivion.

Farley still asked tough questions over their mugs of beer at Cheyenne's, sitting right across from Shawn or Corinne. He seemed more contemplative on the matter than Shawn's own wife. But that's only because Corinne chose to turn her head when it was necessary. Love spanned enormous crevices in the ice fields of life.

"So is our friendly shaman staying home and writing his electronic books, or going up to Frog Pond this week?" asked Farley, his old eyebrows raised in fake suspense.

"You've got the shaman part wrong," replied Shawn, not taking the bait. "But, yes, I'm headed up the trail once again to my little slice of paradise."

"He sure disappears a lot, doesn't he, Corinne? Makes you kinda' wonder, don't you think?"

"You disappear a lot, too," replied Corinne. "I heard you got a gal up there in Sequoia Park."

"Sure, sure, just me an those cuddly old black bears."

"So you've got your bears, and I've got my shaman-like existence," suggested Shawn.

"Someday, I'm going to break this thing wide open, you know," said Farley, with a mocking attempt to sound threatening.

"You bet, Farley. Just call in Bakersfield TV, and we'll all have some fun. Just think how miserable they'd make life in Kernville."

They all laughed over their pints of beer, now almost drained. Cherokee came by a few minutes later to ask them about refills.

"Are you kids getting along okay tonight?" she asked, her gray roots attractively streaking through her still-pretty long braids.

Cherokee had aged gracefully, looking more relaxed these days with her children now fully grown and blended into life in Los Angeles and Bakersfield. Rather than children at home, she now had grandkids in nearby cities – places to visit leisurely, rather than an overwhelming challenge to go home to each night. And now she had

David at home, a younger-than-her husband who managed to prolong her youth. Some things never changed – Cherokee aged for the better.

"We get along okay," said Corinne. "It's just that Farley keeps us on our toes."

"Just doin' my job," replied Farley, trying out his gruff voice.

Corinne too had kept her youth, but there was a little more of it to keep at age 59 than Farley, Cherokee, or even Shawn. She still wore her long blond hair (no gray yet) in a pony-tail, and tonight's sleeveless shirt revealed the fair skin that always made her look like she needed a bit of sun.

Corinne still flew several times a week, using her two-airplane flight school at Kern Valley Airport as her base. Flying had changed less than she would have expected since her days with Apaches and Arrows. They were still building Cessnas in Wichita, so there were a few small airplanes in the sky. She owned a 2025 four-seat Cessna 172R, now over twenty years old, but operating on its second engine. The "R" stood for "Retro," which explained it's classic lines. The 172 had been the Edsel of private aviation, succeeding far beyond the rest of the industry. The only real change in almost a century of production was in the instrument panel and forward of the firewall, where a spiffy diesel replaced the old air-cooled gas guzzler.

She used the 172R for flight training, and leased a more powerful Cessna 182RGR – "RG" for retractable gear, and the second "R" for "Retro." It was similar to Shawn's older 182, upgraded to include a more efficient engine and collision avoidance avionics. Otherwise, a pilot from the turn of the century wouldn't notice any major differences. Small aircraft seemed to have an endless life. Just replace the engine every 3000 hours, and keep on trucking.

"Gotta go, gang," said Shawn, after silence prevailed over their table for a few minutes, making sure Cherokee and Farley saw his genuine smile. "More secret stuff at Frog Pond tomorrow morning, you know."

* * * * *

"**H**ey, Fat, you old fart. How's Miami today?" said Shawn, using his micro-laptop to connect him to his friend, a relationship spanning 4 decades.

Fatius Lane was posed on the small computer screen in front of Shawn, looking as mischievous as ever. Meanwhile, Fatius would be seeing Shawn in a backdrop of tall, healthy green trees, fully recovered from the fire of over 30 years ago.

As they talked, Shawn watched the waterfall plunging into Frog Pond. His 14-foot graphite boat with its tiny electric motor, powered by the sun, was always a comfortable place to be on a summer day. This is where he did much of his thinking, and there was a lot to consider these days.

"Shawn, my honorable shaman of the west, glad to hear from you. It looks nice and sunny there today."

"As beautiful as ever. And I hear Miami is doing good. How about that heat?"

"The temperature or the basketball team? One's hot enough to broil a steak on the pavement. The other's cold as ice. But we're ready to start winning again when the season kicks off."

Shawn laughed. The Miami Heat had lost more than they won for 3 years in a row. Not the Heat empire of times gone by. The other heat – global warming – had threatened to flood the city with an onslaught of rising water from melting polar caps. But Miami had planned well, with an entirely new downtown, and an old town tourist area where modern gondolas plied the waters between restructured foundations.

"Did you see the shaman report from Tokyo?" asked Shawn. "I think it's a bit over the top."

"No doubt. But you gotta' admit it's right along our line of thinking. Gravitons are similar to the Higgs particle, meaning they both produce a field affecting everything, even dark matter. Gravitational waves have an effect like polarization, stretching matter in one direction and contracting it on the opposite side. If we could stop gravity, for even an instant, we'd have some awesome tools for space travel."

"Anti-gravity," said Shawn. "Now that would work for me, especially at my age. Seriously though, both gravitons and the Higgs mediate their own fields when it comes to quantum field theory. Stopping the Higgs field might be easier. Reducing mass to zero seems like less of a challenge than doing away with gravity. Then again, if there's no mass, there goes gravity, too."

"See, that's what I mean," said Fatius. "We could learn from what's going on in Japan. Our concept of a polarization synchrotron could still be a route we want to follow."

"Do you remember when Cornell put out those first news releases years ago? It went right to the top of the Internet as a scientific scam. Now look where that technology has gone. We're still talking about it."

"We've got too many routes to follow here," said Fatius. "We need to narrow things down so we're not chasing our tail. As far as I'm concerned, things keep coming back to spin-zero particles, which lead to quantum tunneling and faster-than-light. We've been using tunnel diodes in computers for half a century, so it's something we can use as a point of reference."

"Think about how this all relates to computers," replied Shawn. "So many things have improved in that area of technology, yet we still don't really understand how they work, like tunnel diodes and quantum computers. They both work just fine, but who really knows how?"

"Good point, Shawn. The way I look at it, we need to build a spaceship that travels faster than light, but we're millions of years from that goal. And we can't wait that long. But there's an alternative, if we can tweak our current computers. Maybe your micro-laptop is our spaceship."

* * * * *

Life in 2049 wasn't much different from life when Shawn first became a Shaman in 2008. Advances in the sciences, especially in the field of computers, were exceptional, and that knowledge had been successfully applied to life's comforts. Still, to Shawn, things didn't seem that different from when he was in college. The human species was still limited to the Earth, except for a few expeditions to Mars. Flight to another galaxy or even another star wasn't even seriously contemplated. Shawn now drove an electric car, but it looked pretty much like his old Edsel, only smaller. Similarly, the rest of the world seemed little changed. Nations still bickered and occasionally fought wars nobody won. If Shawn had guessed what it would be like now when he was in college, he would have contemplated flying cars and spaceships leaving the solar system. He would have been wrong.

Pinging technology originally developed in India was an example of a major leap forward. Over the past 20 years, pinging had lead to the concept called "environmental tracers," but it was now being done with large radio telescopes rather than the optical giants of the past. The VLT in Chile was still active, and even the 200-inch Ritchey-Chretien reflector on top of Mauna Kea was still operational, partly for sentimental reasons (although the government would never admit it). But most of the big optical instruments had been retired long ago in favor of powerful radio telescopes.

Environmental tracers were producing remarkable results, but without the resolution required to see the kind of details Proteus needed to determine the extent of alien life on other worlds. So far, all that had been found was confirmation of the conditions necessary for life, rather than the existence of alien intelligence or even basic life in the form of animals or plants. The "Great Silence" was still a lonely void.

* * * * *

Corinne rode in the right seat, where she felt most comfortable as a flight instructor. Shawn was in his normal position, too, in front of the primary flight instruments on the left side. When they flew together, it was important for them to formally announced who was pilot-in-command, since there's nothing more distracting in times of emergency than two experienced pilots trying to decide who's in charge.

"You've got the airplane," said Shawn, handing over the PIC duties to Corinne. "All's well at eleven thousand feet."

"Thanks for the great opportunity. Especially since George is in charge."

George, the autopilot, had been tracking the centerline of Victor 16 for the last fifty miles. George had been holding their altitude at precisely 11,000 feet since their last altitude change at Palm Springs. George was quite a guy.

"What's the clearance again?" asked Corinne. "Victor 16 to Blythe, then direct Tucson, or was there a STAR?"

"No STAR. Just direct. But George remembers."

Standard Terminal Arrival Routes were still around, but seldom issued any more. Pretty much everything was direct here, direct there, direct everywhere. The old Victor airways were still around, but no longer based on VORs, which had been shut down for over 20 years. Part of the en route airway structure was still based on where VORs used to be, but you got there using GPS. Blythe "VOR," where they were headed now, didn't exist any more, but they were going there anyway, using a set of coordinates the GPS called "Blythe." If you flashed back 50 years, the process of navigation was pretty much the same then, but with equipment that was harder to interpret.

The last of the radar sites had been shut down, too. Good riddance – both Shawn and Corinne had been led down many adrenaline-producing paths by radar, with unreliable coverage in remote areas. Now their own onboard equipment transmitted their position to satellites, which in-turn relayed their location to Albuquerque Center via data-link. Air traffic controllers still sat in front of what looked like radar scopes, but it was really only a computer-generated image, since there was no more radar.

ATC did little talking these days. All airplanes had transponders that communicated with each other, and advised their pilots of traffic conflicts, even how to resolve them. Airliners and military aircraft hardly ever talked to controllers, since clearances were sent by data-link. It all worked pretty well when it worked, until a car goes off the road in Yucca Valley and hits a relay tower, and the ATC computer shuts everything down.

For small aircraft like their Cessna 182RGR, it was more like the old days. At least ATC talked to them on radios, like they used to. Of course, there weren't many Cessnas around any more, except for rich airline pilots who wanted a trip back to the aviation era they grew up in: "Cleared to Tucson via Victor 16, Blythe, direct. Contact Albuquerque now on one-two-eight point seven-five. Have a good day."

The Cessna 182RGR was pretty much the aircraft Corinne had instructed in since 2010, just with a better engine and a glass panel. The cost of diesel fuel had gone out of sight, which explained the dearth of small aircraft these days. And airlines hired pilots with limited flying time, as long as they could handle the simulator, so there wasn't much incentive for companies like Cessna. But Cessna was better off than most. Names like Piper, Mooney, and Beechcraft were only memories of the past.

"So you've never been to Tucson," said Shawn. "What you've been missing!"

"You must like it. You sure spend a lot of time there."

"The University is amazing. Wish I could have gone there for astrophysics rather than UCLA. But scholarships talk."

"Did you play Arizona in football?"

"Sure, part of the PAC-12. But they beat us the year I played. Then again, quite a few teams beat us the year I played."

"And the worst was?..," she paused for dramatic effect, knowing his stock answer.

"USC, of course. I hate those guys."

"Come on, it's been 40 years!"

"And they still beat UCLA nearly every year. I bet the kids in school today still hold the same grudge."

"Well, at least Arizona beats USC in astrophysics," noted Corinne.

"Very true. They don't even have an astrophysics department."

"So there you go," laughed Corinne. "What's more important, football or space science?"

"Football, of course."

Their discussion of football rivalries was interrupted by Albuquerque Center, who gave them their step-down instructions for Tucson. Corinne read back the clearance.

"Roger, Albuquerque. Five-four-niner-three-delta is cleared direct 'Hotter,' descend and maintain seven thousand. Contact Tucson Approach on one-one-eight point two."

"Niner-three-delta, readback correct. See you later."

"Bye now."

Just like the old days, even the part about intersections, still given five letter identifiers. So HOTTR (pronounced "Hotter") was based on old-fashioned VOR airways, with no VORs anywhere to be found.

"Interesting name for an intersection around here," said Shawn. "Hotter."

"At least the FAA still has a sense of humor."

* * * * *

At Dr. Henderson's office, Shawn felt right at home. It was in the same building and even the same floor as Trevor Cantrelli's old office. When Trevor retired, he handed over his favorite shaman contact to Blayne Henderson, who was as prominent in modern astronomy as Trevor had been decades before. According to those currently on staff here, Trevor was still observing several nights a week at his backyard observatory in the foothills west of Tucson. Shawn would love to see him again someday soon.

"You sure came a long way to see results I could have sent you on the Cybernet," said Dr. Henderson.

"Yes, but then I wouldn't have needed to fly a Cessna to get here."

"The airlines must be cheaper," noted Dr. Henderson.

"Quite a bit, in fact. But not nearly as much fun."

"I suppose. Oh, Trevor Cantrelli asked that I give you his greetings. He said to ask you if you've seen the gal called Cassiopeia lately, and it didn't sound like he was talking about the Ethiopian queen."

"It's kind of an inside joke," said Shawn.

"I see. Well Cantrelli always had a good sense of humor. When he turned the extrasolar planet project over to me, he left me a diagram of a human DNA molecule, with a label that said: "When you find this, give me a call.""

"I take it you haven't found it yet."

"Not by a long shot. But the Higgs field approach you're taking might be part of the solution ol' Trevor was hoping for."

"You really think so?"

"Well, atomic physics isn't even close to my field of expertise, but going massless is sure good if you're trying to send a signal somewhere fast."

"We really don't have any alternative to 'fast,' when you consider how far away Zeus is. The GC Project is making a big deal about next year, as if the collision begins in 2050 on a schedule you can set on your watch. But even where we're positioned in our outer spiral arm of the Heavenly Way, it's still a long ways to the nearest stars in Zeus."

"At least 10 thousand light-years, no matter what route you take."

"So instantaneous is what we need," said Shawn. "And the Higgs might be able to do it. It's a spinless particle, you know, and spin-zero is what's needed to travel faster than light, at least as far as most experts tell me."

"But when I think of what you're proposing, from an astronomer's point of view, I'm bothered by any attempt to interfere with the Higgs field. It's not dangerous, I don't think, but I can't see how you can suspend the field long enough to make something massless. And you'll have to do it for more than a few microseconds, since transmitted information is always a complex format, no matter how simple your message. So how do you suspend a field long enough to put together even a basic message?"

"I've been giving that a lot of thought," replied Shawn. "My friend Fat says it might be possible by building a quantum computer that would sort of police itself, building up its own internal program for transmitting while the Higgs field is temporarily suspended."

"Your friend's name is Fat? Is he a computer scientist?"

"Not exactly. He's a remarkable mind who works with me on the GC Project. Fat says we should be looking at quantum tunneling techniques, and I think he's right."

"I'd certainly never argue with a guy named Fat."

"I argue with him all the time, which is how we often make progress. Getting back to the whole faster-than-light communication thing – you know I'm headed that direction only because the obvious solution is to just go there and look, but that technology is way out there, maybe thousands of years."

"You know, that's what everybody says, but I'm not as optimistic. I think it could be millions of years before humans can travel outside our solar system. The scale is simply much greater than most of us realize. As an astronomer, I'm used to the distances involved, and even the distance of a light-year is going to take us a lot longer than most people expect. And that doesn't even get us to the nearest star."

"So you agree then?" asked Shawn. "We'd be better off tackling communication with extrasolar planets as an alternative?"

"Yes, but even that isn't going to work in our lifetime, unless we get some help solving your complex suspended field scenarios."

"And where do we get that help?" asked Shawn.

"You know the answer as well as I do, don't you? We get the help from the very people we're trying to contact. Maybe they're trying to reach us right now, but we're just not looking in the right places."

"Or maybe they're holding off, waiting for us to get a bit closer. We might be sitting right on the edge of their spitting range for communication. A few more years, or a few more light-years, and pretty soon they can spit far enough, and we get their call."

"Now that would be something," said Dr. Henderson. "I sure hope it happens in my lifetime."

Chapter 21

One Tremor, a Million Aftershocks

Why a group of students would dig on the top of an obscure peak near San Diego was probably more related to regional pride than scientific serendipity. A nearby community college advertised an introductory course in archeology in its general education offerings, although there was no archeology department at Palomar Community College. Kurt Santor, the only faculty member who taught the course, drove 20 miles on Thursday nights to teach disinterested students what they needed to know to pass one of Palomar's gaffe courses. Professor Santor's students considered him an easy-going guy who gave away a lot of A's and B's for minimum work. His personal passion was field-work in archeology, and student's could assure themselves a solid passing grade by simply attending one of the semester's two scheduled field trips. These were all-day affairs, which meant giving up a Saturday for the sake of pushing up your grade-point-average.

Kurt Santor knew his reputation as an easy instructor, and he also knew none of his students would likely aspire to a career in science. That was fine with him, since he enjoyed merely teaching the course, and it was a chance to exercise his love for archeology, a degree he earned at the University of North Carolina, but never got to apply in the real world. In his boring everyday life, Kurt worked as a middle-level supervisor at a telecom firm, which verified the career realities of those with a bachelor's degree in the study of artifacts.

Kurt had taught at Palomar College for over 10 years, and loved his Thursday nights at school. Even more, he relished his Saturday field trips, introducing his students to dig sites near the college. He had created all of these sites himself, basic locations that appeared undisturbed in recent decades. It was a good way to introduce students to the tools of archeology, and occasionally an actual find. His students had discovered artifacts hundreds of years old, and occasionally a fossil of prehistoric times. Usually, although nothing substantial was discovered, his students gained perspective on the scientific method in action, which was very self-satisfying for Kurt.

The site of this semester's new dig location was selected for its location near the college, its easy access from the public campground just below the peak, and its name linking it to the school – Mount Palomar.

* * * * *

Shawn was floating in his graphite boat, dozing in the sun between sessions with his micro-laptop, when the chime of an incoming Red Star message caught his attention. It wasn't an unexpected intrusion, since he had told Fatius only a few hours earlier: "Send the report back, with annotations, when you're finished."

The "report" was the latest submission to the *Physics Journal* from a Chinese scientist regarding his experiments in temporarily suspending the Higgs field, and its relationship to dark matter and maybe even dark energy.

Some of the text in the document Fatius returned to Shawn was highlighted in yellow, so he reviewed those portions of the report, along with the electronic post-it comments Fat had tagged nearby.

Near a highlighted section about the Chinese scientist's methodology in turning off the Higgs field, Fatius posted: "We could temporarily shut off a person's Higgs, enabling an individual to travel faster than light. But we'd have to figure out how to turn it back on again upon reaching the destination."

Adjacent to a section about the challenges in turning off the Higgs field, Fat remarked: "Heat is our biggest enemy in a process like this, basically many trillions of degrees. Hotter than Miami."

Near the end of the article, Fatius posted a final comment: "This tells me teleportation from one location to another is possible, although not easy for anything of substantial size. Beam me up, Scotty!"

Just as he was finishing Fatius' review, Shawn's satellite phone icon flashed, incoming from Miami.

"Hey, Fat. You must be a mind reader. I wanted to talk to you about your comments on the Higgs experiments.

"No! No!" exclaimed Fatius, in an unusually excited tone. "Jump over to 'News Reports' to see what just happened!"

"Okay," replied Shawn, simultaneously clicking the header screen for "News" that was already flashing. Somehow he'd missed the blinking icon while reviewing Fatius' comments about the Chinese scientist's research.

"Holy, shit!" yelled Shawn when he saw the science news headline, hollering into the hot mike that he knew Fat could hear. "The 200-inch telescope is at two places at once!"

Fatius replied with a still excited: "Now that's what I call hot!" Then he said nothing more, knowing Shawn was busy scanning the news article.

"This sure changes everything," said Shawn, much calmer now, once he'd read the entire article.

"Sure does! What are your first thoughts, my fellow shaman?"

"First thoughts?" said Shawn slowly. "Well, first of first is that there's a link here. Time isn't the nice even flow we've always assumed, and that could mean time travel, which means faster-than-light in a very different sense."

"This report looks legit," replied Fatius. "The community college teacher who made the original discovery might be suspect, but the follow-up dig by UC Irvine seems conclusive. They found artifacts right near the surface, which is consistent with a telescope 100 years old. It's only a secondary mirror and a few broken pieces of Pyrex, but what was it doing on top of mountain near San Diego? And why would any of Ritchey's stuff be up there."

"What about the original design favoring Palomar until after Hale's death? Maybe they went up there for some preliminary work."

"Not so," said Fatius. "I already Cybernetted everything related to Palomar. Ritchey was never there, and his hyperbolically-curved secondary mirror wasn't built until after they changed their observatory plans to Mauna Kea. It's a very specific optical design, and the archeology seem solid."

"If so, we need to get going right away," said Shawn. "Let's shift our research towards historic anomalies, at least for now. There could be other conflicts in history that we can find, and they could validate time travel, or at least give us some tools for faster-than-light."

"I agree," said Fatius. "It's finally time to play USC."

Shaw thought about that, reflecting back to his interview for his shaman position, with geeky Fatius questioning him about UCLA football. The first thought that came to mind was it was time for David to slay Goliath. His second thought was that it was hopeless, and they were going to get slaughtered again, but at least he'd get some exciting playing time.

* * * * *

Dr. Trevor Cantrelli was 83-years old, now enjoying life in southern Arizona from a place in the desert where the evening skies were a lot less light-polluted than in most of the surrounding region. He used his small telescope a few times each month to enjoy live viewing of many of the objects he had studied with much larger instruments in his earlier days at the University of Arizona. His small home near the base of Kitt Peak was well positioned to look up towards the mountain with fond memories of nights there as a professional astronomer. Today he was at his modest home in the desert, sitting across from an old friend.

"What a great surprise, Shawn. I can't believe you came all the way out here to see me."

"I still spend a lot of time at the University, you know, and I thought that steakhouse might still be here."

"You're kidding, I hope," replied Trevor. "Because the steakhouse has been gone for 20 years."

"Yes, I'm kidding. I just stopped by to see you. It's a great drive from Tucson on a clear day like today. Besides, I figured an old friend might be willing to entertain a few questions."

"Sure, but I'll admit I haven't kept up with most of the professional stuff, except what I read in *Sky and Telescope*. That's more my speed these days."

"There's nothing wrong with *S and T*," replied Shawn. "I hear the Russians used to read it during the Cold War to learn about our latest technologies. Which is what I wanted to ask you about – attitudes toward technology. I've been researching some historic stuff lately, based on the Mount Palomar artifacts, and I'd be interested in your impressions."

"Meaning your shaman investigations relative to faster-than-light travel, or at least instantaneous communication?"

"No shamans around here, as far as I can tell," laughed Shawn. "But if there were such a thing, I bet they'd be interested in time travel."

"I've always been interested in it," said Trevor. "Astronomers are just a bunch of time travel junkies, if you think about it. We thrive in an environment where we're looking back at time from millions of light years away. The farther the better, which means the farther back in time, the more we like it."

"But what they found on Palomar is more like simultaneous time travel, rather than looking back. Two telescopes, or at least parts of two, at the same time in separate places. But we know there was only one 200-inch, and we know it was located on Mauna Kea. So what does that tell us?"

"Maybe it says there really are parallel worlds, and they can get mixed together on occasion. What if – on another world almost exactly like ours – the 200-inch was built on Palomar rather than on a mountain in Hawaii?"

"Okay, Trevor. So it's a somewhat minor glitch in history, but why do we find this discrepancy by digging on Palomar. I mean, who put the mysterious Ritchey optics there for us to find?"

"I suppose God is as good an answer as any, but why would he do it? To me, a better answer is someone from another world who is already here, although we haven't seen him yet."

"Oh, great," said Shawn with a note of disgust in his tone. "The aliens have landed, and they're messing with our minds. Why would they even bother?"

"I doubt they'd bother," replied Trevor. "But maybe they're 'here' only in the sense of trying to communicate with us. Trying to form some sense of mutual language to begin the communication. Or they're just looking around, without revealing themselves on purpose, and we've picked up a clue that they're already here."

"Okay, Trevor, let's just assume that's the case. How do we make contact with them... or it? If they're from a parallel world, wouldn't they speak English anyway?"

"Chinese. Definitely Chinese."

"Very funny. But any language would be easy code to break. If they're keeping quiet on purpose, how do we go about getting them to reveal themselves?"

"Well, since they left some traces for us on Palomar, maybe there are other historic irregularities we can find. Maybe they're all around us right now. Let me put you into contact with a friend of mine from Cal Tech who has a unique background in both history and astrophysics. Maybe he can help."

"Sure, that sound great, Trevor. Thanks."

"Do you have time to go up to the top of Kitt Peak before you go?" asked Trevor. Shawn thought he saw a hopeful look in Trevor's eyes.

"Sure, let's do it. Can we make it before sunset?"

Shawn drove, as Dr. Trevor Cantrelli politely rode in the passenger seat of the small electric car, not criticizing Shawn's driving until the first big curve on the mountain road, where he yelled: "Watch out, Shawn!"

* * * * *

"**D**octor Drake, I appreciate your taking your time to see me today," said Shawn.

"Sure, sure. Any friend of Trevor's is a friend of mine. Please call me 'Marvin.'"

Shawn thought "Marvin" sounded even geekier than "Doctor Drake."

"Okay, Marvin, as Trevor probably told you, I'm researching links to the Mount Palomar archeological discovery, trying to relate it to other possible historic mismatches."

"Well, as a shaman, you must have some knowledge about the variety of things pseudo-professionals have studied in recent decades related to what I call "glitches" in history. Like the Texas School Book Depository shooting in Dallas, and its multiple gunmen theory."

"Did Trevor mention something that led you to believe I'm a shaman?" asked Shawn, feeling uncomfortable about the situation.

"No, he didn't say a thing. But it seems to me you must be one of them secret government shamans associated with the Galactic

Collision Project. Your biography on the Cybernet doesn't match all the scientific contacts you've accumulated. A bachelor's degree in physics from UCLA isn't much to write home about, is it?"

"As good as a history degree from USC," retorted Shawn. He immediately regretted saying it, but he'd already reviewed Dr. Drake's background and knew he held doctorates in history and astrophysics, the history degree from USC.

"Oh, so it's the ol' UCLA versus USC thing," replied Dr. Drake, but he couldn't conceal a smile. "You just wait until the big game in December."

"Sorry," said Shawn. "You're right, I do work for the GC Project, but the whole thing about shamans is just a myth."

"That so?"

"Okay, Marvin. Could you tell me about some of these glitches? It's an area I know almost nothing about."

"Well the Dallas dual gunmen theory isn't the best example, since it has little to do with anything regarding alternative histories. But there have been a few obscure cases that are pretty compelling."

"For example?"

"Well, the one that comes to mind right away involves the bones of a female found on Gardner Island a few years ago. Did you hear about that?"

"It doesn't sound familiar. Where's Gardner?"

"Near Howland Island, one of the places Amelia Earhart landed on her round-the-world trip. An archeologist from the University of Washington claimed he found her bones, which was slammed quickly in the archeology circles, since Earhart died in the United States. They never ran any DNA tests or anything, and it never appeared in any scientific journals, but it still strikes me as a possible glitch.

"So now it's too late for DNA or any other tests?"

"Probably. Some religious fanatic in Minnesota bought the bones."

* * * * *

Shawn turned the bones issue over to Tom Suthers in Washington. Tom was still on the job, preparing for retirement from the GC Project in a few months, but just as involved as ever. His partner, Kent Versace, had already retired, and Tom was running the office with the help of a new young administrator. Within only a few days after receiving Shawn's request, he called back to explain the results regarding the Minnesota investigation.

"He was a real nut case, so it's good you turned it over to me," said Tom. "I didn't have to deal with him personally, of course, but it turned out just as you suspected. DNA results show the bones belong to Amelia Earhart, which causes me to issue one of my few direct orders to a shaman in my entire career."

"I bet I can guess."

"Probably. I need to tell you not to discuss anything about this with anyone, unless you clear it through me first. The public could easily misunderstand, so the President wants to keep this entirely under wraps for time being. To release anything about it might frighten a lot of people. The Palomar discovery is enough for now."

"Sure, I understand. But I do have one name I'd like to run up the flagpole right away. I coordinate with Fatius Lane a lot, and he needs to know about this so we can proceed with our investigation of historic glitches. We think it could lead to instantaneous communication with other planets."

"I'll need to run Fat's name past the President, but I can't see any reason he would refuse. You have no idea how strongly he feels about our whole shaman approach to things."

"Maybe he's hoping he'll be the guy who gets to break the news to the world if we make contact. So far no one has said: 'Take me to your leader.'"

"It's beginning to sound like they haven't made up their minds yet whether they even want to talk to us."

"It does make you wonder, doesn't it?" said Shawn. "It's one of the questions I've been addressing lately."

"I'll call you back later today to confirm Fat is good to go."

"Hey, Tom, when you ask the President, maybe it's best if you refer to Fat as Fatius."

◊ ◊ ◊ ◊ ◊ ◊

Chapter 22

The Big Game

The Great Silence was finally broken. The evidence was scattered over a wide range of disciplines, but Shawn was now convinced Proteus wasn't alone in the universe. He didn't know who it was or where they were from, but the clues kept increasing.

Besides the historic glitches – two of them so far involving the 200-inch telescope and the death of Amelia Earhart – the electromagnetic investigations were getting a lot of attention. Fatius and Shawn quickly theorized there would be evidence of any "visitors" in the electromagnetic spectrum, since any means of communication they started there.

Information was accumulating regarding increases in electromagnetic activity far to the infrared side of the spectrum. These conditions seemed related to locations near national capitals and even in the vicinity of sports stars when they travelled, which seemed a spurious result. Yet teams on the move during this football season in America seemed accompanied by an electromagnetic aura permeating locations where specific national superstars played on Sundays – Indianapolis, Atlanta, Seattle, and other cities where no previous electromagnetic activity of this type had been detected. It grew on Saturdays, peaked on Sundays, and was routinely gone by Monday morning.

None of this was revealed to the public, and it seemed to Shawn that the GC Project had entered a new phase where much more than the identities of shamans was kept secret. It was a change that made him feel uncomfortable, and he expressed it one night to Corinne.

"After all these years, things now seem so closely controlled. Although shamans were always protected, most information they gathered was promptly presented to the public. Everything seemed so open and progressive then. Now it feels like a secret project building higher and higher walls to keep everything in."

"That's because the things you're finding are so controversial. And, of course, it includes hints of alien intelligence manipulating us."

Corinne hadn't pushed Shawn on this topic, but she knew he was dealing with a search for extraterrestrial life right here on Proteus. He never admitted any such conclusions, but it was evident from their routine discussions about the concepts bothering Shawn that his research was headed in that direction. After 30 years of marriage, they saw through each other in ways no government disguise could mask.

"I can't disagree with the classified nature of some of this information, because it could alarm the public unnecessarily," said Shawn. "But I'm worried the government is taking the wrong overall position on the secrecy issue. If they let it pile up too high, what happens when the results are finally disclosed? In some ways, the public might be better off if things were divulged a bit at a time rather than in one fell swoop."

"Isn't there a chance this is all for naught?" suggested Corinne. "Maybe it will all go away, and then the government made a good decision by avoiding the possibility of panic."

"Actually, Cory, I think there's a good chance it will all go away. After all, it now looks like electromagnetic activity we've been monitoring goes back a long ways – over 30 years. We've found some engineering records that pretty much prove it's so. Similarly, the findings that we consider evidence of historic glitches seem to have existed for a long time, but we never discovered them. So one conclusion is any aliens stalking us now have been doing so for decades. If that's the case, why don't they just come out and reveal themselves. Maybe they never plan to do so, for reasons we can't comprehend."

"So you admit it – there really are little green women!" jibed Corinne. "The next thing I know, you'll be revealing all your secrets. It just shows you how good my constant acts of torture has been."

"It's much less than torture, and I know you understand a lot more than I'm supposed to disclose to my spouse or anyone else not involved in the project. But I do appreciate your inputs."

"So here's one more... Suppose you did something that would be noticed by these aliens, something they couldn't ignore? Then they'd either have to reveal themselves or disappear. Either scenario might be better than what we have now."

"The problem is, Cory, we've already done a lot to alert them we know they're here. Just testing for electromagnetic data in specific places where they're active must tell them we have an inkling of what's going on. Yet they're still here, and still hidden. That tells me they haven't made up their minds yet whether they should communicate directly with us, because I'm sure they have the technology."

"Maybe they're listening to what we're saying right now," replied Corinne.

"Maybe. Our primitive knowledge within the field of planetary environmental tracers tells me we could eventually listen in on other planets. Imagine how far environmental tracer technology could be in another thousand years. These aliens could easily be more advanced than that."

"Or how about a society millions or even billions of years old?" suggested Corinne.

"If they haven't already blown themselves up, they'd probably have instantaneous two-way communication capability between planets that's better than our current videophones."

"Hey, Miss Alien," said Corinne, wiggling her fingers in a cute little wave. "I see you. And I know you see me."

* * * * *

Later that night, when Shawn was alone downstairs, working on a summary of the latest electromagnetic intensive areas for Tom Suthers in Washington, a Red Star message came in. When Shawn clicked on the email icon, he was surprised to see it had no return address, which he'd never seen before. But Red Stars could come only from shamans, so he wasn't surprised to see the subject line: "Polarization Synchrotron," which was a topic Fat and he had been discussing a lot lately. The original Cornell device had come a long way, and held promise for faster-than-light communication.

When he clicked open the message, there was nothing in the body except a link to an attachment listed as 19.3 megabytes in size. He thought about this for a few minutes, since it was the perfect set-up for introduction of a computer virus, especially considering the unique lack of a return address. But then he thought some more, and decided any virus would be disabled before it got off the ground by his extensive GC virus-protection software. Plus, all of his data was securely backed up. There was something particularly interesting about this strange Red Star message. After a few more minutes of reflection, he clicked the attachment link, and opened it.

* * * * *

"Okay, Fat, hold onto your hat. Hey, that rhymes."

"So the message had no return address at all, and the attachment was listed as a PDF," clarified Fat. "That format hasn't been around for over 20 years. I'm not sure my computer can even decode it these days. So let me guess, you opened it?"

"You guessed right, and I was able to read it. It's a complete instruction booklet, including detailed blueprints for a device like a polarization synchrotron, but much more elaborate. All made out of common materials you have lying around in the best-equipped laboratories in the world. Not a simple device, but straightforward in its construction detail. It's called a "wave pattern differentiator.""

"And you want to build it, right?"

"Of course we'll build it, Fat. By that I mean Tom Suthers will somehow get it funded for someone to build. Couldn't cost more than a gazillion dollars. It would be nice if we had it by tomorrow."

"That's not asking much."

"I don't think so, if it's our connection to the stars," replied Shawn. "Of course, it could be just a hoax, and a very expensive one, at that. What do you think?"

"Send me the attachment as soon as you can. I should be able to open it, since you did. What's a little computer virus between friends, I always say."

"You know, Fat, I know it's from them. I think I knew it before I even opened the attachment. It's logical – we need help to communicate instantaneously, and they have the technology. So here it is."

"Have you considered why they sent it to you, Shawn. After all, the President of the United States or maybe the Prime Minister of the European Union might have been a good choice."

"Don't forget they've been following sports stars around, so why not shamans?"

* * * * *

Tom Suthers took the proposal directly to the President of the United States, who authorized the immediate construction of the first wave pattern differentiator in the world. Within two weeks, using emergency funding, construction was complete. On September 27, 2049, the first communication contact with an alien intelligence was established from a transmitting antenna on Mountain 99 Road, just off Kern River Highway. The President of the United States authorized this in keeping with the logical assumption that the alien beings had indirectly requested first contact be through a shaman. In a telephone call to Shawn's house the night before, President Donald Curtwell, had asked that Shawn phone the White House as soon as the first communication was complete, regardless of the time of day or night. The President assured Shawn the White House operators would be quick to put his call through. They would know his name and importance when he called, but wouldn't know he was a shaman.

The wave pattern differentiator had been delivered to Shawn's house by government courier, after a C-130 turboprop landed at Kern Valley Airport. Shawn offered the courier a soda, but he said he had to get back to the airport. It was expensive to keep C-130's waiting.

With Fat's help, the two shamans set up the device, using the instructions in the PDF file. This was the first time Fatius Lane had been to Shawn's home, and they had met personally only three times in their 40 years of research together. It was best if shamans weren't seen together very often.

"So it's all ready," said Shawn. "It's hard to believe you just push a 'Start' button. Looks like one of those old-fashioned photocopiers."

"You get to do the honors," replied Fatius.

"Start me up," chimed Shawn, as he pushed the button.

The PDF instructions included a requirement for a personal computer to be positioned within a few feet of the device, and Shawn decided to use his micro-laptop, which he placed on the coffee table in front of them. After a few seconds, a Red Star alert popped up on his screen, another message with no return address and no text in the body. Then, within a few more seconds, words began to appear in plain English, slowly progressing down the screen until four sentences had appeared, followed by the word "END."

"Like old-fashioned instant messaging or text messages," said Fatius as the words slowly appeared. They both hunched forward on the couch to read what it said. Corinne sat patiently to their side on the couch, able to barely read the words if she leaned in close, which she did. The short paragraph was now on the screen.

"Hello, Shawn. My name is Kane, and I'm from a planet in the galaxy you call 'Zeus.' This is a historic day for our planet, contacting an alien intelligence for the first time. You can reply when you are ready by simply typing in a new message box, which I'll leave for you to figure out. END"

"This is a historic first for us, too," typed Kane. "We are glad to meet you on this important day for our planet. Please give us some details about who you are, and your location. END"

"Stupid way to start," said Shawn to Fatius and Corinne. "It's a good thing this isn't being recorded."

"Who says?" replied Fatius. More words came through from Kane.

"We are located in an outer spiral arm of the Zeus Galaxy, which we refer to as the 'Milky Way,' and we call our planet 'Earth.' Our separation distance is approximately 15,000 light-years, although upon merger of our two galaxies, we will be separated by only 5000 light-years, and then thrown apart again by gravitational rebound to a distance of over 40,000 light-years. Here today, gone tomorrow. END"

"Creepy sense of humor," said Fatius. "Ask him if they're going to blow us up." Shawn decided not to ask, but instead inquired about the glitches in history.

"We're aware of the historic oddities that place one of our biggest telescopes at two different locations, and another anomaly indicating one of our most famous aviators died twice in two separate locations. These seem to be related to your recent surveillance of our planet, a fact we knew about. Are you able to explain this flaw in our planet's history? END"

After a few seconds, more text filled the message box.

"We've determined it's not your irregularity in history. Instead, it is ours. We discovered similar discontinuities on our own planet before we made direct contact with you, which still baffles our scientists. We haven't figured it out yet. And yes, we're aware of your specific historic findings, including the bones of Amelia Earhart. END"

"How in tarnation does he know about Earhart?" asked Fatius. "You didn't even mention her by name. Please ask him, Shawn. It might be an important tie to what we're trying to achieve here."

"Kane, a man named Fatius, is here with me, and he wants to know about your knowledge of Amelia Earhart. You speak about her as if you are familiar with her importance in our timeline. Could you explain, please? END"

The next message from Kane was enough to shock them more than anything else communicated that day.

"Shawn, let me bring forward some basic facts before we get too far along. First, your planet and ours are parallel worlds, with histories almost duplicating each other. Except we're almost 5 billion years older than you. We've been studying your planet and its people in detail for 30 years, and have only chosen to make contact now because some things have changed that we didn't expect. Something else will interest you – we'll soon be able to see each other instantaneously, just like we're writing to each other on a common time scale now. And this may sound 'creepy,' as Fatius says, but I'm able to see you right now. So Fatius, in answer to your question: No, we aren't going to blow you up. If you could see me right now, you'd notice I look a lot like anyone else on your planet, and I'm waving my creepy little fingers. So to Corinne, I say: Hey, Miss Alien, I see you. END"

* * * * *

The screen of Shawn's micro-laptop was filled with text for two full hours, as Proteus and Earth exchanged information, mostly one-sided enlightenment from Kane, since no one on Proteus knew anything about Earth before today, but Earth seemed to know everything about Proteus.

Before they finished, Kane explained that Earth had expanded its radius of space travel by ten-fold in the past three decades, a product of scientific progress long hampered by Earth's intense concentration on colonization. The quest for new colonies had sapped all of Earth's energy for billions of years, and now it was time to move forward again. As Kane said: "Because of our initial discovery of your planet, we decided to try another Apollo-scale program. And it worked."

Now, rather than limited to a travel distance of 100 light-years, Earth possessed the technology to travel over 1000 light-years. On that scale, along with expected further enhancements to space technology over the next few years, Earthlings should be capable of nearly instantaneous travel to Proteus within a few decades. Kane then explained, with a sense of hesitation in his words on the screen, that there was even better news. Another planet, not a parallel world but one similar to the living conditions on Earth and Proteus, had been discovered in another spiral arm of the Heavenly Way (which Kane also referred to as 'Andromeda'). This unoccupied planet would be the perfect refuge for an Earth with a dying Sun, and their accelerating space travel technology should get them there before the end of their century.

As for Proteus, Kane explained that his planet would offer some helpful solutions for their current global warming (much of it to be solved by simple thermal alterations to the world's oceans) and even some procedures to drastically decelerate the loss of their natural resources. As Kane put it: "If we knew back then what we know today, it might have all been prevented for us. But at least we can help you now."

"What is your job on Earth?" asked Shawn in one of his last set of textual questions, along with an embarrassing statement he left to last: "All of this seems so one-sided. There's so much you can do for us, and it seems nothing we can do for you."

"Shawn, I work in a position much like yours as shaman. They call me an 'astrophilosopher,' which emphasizes the importance of the merger of the sciences and humanities. We can't progress without dedicated attention to both. My world's government authorized me to be the point of first contact because they are wise enough to recognize that science more than politics is the solution to advancement within a global society. And now that you mention it, there is one little thing you could do for me, if you feel comfortable. It's more of a personal request rather than anything official from my planet. END"

"END?" thought Shawn. It sounds like Kane is actually embarrassed to ask for personal favor. Yet he had listened to Kane's explanation of how Earth had actually considered what they called a "Jump-Off" scenario prior to their discovery of a new uninhabited planet in the Heavenly Way. Shawn could read between the lines: Kane had been instrumental in keeping the politicians in line, a process likely involving great personal sacrifice and risks involving possible loss of his scientific career. Now he was afraid to ask a personal favor of a shaman on Proteus who had become privy to the most momentous decisions in the history of the known intelligent universe.

"Please ask. Whatever, it is, I'll try to help. END"

"There's a current craze on your planet called 'genealogy,' and I need to change something. It will take a minor adjustment to your history records, hopefully without harm to anyone. In the ancient lineage of a person now named Dyanne P. Chertneggen, I'd like to see a minor glitch repaired. We need to find a way to make sure she doesn't end up in a future society called the 'human zoo.' When your planet finally progresses to the point Earth has aged today, I'll be around, and I want to meet her under different circumstances. END"

Shawn looked at Fatius, who replied with a blank expression and raised eyebrows. Corinne, on the other hand, seemed to understand, as indicated by a simple nod of her head. Shawn thought he understood, too.

"Kane, I will do everything in my power as a shaman to take care of it. Of that you can be assured. END"

When they terminated the connection, it was well after midnight. Shawn knew he should telephone the President immediately, even though it would be past 3 am in Washington. But before he phoned, he hugged Corinne like they had just escaped death in a tragic accident, which in a way they had. Then he turned to Fatius, who was now kicked back in his mission-accomplished pose, feet up on the coffee table and hands behind his head, leaned back and enjoying life.

"Fat, I'm curious about the USC game. How did we do?"

"It was a tie."

"There's no such thing as a tie in football," replied Shawn.

"Well, it was a tie, so the game went into sudden-death overtime. That's when we kicked a controversial field goal that hit the cross-bar and went through."

"So we won," stated Shawn with a sense of satisfaction showing on his face, including a scrunched up set of lips in an enormous grin.

"You bet we won, my shaman friend," said Fatius.

Corinne expressed a soft sense of relief: You're right, Fat. Everybody won, and it was a mighty big victory."

Then she smiled at the idle micro-laptop, and wiggled her fingers in a little wave.

About the Author

From 1980 to 2005, Wayne Lutz was Chairman of the Aeronautics Department at Mount San Antonio College in Los Angeles. He also served 20 years as a U.S. Air Force C-130 aircraft maintenance officer. His educational background includes a B.S. degree in physics from the University of Buffalo and an M.S. in systems management from the University of Southern California. The author is a flight instructor with 7000 hours of flying experience.

For the past three decades, he has spent summers in Canada, exploring remote regions in his Piper Arrow, camping next to his airplane. The author resides in a floating cabin on Canada's Powell Lake in all seasons, and occasionally in a city-folk condo in Bellingham, Washington. His writing genres include regional Canadian publications and science fiction.

Books by Wayne J. Lutz

Coastal British Columbia Stories

Up the Lake
Up the Main
Up the Winter Trail
Up the Strait
Up the Airway
Farther Up the Lake
Farther Up the Main
Farther Up the Strait
Cabin Number 5
Off the Grid
Up the Inlet

Science Fiction Titles

Echo of a Distant Planet
Inbound to Earth
When Galaxies Collide
Anomaly at Fortune Lake
Across the Galactic Sea

Order at:
www.PowellRiverBooks.com

Coastal BC Living Blog
PowellRiverBooks.blogspot.com

www.ingramcontent.com/pod-product-compliance
Lightning Source LLC
Chambersburg PA
CBHW071806190726
48292CB00008B/2733

Matchmaking
Cats
of the
Goddesses
I0726624

Now Leaving
ZERO, KANSAS
PLEASE
COME AGAIN!

$$\textit{Chocolate Furnanigans}$$

Chocolate Furnanigans

A PAWSITIVELY PURRFECT SHENANIGANS CROSSOVER STORY

PEPPER MCGRAW

Contents

Cover and inside images from Dreamtime:
Black cat 22 © Svetlana Tyryshkina
Scratching black cat © Bluedarkat
Woman eating chocolate © Melisende
Fire background © Hugolacasse
Paw Prints and Heart © Zsuskaa
Dragon Silhouette © Elena Kozyreva
Pawprints © Fourleaflover
Devil Cat © Roni Markowitz
Cats peeking out of a box © Bluedarkat
Devil Cat with pitchfork © Ania1992

ISBN 978-1-951247-39-3

Edited by J.L. Troughton
PMG Publishing

"SHE'S NOT REALLY a member of the coven," Bygul protested, "which means she's not even on our list. I thought we were going to focus on the necromancer next."

"Are you crazy?" Tivali exclaimed. "I'm hoping if we ignore her, she'll just go away."

"Or find her own matches without our help," Soraya said.

"It's an excellent plan," Muezza agreed.

"It's not excellent at all." Bygul couldn't believe the cowardice of his co-workers. "We're the matchmaking cats of the goddesses! No match is too difficult for us."

"It's not about the difficulty level, Bygul," Tivali said severely. "We matched that grizzly, didn't we? If we could match him, we can match anyone, but that's not the point."

"Then what is the point?"

"Merry deserves a match too," Soraya said.

Bygul sighed. "Then we'll add her to the end of the list, but there are three other witches ahead of her."

"If we wait until the end, she might go back to the Underworld," Tivali protested.

Bygul thought this would be an excellent development. Then, hopefully, they wouldn't have to match her at all. "Look, all I'm saying is, she's wreaking havoc all over Zero and Tempest is about two seconds away from committing sororicide."

"Sorori-what?" Soraya asked.

"She's going to kill her sister," Tivali said impatiently.

"Well, why didn't he just say that?" Soraya twitched her tail in annoyance. "Because then I would have pointed out that Tempest can't kill Merry if she isn't even in Zero anymore."

"Wait, what?" Bygul glared at Soraya. Why was he always the last to hear these things? "Where'd Merry go and why?"

"It was getting a little hostile in Zero for her," Soraya said, "so I figured we could send her to the fairies."

"The fairies?" Bygul, Tivali and Muezza all chorused.

"Yes, the fairies. After all, she is one-quarter fairy."

"I don't know why she couldn't just stay in the Underworld in the first place," Bygul grumbled. "She's half-demon, for goddess' sake!"

"Not demonic enough, I guess," Soraya said cheerfully. "Anyway, I left a brochure in her room about the fairy mall in Jamesville."

"The fairy mall isn't *in* Jamesville," Tivali said.

"No, but the hotel that leads to the fairy realm is."

"Hold on a minute." Bygul felt as if his head was going to explode from all the implications. "You sent a half-demon, quarter-witch, quarter-fairy to Hotel Shenanigans in *Jamesville*? The one that's constantly overrun by goddesses, crazy-ass fairies and *dragons*?"

"Well," Soraya hesitated. "Maybe?"

BEFORE MERRY LEFT THE UNDERWORLD, SHE researched the earth realm and its inhabitants, to try and give herself the best possible chance of experiencing all the wonders Earth had to offer while there.

So far, she had discovered the joys of bowling, roller coasters, movie magic and *audio* books.

Leave it to humans to come up with a way to enjoy books without ever having to actually *read* them.

Unfortunately, she had also discovered the dangers of rollerskating, the monstrous terror of wasps (demonic little creatures that never should have been allowed to migrate from Hell, not that anyone wanted them *there* either) and lima beans (nasty bits of cotton, those).

Thankfully, Merry's adventures in the world of food didn't end with the lima beans.

Humans were truly ingenious when it came to combining ingredients for consumption and she soon discovered the bliss of pizza, ice cream and Dr. Pepper, the latter of which had the unfortunate side effect of making her belch fire.

This didn't stop her from drinking Dr. Pepper, of course. It was simply too delicious to give up, which would explain the slightly scorched status of both the steering wheel and the dash of her car.

Beyond the delights of pizza and ice cream and Dr. Pepper, though, she had discovered the most sublime, wondrous invention of the ages.

Chocolate.

Glorious, divine nectar of the demons.

She was pretty certain Satan had invented chocolate to control the masses. Too bad for him, she was his daughter, and therefore, his ability to control her was pretty much zero.

Which made her think of the town she'd just left.

She winced as she remembered the latest fire she'd set from all the belching.

Tempest had screeched the loudest, shouting that even Pippa, the firestarter of the coven, hadn't caused as much damage in a year as Merry had in a month.

Whatever.

She'd fixed it with her magic, hadn't she? She'd been so quick, in fact, that the human librarian never even discovered the damage, though she had smelled the smoke and caused a bit of a ruckus, trying to track down the source.

Even so, Merry had no idea why her sister had been so upset.

After all, the library was much better than before, if she did say so herself. Not only had she given it a new paint job when she'd fixed the damage, but she'd also created an entire hidden section, devoted to the underworld and demons.

She might also have created a tiny little doorway between the Underworld and that hidden room, just for her and any other demon clever enough to discover it.

She'd made it super tiny though, so really, the only ones that might find it were the pixies. Well, and maybe the hell-kittens.

She thought about that for a moment, then shrugged.

Oh, well.

From what she could see, Zero, Kansas could use a bit of excitement, especially now that she'd left the town in her rearview mirror.

Reaching over for some more of her delicious snacks, Merry was horrified to discover the chocolate covered peanut container was empty.

She tossed it onto the floorboard, where it joined a plethora of empty bags and containers that at one time had been filled with M&Ms, chocolate-covered raisins, candy bars, cookies, brownies, and pretty much every dessert with chocolate she could eat one-handed.

At the beginning of the road trip, she'd tried to eat a giant bowl of chocolate mousse while driving, but found it to be an extremely frustrating experience as the treat didn't always make it into her mouth.

What a tragedy that was.

Now, with barely an hour to go, all the chocolate in the car seemed to be gone.

Except—she grabbed the chocolate shake sitting in her cup holder and tried to suck up the very last dregs of that chocolatey goodness. Sadly, all she got was a bunch of air.

Damn!

One quick detour later and Merry walked out of a gas station with her arms full. She dumped everything onto the front passenger seat, scooped all the trash off the floorboard, glanced around and hoofed it to the bin nearby.

She hesitated for one long moment, arms full of plastic destruction, then dumped it all in the bin, murmuring, "Farewell, you earth-destroying receptacles of delight. You have served me well."

"Mrawr."

She froze two steps away and closed her eyes.

"Mrawr, mrawr."

"Oh, come on!" She glared around her, looking for someone, *anyone,* who might be better suited to handle this horrifying development. Unfortunately, there were no other cars *or* people in sight.

"Mrawr, mrawr, mrawr."

"I can't believe you, Soraya," Tivali said severely, her whiskers quivering in disapproval.

"What? It's not my fault that trucker abandoned a box full of kittens, now is it?"

"That was a hundred miles from here!" Bygul exclaimed.

"I couldn't just leave them there! That parking lot was full of dangers. This one is much less crowded."

"They should have gone to the waiting room for processing," Bygul said. "You're completely ignoring procedures."

"Like you've never done the same," Soraya said.

Bygul let out a growl of frustration. The problem was she was right. In fact, Bygul was *known* for ignoring procedures when necessary.

"Besides," Soraya said. "It was super simple to just move the box from one parking lot to another, and bonus, our target witch was *right* there, so obviously, this was the perfect spot for those kittens to find a home."

"Satan himself failed to convince Merry to adopt a kitten!" Muezza exclaimed.

"Those were hell-kittens. There's a difference," Soraya said. "Besides, I don't get what the problem is. We agreed to match Merry, so obviously, we needed to find the purrfect cats for her. Those kittens were in need and she's less likely to turn away from a bunch of kittens, don't you think?"

"I think that crazy demon-witch-fairy hybrid is not a good candidate for cat motherhood," Bygul said, "which is why we shouldn't be matching her in the first place!"

"I figured we'd just wait until we know who her mate is and then we can match *him* to a cat or two," Muezza said. "It seems the safest option."

"Unless she mates a dragon," Bygul muttered, "or worse, a fairy."

THIS WAS SO UNFAIR.

Merry had spent years turning away the cutest kittens hell had ever spat out, then weeks in Zero, Kansas, pretending not to notice how adorable the coven's familiars were, resisting all temptation to try and score one for herself.

And look what she got for her efforts—an entire boxful of adorable kittens staring her in the face the moment she was on her own, with no one else to manipulate into taking responsibility for them.

Hands on hips, Merry glared down at the box and counted kittens.

She lost count several times due to the kittens' repeated attempts to climb the walls of the box only to tumble back down, usually knocking at least one other kitten down with them.

She thought there were six of them, but worst case scenario, there might actually be eight of the little buggers.

She groaned. "Fine. You can come with me, but don't get too comfortable." She scooped the box up and strode back to the car. "We'll be finding homes for each of you because I'm certainly not in the market for one kitten, let alone all y'all, no matter how adorable you may be."

She opened the passenger door and stood there staring.

Okay, now, this really *wasn't* fair.

The passenger seat was full of the best treats this gas station had to offer, leaving absolutely no room for a box of kittens. And the box was too tall to fit under the dash on the floorboard.

Seriously?

There was no help for it. She was going to have to move her stash because no way was Merry going to put the box of kittens in the backseat.

That would be a recipe for disaster.

She just knew the minute they were out of her sight, they'd somehow escape the box and then it would be invasion of the claws and the cat fur and the hairballs.

No, thank you.

Heaving a sigh of dejection, Merry shoved all the lovely treats onto the floor board and settled the box on the passenger seat. "Don't get used to it," she snarled.

"Mrawr," was the only response.

Grabbing two handfuls of treats, Merry closed the door and stalked around to the driver's side, examining what she held along the way.

Snickers—so good.

Reeses—always fabulous.

Raisinets—under normal circumstances, raisins were disgusting. However, in this case, Raisinets served as proof that chocolate made *everything* better.

Oreos—delicious bits of goodness that got stuck in her teeth, turning them black. Snacks for later!

She settled into the driver's seat, tossed most of the snacks onto the dash, retaining a box that apparently held Milk Duds inside.

She didn't understand the use of the word Dud in relation to chocolate, nor milk, to be honest.

After all, milk was rather disgusting. More proof that chocolate made everything better. Chocolate milk. Yum.

Five minutes down the road and Merry pulled onto the shoulder, executed a u-turn and returned to the gas station.

"Don't look at me like that," she said to the kittens as she climbed back into the car, dumping an armful of Milk Duds on top of the other treats on the floorboard. "If you'd tasted them, you'd have gone back too. Trust me, they're divine. But not good for kittens, which is good news for me, because that means, these are all mine. Paws off, kittens!"

Back on the road, she spent the next hour eating her way through pack after pack of Milk Duds—chewy, divine caramel covered in the greatest substance on earth, *chocolate*—and chatting with the kittens.

"Look, I know some humans are probably going to be terribly disappointed when they go into that gas station and discover that someone bought their entire stock of Milk Duds, but honestly, I deserve them more than any human on earth. After all, I have an entire lifetime of eating these treats to catch up on. How many years is that, anyway?" She thought about it a moment, trying to count, but decided she really just didn't care. "It's a lot of years, all right? And that means, a lot of Milk Duds still to consume before I've caught up to even one eight-year-old human!"

"Mrawr."

"Exactly! Oh, look. It's a sign welcoming us to Jamesville. How polite. Although, there's not much here to see, is there? Just woods and more woods."

According to GPS, if she kept going straight, she'd eventually reach the town square and a bit past that would be Hotel Shenanigans, where she had a reservation waiting.

The only problem was that Merry was more interested in exploring the creepy woods.

"What do you think, kittens? Should we just stay on the nice, safe-looking road or go on an adventure? Oh, look! A turn-off. Adventure calls!"

She turned onto the narrow gravel road and followed it through the very spooky-looking woods. Darkness was just beginning to fall, which gave the towering trees an extra dose of sinister gloom. "Exciting, don't you think?"

A few moments later, she came upon another road and without thinking much about it, made the turn and wasn't even surprised when that road ended in a small parking lot.

Right in the middle of the woods.

"Well, this is rather bold for the humans."

A glance in her rearview mirror showed that darkness had fallen just enough so that she really couldn't even see the road she'd followed anymore.

"Creepy road, check. Spooky woods all around, check."

She glanced around, taking note of the only two cars in the lot. "Deserted parking lot, check. Honestly, this is how every horror novel begins, not to mention horror movies. I'm just thrilled." She leaned forward and grabbed several handfuls of chocolate from the dash and the floorboard, stuffing them into the pockets of her hoodie.

She then hopped out of the car, rounded the hood and grinned when she saw the path just beyond the headlights. It was even paved!

She hurried to the passenger side and opened the door.

Two of the kittens were racing around inside the box, chasing each other, pouncing on each other and wrestling one another to the ground.

The other four—no, five—no, six—were piled in a ball in the corner, sound asleep.

Before she could talk herself out of it, Merry reached into the box and scooped one of the wrestling kittens into her arms. Like all his other siblings, he was pitch black. The minute she drew him close, he started batting at her hair. She chuckled, kissed his forehead, then set him back in the box next to his sister, who pounced on him the minute he was within her reach again.

"If I didn't know any better, I'd think you two were hiding a bit of hell-kitten in your genes, which would be wonderful since it's time for an adventure!" She scooped the box into her arms, bumped the car door closed with her hip and started down the path through the woods. "Good thing we got here when we did, kittens. I might not have noticed this path if it were any darker out. Then again, I do have better-than-average eyesight. It's probably the demon in me."

"Mrawr." One of the kittens leapt for freedom and managed to catch Merry's fingers with her claws before sliding back down the side of the box.

Merry let out a hiss and chuckled. "I think I'm going to call you two Spike and Drusilla, in honor of my favorite fictional vampires. You know, just between you and me, I've met a few vampires in my time here on earth—there's an entire coven in Zero, Kansas— but let me tell you, what a letdown! Oh, look, a building." She started walking around it, chatting the entire way.

"The thing is, I guess my expectations were a little different, on account of the books and the movies and all. I expected the vampires to either be, you know, blood-sucking evil demons, or heroic superheroes fighting the evil in our midst. I don't know what that evil would be, mind you—oil companies, people who don't recycle, dentists maybe—but I definitely expected something *more* from the vampires. But you know what, kittens? They were just kind of *boring*."

She finally reached the front of the building and raised an eyebrow at the neon sign above the door.

Shenanigans.

"Well, this is an excellent development. I didn't expect to find a Shenanigans out in the middle of nowhere. Things are looking up, kittens. Zero didn't have any Shenanigans, though they had plenty of paranormals, so that's a little strange. But here in Jamesville, we've already found two! Well, I guess we haven't technically found the hotel yet, but we know it exists!" She pulled open the door and walked inside, "Maybe we'll meet our first serial killer here! That'd be kind of cool, don't you think?"

"Mrawr."

"Oh, but don't worry, kittens. I'll protect you from the big bad wolves. Promise."

Two

S O MANY CHANGES in little more than a year, Sam thought as he looked around the bar.

Shenanigans itself hadn't changed much, but the lives of its employees and many of its customers had.

Travis and Glory still ran the bar like the black bears they were, letting the local paranormals blow off steam, while also keeping them in line—a task, if Sam was being completely honest, made infinitely more difficult by his own wolf pack.

Wolves.

He grinned. No other shifter he'd rather be.

A burst of laughter caught his attention and his heart tugged at the sight of his alpha, Adam, arm slung around his mate, Gigi, pulling her in for a heated kiss.

A year ago, he would have laughed if anyone had told him his alpha could be so relaxed and happy with a snow leopard mate. With any mate, actually.

If he'd ever thought about it, he'd have bet money that of all the wolves he knew, Adam was the most likely to remain single his entire life.

Instead, among their group of childhood friends, Sam was the only one who remained unmated.

Somehow, despite the events of a year ago, when matings had been thick in the air, Sam had remained unattached.

Like bowling pins, bears, wolves, cougars, even humans had been knocked down one-by-one in a sweep that spanned almost a year.

The black bears had been the first to fall, along with Sam's beta, Max, who had finally claimed Glory for his mate. Then, their childhood friend, Karl, and a couple cougars had hooked up with some witches.

Now *that* was crazy.

It wasn't just the shifters and witches, though.

A human in town mated a fairy of all things. Then, one of the Shenanigans waitresses mated a *dragon* and that set off a whole slew of inter−realm matings.

Thankfully, Sam was too busy working to get caught up in *that* craziness.

He shuddered at the thought of being tied to a

dragon, or *worse*, a fairy. Bad enough to have to travel to another realm to visit the in-laws on a regular basis, but scary fairy ones? While also mated to one? No, thank you.

All things considered, their pack had gotten off easy, considering not one of them was mated to a fairy. In fact, all the pack's mates were, so far, entirely from this realm, and even better, none wanted to live anywhere other than Jamesville.

Even Gigi, who'd shown up a year ago, pregnant with Adam's cubs, had settled into pack life like she'd been born to it. And now their triplets were crawling all over the pack house, wreaking havoc everywhere.

A lot of changes, Sam thought again.

Though he hadn't realized it at the time, as his childhood friends were meeting their mates, one by one, he was subconsciously bracing himself for that moment when his own mate would burst into his life and change his world forever.

Except it never happened.

Instead, the matings had dwindled to nothing earlier that spring, leaving Sam to wonder if what he'd anticipated happening wasn't on the horizon at all.

In the beginning, he'd tried to convince himself he was grateful.

After all, he was too busy for a mate, given how far

out he was booked for his custom furniture business. The good news was that his business was solid with orders showing no signs of slowing down. That was also the bad news, given the nature of his business—custom Sam Warner designs that only he could build.

Just thinking about it exhausted him.

He should be in the shop right now, working on a custom desk order, but it had become harder and harder to ignore the loneliness, especially when constantly surrounded by his happily mated friends.

This was why he was at Shenanigans, attempting to soothe his wolf with pack connections when what his wolf really needed was to find his mate.

In the beginning, that need had been subdued, easy to ignore because he'd expected his turn would eventually come.

Over the past six months, though, with not a single mating in sight, that need had grown into a gaping, hollowed-out desperation, one that warned he would soon be forced to leave his pack and his home, if he ever hoped to find the mate who would make him whole.

He'd spent six months trying to ignore that desperate need. After all, it was a well-known phenomenon that mates were often pulled together by the fates.

He'd seen it happen over and over again in Jamesville.

Glory moved there and found Max.

Phoenix moved there and found Travis

The witches came and found Karl, Cole and Dan.

Gigi came for Adam.

Even beings from other realms found themselves traveling to Jamesville and discovering their mates.

Sam had seen this as a sign. He simply needed to be patient. Eventually, his mate would come.

Only she never did.

Then, about a month ago, he remembered that Gigi was actually the exception.

Sure, she'd come to town to find Adam, but she only did so because she'd been pregnant with his cubs.

A pregnancy that had happened because they'd met while Adam was on vacation.

Away from Jamesville.

Gigi would never have known to come looking for Adam if he hadn't left pack lands in the first place.

"I think I might have to leave Jamesville," Sam said, testing the idea out loud.

"What are you talking about?" Karl asked.

Sam shrugged. He probably shouldn't have mentioned it, but he'd been thinking about it for a month and it was past time to make it happen.

"Why would you leave Jamesville?" Max demanded.

"It worked for Adam," Sam said.

"What worked for me?" Adam grabbed a chair from a neighboring table and shoved his way in between Max and Dan.

Sam glanced over to where he'd last seen Adam and saw that Gigi was now surrounded by the other women of the pack.

"Well?" Adam growled.

"You left the pack to find your mate."

"I most certainly did not," Adam snapped. "My mother manipulated me into going on vacation and I just happened to meet my mate along the way. I did *not* go searching for her."

"Still," Sam said. "The effect remains the same. Gigi wasn't going to come here. She had no reason to, so you had to go out there," he waved an arm to the side, "to find her. Sure you were a dunce and left her behind, but then she got pregnant and the rest is history."

"What's your point?" Adam growled.

"My point is the fates knew what they were doing. First, they pulled you away from the pack so that you could meet Gigi and then when you left her pregnant, the fates sent her here. I've been waiting for the fates to send me my mate, but since it hasn't happened yet, I'm thinking I should leave Jamesville, the way you did, in order to find her."

"I don't think it works that way," Dan said.

"Well, why not?"

"Because none of us were searching for our mates when we found them," Cole said.

"He's right," Adam said.

"Pretty sure that's the entire point," Pete said.

"What do you know about it?" Sam growled. "You got mated at eighteen, the minute you realized Jenny was your mate!"

Pete grinned. "I'm a lucky wolf, it's true."

Sam groaned. "Anyway, the point is, I've met every single shifter, witch and human in Jamesville. So unless we start luring new people in, I have no choice but to leave Jamesville if I want to find my mate."

The door to the bar opened behind him, bringing a chill wind inside and a husky voice that wrapped around Sam and his wolf, bringing them both to attention.

"Maybe we'll meet our first serial killer here! That'd be kind of cool, don't you think?"

As Sam was facing away from the door, he didn't see the owner of that sexy voice, but he did see the way that Adam's eyes widened and Max's jaw dropped, though he wasn't sure whether that was in response to the woman's appearance or her words.

He heard a soft sound, almost like a kitten's meow, but that couldn't possibly be—

"Oh, but don't worry, kittens," the same voice said. "I'll protect you from the big bad wolves. Promise."

Oh, now, this was getting interesting.

Sam slowly turned around in his seat and stared at the woman standing a few feet inside Shenanigans.

The first thing he noticed was her mouth. She had her head tipped back, and her mouth wide open as she spilled the dark contents of a small, yellow box inside, all the while balancing a much larger box in her other arm.

She closed her mouth and let out a sound that made him think of sex. She then tipped her head forward and licked her lips, groaning softly.

Sam shifted uncomfortably, his wolf as riveted as he was.

For a long moment, no one moved, then she lifted that little yellow box again and tipped it once more into her mouth, eyes closed.

She let out a soft, humming sound, a sound that went straight to his dick and made his wolf growl in hunger.

As if she'd heard him, the woman's eyes flew open,

but rather than look his way, she glanced down at the larger box in her arms and said sternly, "Absolutely not. These aren't for the likes of you."

Her words were slightly garbled, probably due to the fact that she was still chewing whatever had been in that yellow box.

"But don't worry, kittens. I'll find you something to eat soon."

Sam shook his head in disbelief. Surely no self-respecting paranormal would bring actual kittens into a shifter bar.

"Just don't get too comfortable because we're not staying and that's that." Having apparently finished what she needed to say to the occupants of the box, she strode forward and set it on a table in the middle of the bar. She then pulled out a chair, plopped down and leaned over the box to continue a whispered conversation that Sam couldn't quite make out.

The woman clearly had no sense of self-preservation whatsoever.

She seemed oblivious to the fact that she had the attention of everyone in the bar, all of them paranormals and most of them predators.

Sam hadn't missed how Travis had prevented Phoenix from immediately approaching the woman, though who could blame him?

After all, she'd come into the bar talking of serial killers and she hadn't exactly been acting stable since then, talking with boxes about kittens.

At that moment, Phoenix apparently lost patience with her mate because she yanked her hand free and stalked over to the woman's table.

"Hi there. Welcome to Shenanigans. What can I —" Phoenix cut off her standard greeting with a squeal. Darting forward, she reached into the box and came out with a literal *armful* of kittens.

Actual kittens.

In a shifter bar.

"Look, Travis," Phoenix squealed as she whirled toward the bar. "*Kittens*!"

Travis just grinned.

Ugh. That bear was ridiculously indulgent with his mate. Sam could totally see the writing on the wall.

If this woman was looking for homes for those kittens, she'd come to the right spot. Clearly they were about to have some bar cats.

"Kittens?" Gigi popped up from where she was sitting across the room and made a beeline for Phoenix and the stranger.

Great. Now they'd not only have bar cats, but pack cats as well. Whoever heard of a wolf pack adopting a bunch of kittens?

"Where'd they come from?" Lara, Karl's witchy mate, asked as she and the other women followed Gigi and Phoenix.

"About an hour west of here. Some jerk left them in a box in a gas station parking lot. I couldn't leave them behind, of course."

"Of course not!" Gigi exclaimed as she scooped yet *another* kitten out of the box.

"How many damn kittens are there?" Adam muttered.

"More than enough for Gigi to claim at least one." Max chuckled.

"I wouldn't laugh too hard," Sam said. "Looks like Glory's joining them."

"That's great news," Adam said. "Glory will put an end to this nonsense. Kittens don't belong in a shifter bar."

Max just groaned and shook his head. "Thanks a lot, Adam. That woman has ears like a bat. She's going to not only let those kittens stay, she'll probably insist on adopting several, just to spite us."

"She wouldn't dare," Adam began, but trailed off as they all watched Glory join the women fawning all over the seemingly endless supply of kittens.

"I THOUGHT YOU SAID YOU WERE SENDING HER
to the fairies!" Bygul exclaimed.

"I was," Soraya said. "I *did*."

"Well, she obviously took a wrong turn somewhere," Muezza grumbled.

"Do you think the kittens will be safe with the
wolves?" Soraya fretted.

"Safer than they would have been with the fairies
and the dragons," Bygul said.

"Besides, we've matched wolves and cats before,
lots of times," Tivali said.

"I suppose," Soraya said. "I just didn't have time to
research these wolves, so I don't really know whether
they're trustworthy."

"They'll be fine," Bygul said. "Those bears are two
of my very first mate-matches."

"Really?" Tivali asked. "What cats did you match
them with?"

"None. These were unintentional matches. I was
working halfway across the country on an entirely
different match and those two black bears kept getting
in the way of what I was trying to accomplish, so I used
goddess magic to send them here, to open their own

Shenanigans bar. That one action set into motion a series of matings I could never have predicted. It's what opened my eyes to the true power of our magic and how we could use it to match more than just cats to their human companions."

"So that's why you added mate-matching to your services," Tivali said.

"That's why. It all started right here in Jamesville."

"You know, Sam," Pete said, "You should go over and introduce yourself."

"What? Why?"

"You *were* just complaining that your mate hasn't shown up yet," Pete said.

"He's right," Adam said. "What if that's your mate over there? What if she just waltzed into your life, exactly the way you've been hoping, but instead of rushing over there, you're just sitting here on your ass, letting the moment pass you by?"

"Are you serious right now?" Sam demanded. "Did you not hear her talking about serial killers when she walked in? Not to mention the boxful of kittens. Why would you wish that kind of mate on me?"

Max snickered. "Maybe we misheard her."

"Yeah," Cole said. "Maybe she said serial *kittens*, not killers."

"Give me a break," Sam groaned. "There's no such thing as a serial kitten and even if there was, you know that's not what she said."

"Still," Karl said. "This could be your chance, dude."

"You should definitely go over and introduce yourself," Max said.

Sam let out a rumble of annoyance, but the truth was, his wolf had been urging him to go to the woman ever since the door first opened, even before she spoke.

That first gust of wind that had blown through the bar had carried with it a scent of something purely divine, something that had caught his wolf's attention and set him to howling for more.

The entire situation made Sam appreciate that old saying about being careful what you wished for. He'd made the wish and now he was knee-deep in the consequences.

Three

"WHAT ARE THEIR names?" The waitress, who had introduced herself as Phoenix, asked.

"I haven't named them yet. Well, except for these two." Merry reached into the box and scooped out the last two kittens who were wrestling inside it. "Meet Spike and Drusilla."

"How in the world can you tell them apart?" Phoenix asked.

"Spike has amber eyes and Drusilla has green ones," Merry explained.

Phoenix examined the kittens she was holding, then protested, "But these four have amber or green eyes too."

"Eh, don't know what to tell you." Merry wasn't

about to admit that she couldn't tell them apart to save her life. She'd just done a quick check when lifting the kittens into her arms to make sure one was a boy and the other a girl and since they were—Spike and Drusilla!

Tomorrow, it was entirely possible two different kittens would have those names.

"Phoenix, stop hogging all the kittens." One of the women stole two from Phoenix, cuddling them close for a moment before passing them to two other women standing nearby.

She then took a third kitten for herself, leaving Phoenix with only one.

Phoenix scowled, then cuddled the remaining kitten close. "Don't worry, little guy, I won't let her steal you like she did your siblings."

"You're so adorable," the thief crooned to the kitten in her arms.

"No, Lara." A man stomped across the bar and glared at her.

Something about the way he moved and the growl in his voice screamed shifter to Merry.

"And no to your sisters too." He transferred his glare to the other women. "We've already got three cats running around the apartment. We don't need any more."

"But, they're so cute, Karl. Look at them!" Lara and her sisters held up their kittens, but Karl just growled at them.

Definitely a shifter.

Lara sighed. "I suppose you're right. Ash probably wouldn't appreciate me bringing home another familiar." She returned her kitten to the box and Phoenix promptly reclaimed him.

Lara turned to her sisters. "Maybe we can get Aunt Dory to adopt a couple."

"Seriously?" Karl exclaimed. "Do you *want* those kittens to get mauled?"

One of the other women groaned. "He's right. Aunt Dory's cats are *so* territorial." She whirled and called across the room, "Cole—"

"No!" One of the men shouted back.

"Damnit. Fine. They're so cute, though." She gave one last cuddle to the kitten in her arms before returning him to the box. Her sister did the same.

Phoenix scooped them both up again.

"Thanks for letting us pet them, Merry," Lara said.

"Yes, thanks," her sisters chorused.

The three turned and walked away, talking loudly about their mates owing them big-time for giving up those adorable, precious little babies.

Karl rolled his eyes, hesitated, glanced at the

women walking away, then reached out and gave each kitten a surreptitious scratch on the head.

"I saw that," Lara called without turning around.

Karl let out a low growl, muttering, "Just my luck to have a witch for mate," then hurried after her.

"I love these kittens," Phoenix exclaimed. "They're so soft and playful. Can I have them, Merry? Please?"

Merry shrugged. "I suppose. If you really want them."

"Yay!" Phoenix whirled to face the bar. "Travis, we're adopting four kittens!"

The bartender just grinned back at her.

"Unless—" She whirled back around. "Gigi—"

"Sorry, but no." Gigi was sitting at the table, playing with one of the kittens.

"Oh, but—"

"I'm adopting this one," Gigi said quietly.

"But what about JoJo?"

"Who's JoJo?" Merry asked.

"Her adorable, precious *puppy!*" Phoenix squealed.

"JoJo won't mind. She likes cats."

Phoenix let out a huff of exasperation, then turned toward the other women sitting at the table.

"No," the woman said without without looking up from the two kittens she was playing with.

Merry did a double-take, then started counting

kittens. She could have sworn there'd only been eight when she'd walked into the bar, but now, with the four in Phoenix's hands, the one with Gigi, the two with Glory *plus* Spike and Drusilla...

"But Glory," Phoenix began.

"You've already claimed four, Phoenix," Glory said. "These two kittens are mine."

"Damnit!" Someone roared from across the room. "I blame you, Adam!"

Phoenix pouted, then turned to Merry, a speculative look on her face.

Before Merry could offer her Spike and Drusilla, the door behind her opened and a voice called out, "We heard there were kittens!" and in a rush of movement, Merry found herself surrounded by three older women, who instantly reached into the empty box and started pulling out *more* black kittens.

"What in all the Realms of Hell is going on?" Merry muttered.

"WHAT'S GOING ON WITH THAT BOX OF kittens?" Bygul growled.

"Is it my imagination or are those kittens multiplying?" Tivali asked.

"They're not multiplying," Soraya giggled. "We have seventy-three kittens on our caseload and I figured we might as well take advantage and place some with the shifters. I mean, look at those women! They're clearly cat people."

"They're *wolves*, Soraya," Muezza said severely.

"So?"

"So wolves are *dog* people," Bygul said. "Sure, we've had the occasional success with them, but you can't expect *all* wolves to—" He fell silent as the new arrivals started squealing and fawning all over the kittens, petting, cuddling and playing with them, all while arguing over who was going to adopt which one.

"Obviously, I can," Soraya said. "Besides, the snow leopard has a dog companion."

"What does that have to do with wolves and cats?" Tivali asked exasperatedly.

"Cats are way less accepting than dogs," Soraya said. "So if a snow leopard can accept a dog, I figure these wolves should have no problems accepting a few *adorable* kittens."

"A few?" Bygul asked incredulously.

"Well, she's got a point," Muezza said. "About the kittens being adorable anyway."

"Regardless of how cute they are, you can't send all seventy-three kittens to Jamesville," Bygul said. "The wolves would riot."

"I'm not planning to send *all* of them," Soraya said. "Just the black ones. They're so difficult to place."

"Uh-huh," Tivali said. "And exactly how many black kittens are on the caseload?"

"Forty-one, I think. Or maybe it's forty-two."

"You can't send that many cats to the wolves," Bygul exclaimed.

MERRY COUNTED THE KITTENS RACING around the bar. The women had decided to let the kittens down to play and from that point on, chaos reigned.

Just when Merry thought she had a handle on the number of kittens, she'd lose count and have to start again.

It wasn't easy counting kittens who refused to sit still and who looked so much alike.

However, Merry was pretty sure the count was up to fifteen, which made absolutely no sense. She knew for a fact there'd been no more than eight, maybe ten

at the most, in the box when she'd walked into
Shenanigans.

Yet, now there were fifteen. Maybe even sixteen,
since she was pretty sure she hadn't counted that
one yet.

She stared as a black kitten with one white paw
went racing by, then reached into her pocket to drag
out a candy bar.

She devoured it in about two seconds, then pulled
out another one.

This was a nightmare!

Thank the demons for chocolate.

Chocolate made everything better, even when
faced with an unknown number of homeless kittens.

The only good news was that Merry was pretty
certain the majority of the kittens would not be accompanying her back to the hotel that night. Thank the
demons.

"So, you like kittens, eh?"

Merry froze as the scent that accompanied that
gravelly voice washed over her. She crouched down to
place Drusilla, or maybe it was Spike, on the floor—no,
that was definitely Drusilla.

Standing back up, she slowly turned to face the
owner of that voice.

By the flames of Hell, the man was *hot*.

Merry was quite tall for both females *and* males in the Earth realm, though rather short for Hell, but this man stood eye-to-eye with her.

And what gorgeous eyes they were. Dark and intense, they were trained on her face, waiting for her to answer.

Merry cleared her throat. "Not really."

A look of confusion crossed his face. "Not really what?"

"I'm not really that fond of kittens, though I have to admit, they are rather cute." Cute, but so tiny and fragile, at least compared to the Hell-Kittens her father always had running around the Nine Realms of Hell.

She eyed the box that had somehow made its way to the floor and was now sitting tipped on its side, spewing yet another kitten from its depths.

This was probably the work of Satan, that nosy, interfering bastard.

"If you're not that fond of kittens, how in the world did you end up with twenty of them?"

"Twenty!" Bygul exclaimed. "Soraya, I said to stop sending them kittens!"

"I'm trying to stop it, but the portal seems to be stuck."

"*Portal?*" Bygul, Tivali and Muezza chorused.

"You opened a portal in the bar?" Tivali demanded. "What were you thinking?"

"Not the bar," Soraya exclaimed. "I would never do that! No, the *box* is the portal."

The box that was spewing out three more kittens, even as they watched.

"For goddess' sake, Soraya!" Bygul exclaimed. "What's on the other end of the portal?"

"The waiting room, of course."

The rest of them groaned.

The waiting room was where they transported the kittens on their caseload to keep them safe until they were ready for delivery to their new human companions.

It was a place outside of time, near their home realm of the goddesses, but not quite in it, and it wasn't to be messed with at all.

"There must be *thousands* of cats and kittens in the waiting room!" Tivali exclaimed.

"Oh, don't worry," Soraya said. "I programmed the portal with very specific requirements. Only black kittens on *our* caseload can use it. For all the other cats, it's just a regular old box."

"Well, this is a nightmare," Muezza observed. "If we don't do something fast, all forty-plus black kittens are going to end up running around that Shenanigans in Jamesville."

SAM TOOK ADVANTAGE OF THE CHAOS IN THE room, what with all the kittens—he'd lost count at twenty—to approach the woman Phoenix called Merry.

An unlikely name, he thought, for someone who seemed so serious.

Not a single smile had crossed her face since entering the bar, not even when one kitten started playing with the strands of hair escaping from the strange balls sitting on the sides of her head. Not quite Princess Leia buns, but close.

Even when speaking with the kittens, she wasn't smiling or crooning the way the other women were.

No. She just spoke in a quiet, serious voice, with no real inflection to it at all, almost as if the kittens were human rather than non-shifting animals.

It was disconcerting, to say the least.

Nevertheless, both Sam and his wolf were intrigued.

And that was before he approached closely enough to catch her scent, which was when his wolf lunged forward and started to howl.

Great.

This strange, serious woman, who spoke of serial killers and carried around boxes full of kittens, was his mate.

He was doomed.

Twenty!

Merry whirled and started counting cats again. "There can't be that many, can there?"

"I'm pretty sure there are more."

She scowled as three cats raced by. Damn! She lost track again. "So, who are you?"

"Sam Warner. And you are?"

"Merry. Merry B-adness, those are a lot of cats."

"Merry Badness?"

She glanced at him from the corner of her eye. It was really all she could manage without wrestling him to the nearest flat surface for a bit of sin and fun. The man was just too beautiful for his own good. In a rugged, down-to-hell, shifter kind of way.

The room was full of shifters and witches, and for the most part, she couldn't tell one from the next.

Though she was pretty sure the waitress was different from the other shifters in the room and her bartender boyfriend was definitely a bear. There was just something about the way he dragged her across the bar for a kiss that absolutely screamed bear.

Merry eyed Sam Warner speculatively, still not facing him straight-on, but enjoying the thought of *him* hauling *her* across the bar.

Yep.

He definitely had the muscles for it and now she was imagining all kinds of blissful things they could do together.

Damn.

She searched her pockets and found one minuscule bar of chocolate left.

This was a disaster!

She tore it open and popped the entire thing in her mouth, all at once.

She closed her eyes and just held the chocolate there, on her tongue, letting it melt slowly. She let out a soft groan of delight.

Delicious!

Chocolate was perhaps even more sinfully delightful than sex.

She opened her eyes and peeked at Sam Warner again.

Well. Maybe not more than, but definitely *as* delightful.

Then again, maybe she should conduct a little experiment.

No. A clinical trial.

Yes! She'd conduct clinical trials involving chocolate and sex and this human at her side, this Sam Warner, could be her first participant. Subject. Whatever.

"So." She turned to face him straight on as the last of the chocolate melted in her mouth. "You want to have sex?"

Four

"WAIT. WHAT JUST happened?" Bygul demanded.

"I have no idea," Tivali said.

"I moved the box!" Soraya exclaimed.

"Moved it where?" Muezza asked.

"Back to the waiting room. Now when the black kittens go in, they just portal right back out into the same room. Don't worry. I replaced it with a perfectly ordinary box. The humans won't even notice the difference."

"If you say so," Bygul muttered, "but that wasn't what I was talking about."

"Oh? What happened? I was a bit busy moving the portal box."

"The demon-witch-fairy just asked the wolf for sex," Muezza said.

"Just like that?" Soraya asked.

"Just like that," Tivali said.

"I had no idea demon-witch-fairies were so forthright," Soraya exclaimed.

"It's gotta be the fairy in her," Bygul muttered.

"Definitely," Tivali agreed. "They're way worse than demons."

SAM WAS TRYING TO FIGURE OUT HOW TO GET his pretty mate to look at him when she abruptly turned and asked if he wanted to have sex.

Or at least that's what he thought she said.

He was having trouble believing it though.

"I'm sorry." He shook his head at the squeaky sound of his voice, cleared his throat and tried again. "What did you just say?"

"I asked if you wanted to have sex. I'm conducting an experiment, you see. Oh, Phoenix!" She whirled to catch Phoenix's attention as she walked by.

"Yes, Merry?" Phoenix had a huge smile on her face, and two kittens, one on each shoulder, were batting at her dangling, snowflake earrings. "Can I get you something? What's your favorite drink? You've made me so happy with these kittens. I know a drink can't possibly be enough to repay you, but I'd like to try anyway."

"Do you have anything with chocolate in it? *Lots* of chocolate?"

"Hmm. Let me go see what I can find. Come on, my loves." Phoenix turned and headed back to the bar. As she walked, two more kittens raced after her, chasing her feet and batting at her shoelaces.

"This place is nuttier than a fruitcake," Sam muttered.

Merry looked at him quizzically. "Why would a cake have nuts in it? For that matter, why would a fruit have cake? You're not making any sense."

"It's just a saying."

"Right. So back to my question. Do you want to have sex? I need chocolate first, though."

Sam raised his eyebrows at that. "You need chocolate for sex? Is it for courage?"

Merry let out a peel of laughter.

Whoa.

He'd never heard a laugh like that. There really was no describing it. It should have made everyone around them smile in response, except it sounded kind of dark.

And evil.

He'd just been thinking that she hadn't smiled since entering the bar and now he was thinking he hoped to never see her smile again.

And the laugh was so much worse.

He glanced over at his pack and saw them all staring back at him, wide-eyed, with worried looks on their faces.

"Serial killer," his brother, Karl, mouthed slowly.

"Sam, my baby, did you see all these precious kittens?"

Sam stiffened in horror. He'd forgotten their *mother* was in the building. Worse, she was with the *alpha's* mother and aunt.

Before he could even think of running, his mother was right there, pulling him down to pinch his cheeks and ruffle his hair. "Hello, my sweet boy. How many kittens are you going to adopt?"

"Uh."

Could this night get any worse?

First, his mate showed up, talking of serial killers and handing out kittens like some kind of feline-dealer from hell.

Then, she propositioned him, which might have been the highlight of his night if she hadn't *laughed* when he asked a simple question, making it clear he had his very own special spot on her list of victims, a fact that had chills racing up and down his spine.

And now, his *mother* was there, talking about him adopting kittens as if *that* were a foregone conclusion. Ridiculous!

Before he could even think of an answer, one that would get him out of this entire situation, his mother whirled and said, "Well? What's wrong with you, boy? Introduce us to your girl!"

The answer was yes.

It *could* get worse.

Dragging in a deep breath, Sam said quietly, "Mom, this is Merry. Merry this is my mother, Francine."

"Lovely to meet you, my dear." Francine grabbed Merry's hands in hers and clasped them tightly. "I am so excited about the kittens. The minute I heard a young woman had shown up at Shenanigans with a boxful of kittens, I just knew you were going to be an amazing addition to the pack."

Merry's eyes widened and she sent him a panicked look, as if he might be able to stop the steamroller that was his mother.

Sam just shrugged helplessly back. He had no idea what Merry expected him to do. His mother was one of the infamous Alpha Six. There was absolutely no stopping her once she got started.

"I mean, how could you be anything less than perfection when you come bearing kittens?"

Sam swallowed the snort he was desperate to release. No way did he want these women angry at him.

"Anyway, since my son can't seem to find his words to complete these introductions, I'll just have to take care of that myself." Francine dragged Merry a couple feet away where—horrors—the mothers of the alpha *and* the beta were apparently waiting their turn.

"This is Agatha," Francine said. "She's Adam's mom. He's our pack alpha, and Gigi's mate. You've met Gigi, haven't you?"

Merry started to nod, but then Francine added, "And JoJo, of course?" so then Merry shook her head, looking a bit confused, which Sam completely related to.

"And this is Betina," Francine went on, not even seeming to register Merry's confusion (or her answers for that matter). "She's Max's mother. He's our pack beta and he mated Glory. You've met Glory, right?"

Without even waiting for Merry's answer, Francine continued, "It's really quite shocking, you know, that our pack alpha *and* our pack beta mated non-wolves.

We're becoming wonderfully diverse, don't you think?"

Still without waiting for a reply, or for Agatha and Betina to acknowledge Merry, Francine whirled and dragged her back to Sam's side. "So. How many kittens are you adopting, son?"

"Uh."

"We haven't quite decided yet," Merry said. "A number of the kittens are already spoken for and I'd hate to promise Sam he'd get one, only to discover there are none left."

"Oh." Francine looked disappointed. "Does that mean we're too late to adopt as well?" She indicated herself, Agatha and Betina.

"Not at all," Merry assured her. "Glory is handling all the adoptions for me, and she knew you three would be interested. I bet she's already got specific kittens in mind for each of you."

"I knew I loved Glory for a reason," Betina declared.

"Besides the fact that she's your son's mate?" Agatha asked dryly.

"And makes him incredibly happy?" Francine asked, then turned to glare at Sam.

Sam jerked back in shock. "What'd I do?"

"Nothing and that's the point. You need to stop messing around and find your mate, young man!"

It was all Sam could do not to proclaim loud and clear that he'd already found her and she was was standing right beside him, thank you very much, and if his mother would stop interfering in his life, he'd maybe get down to the business of *wooing* his mate.

Except he was currently rather terrified of his mate and wasn't quite sure he *wanted* to woo her.

His wolf didn't like that thought at all because it howled, then lunged for his mate. It took all of Sam's strength and control to keep from shifting entirely.

The look on Merry's face told him she was aware something had just happened, or almost happened, but she hadn't flinched at all. She simply eyed him with a curious look on her face, then watched as Francine hooked arms with Agatha and Betina and walked across the room toward where Glory was herding cats out from behind the bar.

"Glory!" Betina called.

Even from clear across the bar, Sam could see Glory's shoulders hunch a bit, before she shook it off and turned to face her mother-in-law. "Hello, Betina. How are you?"

"Excited to adopt a kitten. Merry says you're handling the adoptions for her."

Glory's head jerked around and she glared at Merry, who let out such an evil-sounding chuckle that Sam had sidled two steps away before he realized what he was doing and hurried back to his mate's side.

"You just threw Glory under the bus, didn't you?" He asked Merry.

"There's no bus in here and even if there were, I don't see why I would want to do that. Sounds rather dangerous."

"It means, Glory had no idea she was going to be handling those adoptions, did she?"

"Of course not. Why would I warn her that I was pawning the duty off onto her?" Merry asked. "If she knew in advance, she might have found a way to thwart my efforts. Now, she's stuck."

"Announcing it to her in-laws was pure genius."

"No, that was just luck," Merry said. "I'd already chosen Glory when they showed up. It was between her and Gigi."

"Not Phoenix?"

Merry snorted. "Of course not. She'd have just let herself adopt them all, then her bartender boyfriend would be cleaning litter boxes for the rest of his natural life and that would probably be the end of that relationship."

Sam snickered. "Mate."

"What's that?"

"He's her mate."

"Well, that's disappointing."

"It is?" Sam scowled at the thought that his mate might be lusting after Travis. How annoying!

"Well, yes. Because bartender mate doesn't have quite the same ring to it as bartender boyfriend."

"I mean, you're not wrong."

"I'm never wrong."

Sam glanced over to see if she was joking, but he simply couldn't tell. Her face was completely expressionless, not a single smile or twitch of the mouth in sight.

At that moment, Phoenix came rushing across the floor toward them. Her arms were full and as they watched, she dumped everything in her arms on the table in front of them.

"I brought you every bit of chocolate I could find," Phoenix began, but Merry was already helping herself.

She snatched up a candy bar and had it stripped of its wrapping and was devouring it in seconds. "Delicious," she mumbled as she grabbed a jar of chocolate syrup. She tipped her head back, opened her mouth wide and started pouring in the syrup.

Sam glanced at Phoenix and saw she was beaming. What the hell?

He glanced back at Merry and saw that she'd set the bottle aside and was now opening a bag of chocolate covered raisins.

Gross.

"These are so marvelous," Merry said around a mouthful of chocolate. "I've never tasted anything so wonderful in my entire life. Well, except for chocolate brownies. And chocolate cake. Chocolate ice cream. Ohh, but chocolate ice cream with bits of chocolate brownies and a swirl of fudge. Mmmm."

She closed her eyes and swayed as she continued to shove chocolate candy, baked goods and other chocolate concoctions in her mouth.

"This can't be healthy," Sam muttered. "Maybe she has an eating disorder." At this rate, the chocolate would all be gone in the next five minutes.

"Eh, it's perfectly normal for demon hybrids," Travis said as he came up behind Phoenix. "Used to see it all the time in Seattle where there was a huge demon population."

"Wait. What?"

His mate was a *demon*?

Wait a minute.

Travis hadn't said demon.

He'd said demon *hybrid*.

This was a nightmare! Everyone knew hybrids were

unstable and that demon hybrids were the worst of the lot.

Well.

Except for *fairy* hybrids.

They were even scarier, but still!

All he'd ever wanted was a nice, sweet, calm, loving mate, and instead, he'd gotten one of the most terrifying beings in all the realms!

Five

RESCUING THOSE KITTENS was the best decision Merry had ever made.

Phoenix loved them and was thanking Merry with chocolate! It was by far, the most wonderful consequence she could have ever imagined.

Merry sifted through the remaining chocolate on the table—it was mostly wrappers now—and grabbed a small box of something called Cocoa Puffs and started eating.

Ohhh my.

She was peripherally aware that Sam and the bartender boyfriend were still chatting beside her, but she was too engrossed in her chocolate fantasies to pay any attention.

"Oh, Merry, Merry!" Francine's voice was getting

louder as she rushed closer to Merry's private chocolate party.

With a sigh, she opened her eyes, if only to keep an eye on Francine, to make sure she didn't steal the last of her delicious chocolate.

Agatha and Betina were right behind Francine, so it was a good thing Merry's eyes were open. She was absolutely certain she'd have to protect her dwindling stash of chocolate wonders from these three.

"Where are you staying, Merry?" Francine asked.

Now this was interesting.

It occurred to Merry that she would make an excellent serial killer's victim.

After all, she'd managed to wander deep into the woods, where she knew absolutely no one in the area, and now Francine wanted to know where she would be sleeping that night.

This was truly the perfect setup for a slasher film.

It would be even better if it turned out these three, sweet ladies were actually serial killers.

It'd be genius. No one would ever suspect them.

Merry couldn't think of a better way to find out whether they were serial killers, than to answer Francine's question. "I'm staying at Hotel Shenanigans. I don't know the room number yet, but I'm sure you can find me—"

"Oh, no. That won't do at all," Francine interrupted. "It's the holidays, dear. You can't stay alone in a hotel over the holidays."

"I can't? I didn't know that. The man I spoke with didn't say anything when I made the reservation."

"Francine just means that you should be with family this time of the year," Agatha said.

Merry made a face. What a *horrible* thought that was.

She'd never actually celebrated the holidays—*any* holiday, really—but it sounded like they were supposed to be *joyful, happy* events.

Shudder.

Even worse if they were meant to be experienced with *family*.

Double shudder.

"Yeah, I'm basically here to escape my family, so—"

"Oh, dear," Betina said. "Are they really that bad?"

"I mean, no, not exactly. It's just my dad's really busy with his job and my sister's kind of, frankly, a pain in the ass, and well—my mom washed her hands of me when I was still a baby, so, trust me. This is the best case scenario for me. Away from my family, free at last. It's a wonderful feeling."

"Won't your father and sister miss you at the holidays?" Betina asked.

"Please. It's not like they'll be celebrating together."

"Well, that decides it," Agatha said. "You'll just have to come home with us."

"What?" Sam and Merry chorused.

"We have the perfect cabin for you on pack lands. Gigi used to stay there before she moved into the pack house with Adam," Agatha said.

"That was back when my nephew was being a dick," Betina said.

"Oh, but—" Merry wasn't exactly sure what she was going to say, but she didn't get a chance to find out because Francine whirled and called out, "Karl, call Harry and cancel Merry's reservation. Tell him she'll be staying with the pack."

Karl was a couple tables over, sitting with some other men and looked entirely put out at the request. "Mom, you know Lily hates it when we do that. She accuses us of stealing their clients."

"We've only done it once before," Agatha protested.

"And Lily *still* hasn't forgiven us," Karl said. "When she found out that Gigi owned a hair salon and was giving free manicures and pedicures to all the women of the pack, not to mention dyeing their hair for free, well—let's just say threats against the entire pack were made," Karl said.

"So that's why we keep getting invoices from the hotel!" Another man exclaimed.

"That's Adam," Sam murmured, "the alpha of our pack."

"You're getting invoices?" Karl asked.

"Yes, and I keep throwing them away because they don't make any sense."

"What do they say?"

"They're all these weird charges, like the denial of beauty enhancement opportunities and fines for thievery and corporate espionage.

Sam snickered and muttered under his breath, "Crazy fairy," which reminded Merry.

As entertaining as this pit stop had become, she had an actual reason for being in Jamesville and it had nothing to do with kittens or the sexy wolf she'd hoped to conscript into volunteering for her clinical sex trials.

Sex and chocolate trials.

Clinical sex and chocolate trials.

The title still needed some work.

"Fairies," Merry announced.

"What's that, dear?" Francine asked.

"I was planning to stay at the hotel so I could meet some of the fairies."

"Oh, dear," Betina said.

"They're not exactly the friendly type, you know, and they're not very welcoming of tourists," Agatha said. "Well, unless you're spending a lot of money at one of their hotels or in the mall."

"Ooh, I've heard all about the fairy mall," Merry said. "Have you guys been to it?"

"Oh, yes, and it's glorious," Phoenix said as she walked by, balancing a tray full of drinks.

That sounded promising.

"Mom." Karl called from his table, holding out his cell phone. "It's Lily and she wants to speak with you."

Francine made a face, then walked over to grab the phone. "Lily? It's Francine. Yes, yes, well I certainly understand, but—uh-huh, uh-huh." Francine let out a huge sigh and held the phone away from her ear.

Everyone winced at the shrill sound of Lily's voice as she raged and shouted.

"Come along, Francine," Agatha said. "Let's just go to the hotel and sort things out from there."

Francine nodded, still holding the phone away from her ear. She started to follow Agatha and Betina out of the bar, but then whirled, pointed at Sam and said, "When Merry's ready, take her to the old cabin. Do *not* let her go to the hotel. She's ours, not theirs, and we're not going to share, at least not until she's decided to stay." With that, she turned and slammed out of the bar.

"So," Sam drawled out the word slowly. "Why are you interested in meeting the fairies again?"

"Abort, abort!" Bygul exclaimed. "Someone *do* something."

"Why? What's wrong?" Tivali asked.

"The minute she starts talking about the fairies, it's all over," Bygul said. "Look at that wolf. He's already on the fence about his mate. Did you see his face when the bartender boyfriend announced she's a demon hybrid?"

Muezza snorted. "You do know his name is Travis, right?"

Bygul twitched his tail in dismissal. "Merry's right. Bartender boyfriend has a fabulous ring to it. Actually, I think I'll call him Triple B for Bartender Boyfriend Bear or maybe Beary Boyfriend Bartender. Hm. I'm not quite sure of the order just yet, but that's beside the point."

"Then, what is the point?" Tivali asked.

"The point is the wolf needs to claim his mate

before he discovers the truth about her."

"And what truth is that?" Tivali asked.

"That she's a demon-fairy-witch hybrid, of course."

"No worries!" Soraya popped back from wherever she'd disappeared to a while back. "I've pretty much filled the bar's cabinets with chocolate."

"And what's that going to accomplish?" Bygul asked.

"*Hello*. Did you not hear Merry going on about conducting sexy chocolate experiments with the wolf? All we have to do is get her some more chocolate and she'll remember her plans and then, boom, sexy, mating times."

"Huh. That's not a bad plan, Soraya." Bygul was pretty amazed. Then again, he *was* an excellent trainer and team leader.

SAM WAS STARING AT MERRY EXPECTANTLY, so she said, "Well, it's kind of a long story."

"I *love* long stories," Lara said as she pulled out a chair and plopped down at Merry's chocolate table.

"Me too," Gigi said, as she walked up, a purple,

poofy dog at her side, with one of the kittens in her arms. "JoJo, meet Merry. Merry brought Koko into our lives."

JoJo let out a little bark, which made Lara giggle.

"Merry," Gigi continued, "this is JoJo and Koko."

"Cocoa, yum," Merry said.

"K-o-k-o," Gigi spelled out the name.

"Oh. Well, that's cute too," Merry said. Not as cute as Cocoa, of course.

"JoJo and Koko?" Phoenix squealed as she walked by again, this time heading back to the bar. "That's adorable!"

"It's ridiculous is what it is." Adam stood, grabbed the table the men were at and dragged it over to where they were all seated. "I'm Adam," he said to Merry as he settled into a chair. "I hear you're moving onto our pack lands."

Merry shrugged. "That's the rumor anyway."

"Well, I'm the pack's alpha and Max here is the beta."

Max nodded to Merry as he pulled out a chair.

"So if you need anything," Adam continued, "don't hesitate to ask."

Well, that was surprising. "Okay. Um, thanks."

"And I'm Cole." A third man plopped into a seat and grinned at Merry. "I'm not a wolf, and I'm mated to a witch, so I can't really help with anything pack-related, but I can definitely help with all these brownies. Yum!" He reached for the plate of brownies and Merry lunged forward.

"Mine!" She snarled as she dragged all the chocolates closer to her side of the table.

Cole froze, then slowly sat back, wide-eyed.

"Dude, don't mess with the demon hybrid," the bartender boyfriend called from across the room.

Phoenix giggled as she arrived with another armload of chocolates, which she dumped into the middle of their table. "You're not going to believe this, but I found a bunch of chocolate hiding in the back storage room."

"I love you," Merry said as she grabbed a couple candy bars and started eating.

Phoenix giggled as she wandered away again.

"So," Sam said. "Fairies?"

"Right. Fairies. Well, you see—are you sure you want to hear this?"

"Definitely," Sam said decisively.

Merry drew in a deep breath. This was going to take a while. "Okay, so I guess this story begins in Hell."

"Wait. Hell-hell?" Karl asked.

Merry paused and glanced around the table. "Um, yeah. You know, the Nine Realms of Hell. That Hell."

"Right," Karl drawled. "Okay, go on."

"So, anyway, I was kind of kicked out of Hell. I mean, not really, because I was still *in* Hell, just not in the main part of it. I was on the outskirts, you could say. Mostly because, according to my dad, I tend to rile up the demons. But I maintain that he's full of shit. I mean, they're demons. They're supposed to be riled up. Pretty much all the time, right?"

SAM NODDED HURRIEDLY WHEN MERRY glanced at him, but all he could think was that he was mated to a demon hybrid who was known for riling up others of her kind.

What had he done to deserve this?

"My dad accused me of always picking fights with the demons, especially the pixies, but I maintain that it was self-defense. After all, they always threw the first punch. Anyway, so my dad decided he needed me to be somewhere demons weren't likely to go, so he put me in charge of the stupid Bed & Breakfast in Hell, but I'm sorry, that's just ridiculous. I mean, sure the B&B

in Hell is mostly for tourists from other realms who come for a little visit, and sure, I had a lot less interactions with the demons as a result; after all, they had no reason to stay at the B&B, but—"

"I'm sorry," Adam interrupted. "So you're saying there's a Bed & Breakfast in Hell?"

"Well, sure, I mean, Hell's a destination vacation, after all. There should probably be a lot more B&Bs, but Satan's territorial and he insists that it's *his* B&B or no B&B."

"Hold on. *Satan* owns the B&B?" Sam asked.

"Well, part of it anyway. It's kind of a family business."

"Family business," Sam repeated faintly. He was feeling a little woozy, as if the world was spinning off-kilter a bit.

"So anyway," Merry continued, "There I was, bored out of my mind, because let's face it, I am *not* the Bed & Breakfast manager type, and I was desperate to get out of Hell. Seriously. I needed a Get Out of Hell Free card.

"Then I had a brilliant idea, but let's not talk about the crazy things I did to lure an unsuspecting troll to Hell to temporarily manage that Bed & Breakfast for me. Instead, let's just focus on the fact that it worked!"

"Wait. There are trolls in this story?" Gigi asked.

"Who cares about the story?" Cole said. "I'm stuck on the fact that there are trolls at all."

"Yes, there are trolls. They live in the troll realm," Merry said. "Turns out they're a lot smaller than I expected, but I guess in their realm, they're huge. Anyway, despite their size, they are *mean*. Which makes them perfect for running a B&B in Hell, right? But that's all beside the point, because no, Gigi, there are no trolls in this story. The troll arrived and I made good on my escape. I have no idea how things are going with the troll and the B&B back in hell, but it doesn't really matter since like I said, the troll's only temporary. I've got long-range plans in place and they're just starting to heat up."

The entire time Merry was speaking, she was working her way through an amazing amount of chocolate. Despite talking non-stop *and* eating non-stop, she never seemed to be doing both at the same time.

Even though he watched the chocolate going into her mouth and disappearing at a rapid rate, Sam never saw any evidence of food in her mouth. How was she doing this?

"So my dad and I made a deal. Since I'd found someone to care for the Bed & Breakfast, he would let me leave Hell, but only if I agreed to stay with my sister and her coven for a while. Except, you know what? I may be a quarter-witch, but that doesn't mean I belong with the witches, if you know what I mean."

"Wait, you're also a witch?" Sam asked. Was it getting a little hard to breathe in the bar?

"Well, technically, yes, I am, but I don't really feel like one. I mean, okay, I do know how to cast a spell or two, or a couple thousand, but that doesn't really mean anything. After all, I knew almost immediately that the coven wasn't the place for me, and maybe that had more to do with sisters than with witches, since Tempest and me, we don't really get along all that great.

"I mean, I guess we do, I love her, of course, since she's my sister and all—well, half-sister really—but the thing is, she's kind of got that big-sister, I-know-better-than-you thing going on, and ever since she found her coven of sister-witches, well, I guess there's a brother-witch too, but regardless, ever since she found her coven, it's like she doesn't need me anymore—not that she ever did.

"Seeing as her coven was already complete when I arrived, though, I felt somewhat superfluous, kind of like that eighth pixie *no one* ever needs. I mean, it could have been worse, I suppose. I could have been the eleventh or twelfth pixie, on account of some of the witches being mated by then, but since their mates aren't witches, I was all about pretending that I was just the eighth pixie, not some super inflated, horrid number like eleven or twelve.

"*Anyway*, the point is I didn't feel like I belonged with the witches either, so I was like, where can I go where maybe I'll fit in for once in my life?

"I mean, I don't fit in with the demons because apparently I'm always riling them up, according to my father, but what does he know? It's not like he's an expert on demons, just because he's the Lord of the Nine Realms and the Prince of Darkness. I mean, how ridiculous is that?"

"Wait, what's that about your father?" Sam asked, but she kept barreling on, not even pausing at his question.

"So basically, I'm not demonic enough for Hell, or *too* demonic for Hell as the case may be, I mean, that's really what the situation is, and not witchy enough for the witches, or maybe just *too* witchy for my sister to manage to live in the same town with me.

"So that's how I decided I should keep looking for a place where I belong, and honestly, the fairies seemed the right place to start, considering I'm also a quarter-fairy."

"Hold on a minute, hold up. You're a what now?" Sam demanded.

"I'm a quarter-fairy."

"I feel faint," Sam said.

"Let me get this straight," Adam said slowly, a huge grin on his face. "You're half-demon, one-quarter witch and one-quarter fairy."

"Yep. It's a pretty awesome combination if you asked me."

"This is the most entertainment we've had around here in a long time," Cole observed.

"I feel faint," Sam repeated.

"What's wrong with you, Sam?" Merry asked.

"Oh, nothing. Nothing at all. I'm just a little, uh, overwhelmed."

"Huh. I can't imagine why."

"The wolf looks like he's going to bolt," Bygul observed.

"Well, that won't do," Tivali said.

"Not if he's her mate," Muezza said. "Someone needs to remind him of why she's worth it."

"Oh, don't worry," Soraya flicked her tail. "I

opened the door to the pudding cabinet right before Phoenix stepped into the kitchen. She's back there now, chilling it to perfection."

"And how is that going to help?" TIvali demanded.

"Do you not remember the polar bear's response when Tessa was devouring all those desserts? Orgasm on a plate, I think she called them."

"Oh, yeah," Bygul said. "Didn't he drag her—"

"Into a closet for some sexy times? Yes, he did," Soraya said. "I'm counting on a similar reaction from the wolf."

"But she's been eating desserts in front of him this entire time," Muezza protested. "How is pudding going to be any different?"

"Trust me," Soraya said. "Apparently, it's all about the spoon."

"I've said it before and I'll say it again," Bygul said.

"Humans are so weird," the four cats chorused together.

STORY FINISHED, MERRY EXAMINED THE table, pondering her chocolate choices. Eventually, she selected a brownie and some truffles.

She then spent a long moment, looking back and forth between the brownie in one hand and the package of truffles in the other, trying to decide which to taste first.

Decisions, decisions.

As she was pondering her options, Phoenix set a giant bowl in front of her. "I've never made chocolate pudding before, but it was super easy—it barely took ten minutes from start to finish—and I have to say, I taste tested it and it's delicious. Enjoy!"

Letting out a little growl of delight, Merry dragged the bowl closer, set the brownie directly in the center, and, with truffles clutched in her left hand, began spooning up brownie pudding with her right.

"Mmmmm," she groaned after the first bite. "Soooo good."

Six

"I DON'T GET it," Karl said. "What's the deal with all the chocolate?"

Sam was too busy watching his mate as she practically made love to the spoon, licking every drop from it before going in for another bite, to bother answering.

"It's delicious, man. What's not to get?" Cole scowled. "I do think she could have shared at least one brownie, though."

"Do you know *nothing* of demon hybrids?" Glory exclaimed as she walked by.

"Just that they're a little unstable," Cole said.

"Who cares about unstable?" Glory said. "We're all a little unstable, for shift's sake. It's their obsessive personalities you have to watch out for, plus they're extremely possessive. The minute Phoenix gave those chocolates to Merry, they became hers, and no one, not even her mate, could convince her to give them away. The situation is even more dire since it appears she's a little attached to the taste of chocolate. So, yeah, best not be messing with her current chocolate obsession."

"You know, all these years, you've talked about brownies and chocolate cake and I've never really regretted that I couldn't eat the wonders of chocolate with you," Karl said. "After all, there's plenty of other sweets and delicious things in the world. But now, seeing the look of bliss on Merry's face as she eats her weight in chocolate, I'm really sad that I'm never going to know its taste."

Merry's eyes flew open. "Wait. What? You've never tasted chocolate?"

"It's poisonous to wolves," Karl said.

Merry whipped her head to the side and stared at Sam, wide-eyed. "Really?"

He made a face. "I mean, it won't kill us, but it has been known to make dogs terribly ill."

"But you're not dogs, you're wolves."

"Yeah, but it'll probably have the same effect."

"So you've never tried it? You don't actually know what it'll do to you?"

Sam shrugged. "Never really felt the need to find

out." Though he agreed with Karl, now that he'd seen the look on Merry's face while she was eating chocolate, he had an unexpected desire to taste test it.

"Right." Merry stood abruptly, spun in a circle, then grabbed the box the kittens had all come in. She stared at it for a long moment.

"Merry?" Sam asked.

She blinked at him. "I'm pretty sure this isn't the box I brought the kittens in. The walls are too low. They would have all escaped in my car long before I made it here." She stared at it another moment, then shrugged. "Oh, well. It'll do the job anyway." She whirled and started scooping all the chocolate—candy bars, cereals, baked goods—into the box. As soon as everything was packed away, she handed the box to Sam, grabbed the giant bowl of pudding, and said, "Time to go."

"Go?" He felt as if he were three steps behind, completely uncertain as to what was happening.

"Yes, Sam. Time to go. It's time for our little experiment."

"Experi—ohhhh. Right. We're out of here. See you guys later."

As he walked out the door, a box of chocolates in his arms, and his slightly feral mate at his side, Sam heard Karl exclaim, "Can you believe she took all the chocolate? I was going to taste test a couple things, just to see."

SAM THREW OPEN THE DOOR TO THE CABIN where Merry would be staying for the foreseeable future. He'd debated taking her to his cabin, which wasn't far from this one, but he was concerned if he did that, she might not stay in the morning.

This way she had her own place and it was on pack lands, close enough to keep his wolf satisfied.

The moment they stepped inside, Merry set the bowl of pudding on a side table, grabbed the box from his hands and set it on the floor, backed him up against the door and kissed him.

Heat blasted through them both and he clutched her closer, his wolf howling in delight.

She dragged his flannel down his arms, then shoved her hands beneath his t-shirt to run up his torso.

Shivers of delight wracked his body as he dipped his face into her neck and inhaled her scent. "You are so delicious," he groaned as he scraped his fangs against the vein there, then caught her skin between his lips and sucked.

She shuddered in his arms and growled.

The feral sound made his wolf howl again.

Sweet hell, she was potent.

Merry pulled back, twisted her fist in his shirt and pulled him down for another searing kiss.

Long moments later, she shoved him back, turned and grabbed the bowl of pudding from the table, then walked further into the house. "Bring the box of chocolates," she ordered.

He grabbed the box and followed where she led.

Moments later, he was flat on his back in a bed, with Merry crouched over him, the bowl of pudding in her hands.

"Take off your shirt," she ordered.

He did a half-crunch to pull the t-shirt over his head, then tossed it away.

Her eyes lit up as he settled back on the bed.

She scooped three fingers of pudding from the bowl and smeared chocolate around his nipples. She then leaned down and slowly licked and sucked them clean.

He let out a growl of pure need and reached for her, but she leaned back and shook her head. "Naughty, naughty. I haven't gotten my chocolate fix yet, so you just lie back and enjoy." She smeared more chocolate on his nipples, and proceeded to lick them clean once more.

Time passed in a haze of maddening lust and desire as Merry explored his body with fingers and hands covered in chocolate, then devoured him and the chocolate in long, slow strokes of her tongue.

By the time they were both naked, Sam was lost in a haze of madness, desperate to claim his mate.

IN AN INSTANT, MERRY WENT FROM HOVERING over Sam, contemplating which part of his body to cover in chocolate next, to flat on her back with Sam settling on top of her, making them both gasp at the feel of their naked bodies rubbing against one another.

She arched her back at the sensation and clutched at his shoulders. "Sam."

"Ah, sweet Merry, you've driven me to the very edge of madness."

She grinned. "And I had fun doing it."

"Let's see if I can return the pleasure." He lifted up and slowly traced his fingers across her breast.

Merry scowled when she realized he was using

chocolate—*her* chocolate—to paint her nipples. She'd never be able to eat the chocolate from this angle!

She lifted her hands, intending to try and rescue some of that precious chocolate for herself when her eyes rolled back in her head.

Sam's mouth was clamped around her right breast, his tongue swirling, mouth sucking, teeth nipping and pulling.

Her mind shut down as sensation took over everything.

She managed to get her left hand to her left breast, but then Sam's hand was there, brushing hers aside as he rolled and manipulated her nipple, making it bud so tight, she could barely breathe.

He then switched sides, mouth clamped to her left breast, fingers working the right.

"Sam," she groaned, sliding her fingers through his hair and trying to pull his head back.

He resisted all efforts, though, just continued to work her breasts until she was writhing and panting with need.

"Sam!"

He lifted just enough to settle exactly where she needed him to go.

She hooked her legs around his hips and yanked him forward.

They both groaned as he plunged deep. The friction as he filled every available space sent shudders through Merry's frame.

Long moments later, they hung on a precipice, neither daring to move, knowing one small movement would send them both plunging over the edge.

Eventually, the need to move became too great and Sam slowly pulled back, then surged forward again. He pulled back once more, changed his angle slightly and slid deep once more, this time rubbing something inside that made Merry cry out in ecstasy.

As if that was the signal he'd been waiting for, he picked up the pace, moving forward and back, every slide and move rubbing that perfect spot, so that everything coiled tighter and tighter, and then, with one final plunge, everything exploded and the world disappeared in a flash of heat and light.

"TOLD YOU IT WOULD WORK," SORAYA crowed as Merry dragged the wolf from the bar.

"It really was the spoon," Muezza marveled.

"Weird," Bygul said.

"Let's just hope the wolf doesn't touch her chocolate," Tivali said.

Bygul flattened his ears. "Why would you even mention that?"

"You know that words have power, Tivali," Soraya said.

"Oh, please. Surely the wolf is smarter than that."

"You ate my pudding," Merry said grumpily as she stared into the empty bowl.

Sam chuckled. "It seemed the right thing to do at the time."

"I was saving that last bit for later." She pouted at him.

"There's a whole box of chocolates over there." He waved a lazy arm toward the floor.

"But none of that is pudding."

"I'll ask Phoenix to make you another batch, how's that sound?"

She set aside the bowl and pounced on him. "Yes!" She peppered his face with kisses. "That would be great. How soon do you think she could make us a batch?"

"Us?"

"Well, I didn't get to finish my explorations."

He grinned. "How about we try to explore without pudding for now?"

"I suppose we can use the raisins." She turned around and stretched, almost falling off the bed in her eagerness to grab the box.

Sam let out a growl behind her and she glanced back, grinning at the look on his face as he stared straight between her legs.

She wiggled her butt. "See something you like?"

He caught her around her waist, flipped her over so that she landed on top of him and kissed her breathless.

Things progressed from there and she never did snag any of those raisins, though she supposed in the end, the sexy times were a fair trade for the chocolate.

She thought about that for a while, as she lay on Sam's chest, listening to his heart thud after a particularly vigorous bout of sexy times.

"You know, I'm hard-pressed to say the results of these experiments. I guess the answer is that the only thing better than chocolate and the only thing better than sex is chocolatey sex."

Sam let out a bark of laughter.

"Here's the weird thing, though. At first, I wanted

the chocolate with our sex, but once we got going, I didn't really miss it, mostly because I forgot all about it."

"I'll take that as a compliment." Sam grinned.

"Well, considering I'm fairly certain not every male would be capable of making me forget that chocolate even exists, yes, you should definitely take that as a compliment."

"I don't really know how to react to that."

"The thing is, the experiment will not be complete until I have some chocolate pudding without the sex. Because the question now is, will I miss the sex while eating the chocolate?"

"You'd damn well better," Sam said.

Merry started to laugh, then quickly put a hand over her mouth. "Sorry."

"Why?"

"Well, you know, the demons don't really like my laugh. They say I sound too demonic, which doesn't make any sense. How can a half-demon be *too* demonic? Anyway, that was one of the rules my dad always set for me—no laughing around demons. Or in Hell anywhere. Which pretty much meant no laughing."

"Well, that's some shitty parenting," Sam said. "What kind of father forbids his kid from laughing?"

"Well, you have to understand, anytime I laughed, it freaked out the demons and they would just attack because well, that's what demons do when they're afraid. So, there I was, this little toddler being attacked by full-grown, scary-ass demons. Yeah, my dad didn't know what to do, so he had a witch cast a spell binding my laughter."

Sam looked horrified.

"Oh, don't worry, the binding spell dissipated when I turned ten. It was just, you know, to get me through the vulnerable years."

"Well, you never have to worry about that with me. I love the sound of your laughter."

MERRY SENT HIM A LOOK THAT SEEMED TO BE a mix of skepticism and hope.

"It's true," he insisted, injecting as much sincerity in his voice as he could.

Okay, so he wasn't sure how he managed that exactly, but now that he knew how everyone *else* had reacted to the sound of his mate's laughter, he was determined to be different.

Never mind that the sound still gave him chills.

And that's when it happened.

Merry *smiled*.

Dear shifter gods, it was a scary smile, but it was also special because it was meant for him and from what Sam had seen so far, those smiles were few and far between. So few, in fact, that he might be the only one on earth ever blessed with one.

"I'm so happy you're my mate," he blurted out.

And just like that, the smile disappeared.

"Wait? What?" Merry scrambled off the bed. "That's not possible. Is it?"

"Of course, it is."

"I would know, wouldn't I?"

"I don't know. Do demons have fated mates?"

She shook her head. "Well, maybe, but if they do, it never ends well. No one actually knows because demons mostly have short-term liaisons. But that's not the point. I'm also a witch."

"Witches don't know," Sam said decisively. "They just have to guess, like humans."

"I'm also part fairy. Don't forget the fairy part."

As if he could *ever* do that.

"Yeah, I don't think fairies know when they meet their mates either."

"So what you're saying is I just have to trust that you're right and we're mates."

Sam had enough self-preservation to realize that ranting about how he would never have willingly chosen a demon hybrid, let alone a fairy one for his mate, thus *obviously*, he was telling the truth, was definitely *not* the way to convince her. "The truth is most shifters would never lie about this because to do so would be to give up on their true mate, so yeah, I kind of hope that you'll believe me."

"It's not that I don't believe you. I just can't believe the fates would be so *cruel*."

Sam reared back in shock. Okay, that was unexpected and if he were being truthful, kind of hurtful.

"Oh, don't be so sensitive," Merry said. "I'm just saying it doesn't make any sense."

Sam growled and settled back to sulk while she paced and protested the very idea of their mating.

This went on for a while until Sam got bored of listening to her mutterings and tumbled her back to the bed, where he did his best to show her the many benefits of being mated to a wolf.

Seven

"S HE'S NOT EXACTLY receptive to the idea that the wolf is her mate," Tivali fretted.

"Yeah, I'm telling you, fairy hybrids are the *worst*," Bygul said.

"Don't worry. I've got it all in hand," Soraya said.

"I don't see how," Muezza said. "The only way this could get any worse was if her father showed up."

"Oh, I'm totally counting on it," Soraya said. "In fact, I dropped him a couple clues since he was having such a difficult time figuring out where Merry had gone."

"Seriously?" Bygul, Tivali and Muezza chorused.

"Why would you do that?" Tivali wailed.

"What if he brings the Hell-Kittens with him?" Bygul demanded.

Soraya licked her paw daintily, then said, "Oh, I wouldn't worry about that. After all, the Hell-Kittens are already in Jamesville."

"What?" the other three cats shouted, but Soraya just kept grooming herself, completely unperturbed.

MERRY WOKE TO AN ANVIL SITTING ON HER chest.

She opened one eye and found herself staring at a monstrous cat's butt.

Like seriously huge.

For one long, disorienting moment, Merry thought the sexy wolf had somehow shifted into a panther, but then she realized Sam's very human arm was slung around her waist and he was lying next to her, definitely *not* the owner of the cat's butt.

That's when she realized that even though Sam was lying on her left side, something was pinning down her hair on the right.

And it wasn't the same cat sitting on her chest.

That cat was so big, his front paws were lying right on top of her very delicate bits, and yes, she could feel him making that strange kneading movement that cats loved to make when they were super content.

"I'm happy you're happy, big guy, but try not to cause any permanent damage, okay?" She winced as his claws pricked sensitive flesh.

Shifting slightly, she glanced to the right and saw a second cat was curled up on top of her hair.

As if it sensed her watching, the cat's eyes slowly blinked open, showing off exceptionally bright, green eyes with tiny flecks of silver scattered throughout the green.

"Drusilla, is that you?"

Drusilla yawned, then stood up, stretching so slowly, Merry almost missed the way she grew as she stretched.

Seriously?

How in all of Hell had her father managed to slip two hell-kittens into that box without her knowing?

"So this is where you've been hiding, daughter."

Merry yelped as both hell-cats launched off the bed into Lucifer's arms with yowls of welcome.

"What the—" Sam came flying out of bed in response to the yowls that sounded as if they came from the bowels of Hell.

A man was standing in the doorway, glaring at him. "Who are you?"

"Dad!" Merry jumped from the bed, wrapped a sheet around her and came to stand in front of Sam. "You can't just come barging into my bedroom! Out!"

"Well, I wouldn't have to if you kept your father informed of your whereabouts, now would I?"

"Like you haven't known all along! Don't think I didn't notice you slipped two hell-kittens into my car."

"Actually, I had nothing to do with these two stow-aways." He rocked the two monstrous cats back and forth in his arms. "I can't believe they found you before I did. Smart, aren't they?"

"Whatever. Would you please go into the living room so we can get dressed?"

"Yeah, yeah, hurry it up though. I've got things to do, places to be." With one last glare at Sam, her father turned and stomped off.

"That's your dad?" Sam asked faintly. The man was scary. Like seriously scary. He gave off dark vibes that Sam couldn't even begin to process. "I'm guessing he's the one responsible for your half-demon blood."

"Oh, yeah. My mom was half-witch, half-fairy.

Kudos to dear old dad for having the courage to take that risk, you know?"

Sam shuddered just *thinking* about it. Only then he realized—*he* was taking that risk!

"Just be glad you missed his entrance," Merry said as they set about getting dressed.

"What? Why?"

"Eh, I think we'll save that for his next visit."

"Next visit?"

"Sure. I am his daughter, after all. As much as I'd like to pretend this is a one-off occasion, chances are he'll be visiting a lot."

Sam had to sit down at the thought of frequent visits from that scary man, who just so happened to be his mate's father.

What had he done to deserve this?

A few moments later, Merry dragged him into the living room and set about introducing her father to Sam.

Unfortunately, Sam lost the ability to see and hear the minute he heard the names of his future father-in-law.

"Sam, this is my father, Lucifer, otherwise known as Satan, the Prince of Darkness, Lord of the Nine Realms of Hell, and The Beast. Dad, this is my—Sam? Sam? Are you okay? Sam?"

Sam blinked and discovered he was lying flat on his back in the middle of the floor. "What happened?"

"You fainted, son."

He heard the words, but they didn't quite compute. "Wolves don't faint."

"Well, then, you fell down rather abruptly," Merry said, "and right in the middle of introductions too."

That's when memory rushed back in to fill all the blank spaces in Sam's head.

Lucifer.

Satan.

Prince of Darkness.

Lord of the Nine Realms of Hell.

The Beast.

Was.

His.

Future.

Father.

In.

Law.

Everything went dark again.

"Sam? Sam?"

"Just leave him there, Merry. He'll come around when he's ready."

"It seems a bit mean to just leave him on the floor."

"Eh, the cats will keep him warm. Besides, this

gives me a chance to catch up on what's going on in your life. Come on over here and tell me all about this sad, fragile, wee little wolf you've been shacking up with."

"Dad! We're not shacking up. We're just—enjoying ourselves."

"Mates," Sam muttered.

"Did you hear that, Dad?"

"Nope. Didn't hear a thing."

"Mates." Sam managed to get the word out a bit more forcefully that time. He struggled to sit up, then slowly climbed to his knees.

Why was it so dark in here?

Oh, right.

He cracked his eyes open just a tiny bit and found himself staring into the amber eyes of a giant, feral cat.

He scrambled back. "What is that?"

"Oh, that's Spike," Merry said as she rushed over from the couch where she'd been sitting with her *father*. The freaking devil himself. "I'm so happy you're awake, Sam. I was worried."

Yeah. So worried she was sitting on the couch, leaving him to the tender mercies of a terrifying creature called Spike.

Something huge and black settled on his left shoulder. A peek to the left showed another cat, just as huge as Spike, resting its head there. He could feel its whiskers brushing across his cheek.

"Aw, Drusilla likes you."

Those names, Spike and Drusilla, had a visceral effect on him, sending ice sliding down his spine.

Where did he know those names from?

Slowly pulling away from Drusilla, he allowed Merry to help him to his feet. He staggered over to one of the armchairs and collapsed in it.

"So. You're courting my daughter."

"She's my mate," Sam said, "so, yes, I'm courting her."

"Are you serious right now, daughter?"

"What?" Merry exclaimed.

"You seriously expect me to believe you're mated to this fragile wolf?"

"I'm not fragile!" Sam had never been so offended in his life.

"You fainted twice in my presence," Lucifer said.

No.

Absolutely not.

He could *not* handle calling his future father-in-law Lucifer, not even in his head.

It completely freaked him out!

Sam cleared his throat. "I'm sure it had nothing to do with your presence, Lucy."

Merry let out a truly evil-sounding laugh, which made Sam grin.

Yes, he could handle this.

Lucy.

His father-in-law was just Lucy, a benign, not scary at all, regular old human.

Lucy scowled. "This is absolutely unacceptable, Merry."

"What's unacceptable is you thinking you can just waltz in here and dictate who I can and cannot mate."

Ooh, unexpected bonus.

Family drama suddenly made this mating more palatable for his mate.

Sam grinned.

"Hm." Lucy glared at the two of them, then abruptly waved his hand and said, "Fine. But you have to keep the two hell-kittens."

Say what now?

"You're constantly trying to pawn these kitties off on me and it's just not going to work, Dad."

"Well, in this case, it has to. You need a familiar for your demon side and another one for your witch side. Since you've got all that fairy blood, no earthbound familiars will do. So it's hell-kitties or back to Hell with you."

Merry let out a feral-sounding growl. "Fine. Fine. They can stay."

"Excellent. I expect updates on the mating situation." Lucy stood and held out his arms to the hell-cats who raced toward him and leaping, shrank down to normal, kitten sizes. He ruffled their fur, kissed their heads and murmured, "Be good for Merry, my loves."

The cats jumped down and raced out of the room, heading who knows where.

Lucy whirled and pointed at Sam, though he directed his words to Merry. "He's expected at our monthly family dinner in Hell. Don't be late."

Then, in a burst of actual, real-life, as in Sam could feel the heat, fiery flames, Lucy disappeared.

"Not bad, Soraya," Tivali said. "How'd you know Satan would get her all riled up about her right to choose?"

"Eh, these humans are pretty predictable when you get right down to it, even the demonic, fairy ones."

"I'm not convinced Merry's going to give in just yet," Bygul said, "but she's definitely on the right path.

Although I am *not* happy about those hell-kitties. There are entirely too many earthbound cats who need homes for us to be placing cats from other realms there."

"Okay, so maybe we didn't place any earthbound cats with our target demon-witch-fairy," Soraya said, "but we *did* place a ton of earthbound cats with the other shifters."

"She's right," Muezza said. "It doesn't happen often."

"Hey!"

"But this is a real success story, Soraya," Muezza continued.

"Aw, thanks."

"More than that," Tivali said. "This was the most successful cat placement event of our careers. So far anyway."

"Indeed," Bygul said. "Nice job, Soraya. Now let's get this mating nailed down so we can move on to our next target witch."

THE MINUTE HER FATHER WAS GONE, MERRY whirled on Sam. "Don't be getting any big ideas. I'm still not admitting we're mates. I just refuse to have my father dictating my life choices, you know?"

"Hmm," was all that Sam could say in response to that.

He was still pretty much in shock from all the big reveals.

Satan for a father-in-law *and* Hell-Kittens? The fates were asking an awful lot of a down-to-earth, working wolf.

Sam eyed Merry.

Of course, there *were* some perks involved.

Time to convince them both.

With a lunge, he swept her into his arms and carried her into the bedroom, where they wrestled and laughed (her laughs still gave him chills, but he was getting better at hiding it) and loved the day away.

Later that evening, Merry was still insisting they weren't mates as they walked through pack lands, on their way to the weekly family dinner the Alpha Six insisted was obligatory. No excuses allowed.

Sam had no idea how he'd managed to get roped into such a thing, but the mothers had instituted it back when Karl and Max got mated, one after the other.

Then, when Adam met Gigi, the weekly dinner moved from Francine's house to the pack house and now there was never any predicting who might show up for the weekly, "family" dinners.

Frankly, as one of the few unmated adult members of the pack, the dinners tended to be torture for Sam, considering the Alpha Six hounded him about finding his mate every single week.

This was why Sam was thrilled to finally have a mate to drag along with him.

Of course, Merry was horrified at the idea of attending a family dinner, but when Sam pointed out that he was expected to journey to Hell for dinner with *Satan*, she relented, though she still tried to point out that Sam's family dinners were once a week while hers were only once a month.

"In *Hell*," Sam repeated and that pretty much ended that argument.

Of course, as they were were getting ready to leave, Merry started fretting about the impression they might be giving by attending together.

"And what impression would that be?" Sam demanded.

"That we're mates, of course."

"But we *are* mates, Merry."

He should have known better since that statement just started another argument over whether they were mates or not, which ended, as usual, in a truly exceptional round of lovemaking.

As they were getting dressed (again), Merry asked if chocolate would be on the menu and Sam had to admit that he wasn't sure.

This, of course, led to Merry filling her pockets and his with the chocolate stash she'd found in the kitchen cabinets.

Sam had no idea how the chocolate had gotten there because he was pretty certain Gigi had taken everything with her when she moved into the pack house and no one had lived there since. It was just one of the many mysteries surrounding his mate. If he had to guess, though, he'd put his money on his mate having cast a spell that activated everywhere she went, so that she never ran out of chocolate.

"We're late, Merry."

"I know, I'm coming." She ran into the living with a handful of candy bars that she started shoving into his jeans pockets.

"They're going to get all melty in there, you know."

"Yum. Melted chocolate."

Sam rolled his eyes. "Right. Let's go already."

Of course, as they walked across pack lands, Merry started fretting again, which led to her sharing, one more time, all the reasons they couldn't possibly be mates.

"I'm just saying it doesn't make any sense," Merry said as they walked into the pack house. She paused in the entryway to tip her head back and pour into her mouth the last of the chocolate candies from the two bags she'd consumed on their way there.

"It's not because of who you are or anything you did," she said, "but if you think about it, you'll understand that I'm right."

Sam just rolled his eyes and led the way into the pack dining room where of course, everyone was already seated and eating.

The minute they stepped inside, Glory snarled at them, causing Sam to rear back in shock, but Merry didn't even flinch.

"I mean, imagine the poor kids we'd have," Merry continued, scrounging in her pockets for more chocolate. She'd just reached the table and was pulling out a bag of mini candy bars, when Glory let out an actual, full-on bear roar.

Sam, along with most of the other shifters in the room, dropped to the floor, crawling under the table or out of the room entirely.

Even their pack alpha, Adam, leapt away from the

table, though he was still on his feet, glaring at Glory, with his mate, Gigi behind him.

"Merry, get down here," Sam hissed at her, tugging on her jeans.

Merry leaned over and stared under the table at him and the others. "What are you doing under there?"

A deep rumble sounded above them and Sam cowered. "Merry, I'm telling you. Get your ass down here before that bear rips you limb from limb."

Eight

"Oh, that sounds intriguing." Merry straightened and glanced at Glory, who stood on the other side of the table, glaring at her. "You know, I had my money on Francine, Agatha or Betina. Maybe even all three of them together. It's always the quiet ones you have to watch out for."

"What are you talking about?" Glory snarled.

"For the role of serial killer. I applaud you for your choice of setting. These woods are ideal for stalking your prey and stabbing them a thousand times before they even know you're there."

"I'm never going to look at the woods the same way again," someone muttered under the table. It sounded like Sam's brother, Karl.

"Though I must warn you," Merry continued, "if you'd hoped to continue incognito, well, I'm afraid choosing to attack your next victim while at the family dinner table probably isn't the way to go."

"I'm not a serial killer," Glory snapped.

"No? My mistake," Merry said. "I just thought what with the claws and the vein popping right here." She tapped her temple, which made her realize she was still holding that unopened bag of mini chocolate bars.

She couldn't believe the bear had actually distracted her from her chocolate. She ripped it open and that's when the bear let loose a truly awesome-sounding growl.

"You sound so fierce. I love it!" Merry grinned, but then it occurred to her *why* the bear might be growling and her grin instantly turned into a scowl. "But no, I don't care how fierce you are, I am *not* sharing my chocolate. You'll have to wrestle me for it and I promise you, I'll win."

"I don't want you to share it," Glory snarled. "I want you to destroy it! I want it banned from Jamesville entirely, but *especially* from the pack lands and surrounding woods."

Merry gasped in horror. "You monster! Why would you ban chocolate?"

"Because our cabin smells like ass! I was going to move back into the apartment above the bar, just to escape Max's revolting new chocolate habit, but the bar stinks even worse. You know why?"

Merry shook her head, speechless.

"Because the wolves' systems can't handle the chocolate, but now that they've all tasted it, *thanks to you,* they also can't resist it. So it's a disgusting, fumigation nightmare in the bar right now!"

"Interesting. On the bright side, at least they've finally experienced the joy of chocolate, right?"

Glory let out a growl of annoyance.

"Just kick him out of the cabin, Glory." One of the witches popped her head out from under the table. "We made Karl sleep in the woods last night and he's not allowed back if he has even one bite of chocolate during the day."

"Also, you own Shenanigans," Gigi pointed out from clear across the room.

Merry had no idea why she was all the way over there or why Adam was standing in front of her like he expected her to be attacked at any moment. Merry eyed Glory. Maybe she really *was* a serial killer and Adam knew it.

"She's right," the witch said, climbing out from

under the table, swatting away Karl's attempts to drag her back. "You could totally ban chocolate from Shenanigans if you wanted to."

"Do you know what Phoenix would do to me if I banned chocolate, Lara?" Glory demanded. "Chocolate that her new best friend, Kitten-Dealer here, is obsessed with?"

Merry rolled her eyes. "Banning chocolate would be like banning crime or alcohol or sex. People will always find a way to get some anyway."

Glory let out a huff of annoyance. "I suppose that's true, but I still blame you. The wolves never *thought* to try chocolate until you showed up."

"And what a terrible state of affairs that was," Merry said as Sam and the rest of his family climbed out from under the table or reappeared from wherever they'd been hiding.

Francine caught Merry's attention as she took a seat across from her, glaring all the while.

Merry raised an eyebrow at the woman, wondering why Sam's mother looked so put out.

"Really? You thought I was a serial killer?" she burst out.

Merry shrugged. "You insisted I stay on pack lands."

"I was being nice!"

"Exactly," Merry said. "It's always the nice ones in slasher films and true crime podcasts."

"That can't be true," Francine said. "Can it?"

"Personally, I'm flattered," Agatha announced.

"Of course, you are," Adam muttered.

"My son's mate can't go around thinking I'm a serial killer, Agatha!" Francine exclaimed.

"I don't see why not," Agatha said. "Think of the benefits."

"Benefits? What benefits could there possibly be?"

"Oh, there would be *so* many benefits," Merry said. "Think about it. Serial killers are *always* respected."

"I think you're confusing respect with fear," Karl said dryly.

"Am I?"

"But what about the kids?" Francine wailed.

"Kids?" Merry exclaimed, horrified. "What kids?"

"My grandbabies! Admit it—you'd *never* trust a serial killer with your children."

"Eh, I guess it would depend on the serial killer," Merry said.

S AM COULDN'T DECIDE WHETHER HE WAS impressed or terrified. Probably a bit of both.

After all, his mate had stood up to a freaking bear!

She'd even challenged Glory to a wrestling match. Over chocolate!

He was busy trying to convince himself that if, by chance, the bear had decided to attack Merry, he would have come out from under the table to defend her— right?—when the sound of her voice caught his attention.

"I guess it would depend on the serial killer," Merry said.

Sam's wolf let out a snort of amusement in response to the wide-eyed looks he was getting from his pack.

Taking note of Merry's empty plate, he started filling it with actual, real food. After all, if left to her own devices, the only thing Merry would eat would be the chocolate she was downing at a truly impressive rate.

"And let's be clear, Francine. Sam and I will never have any kids because we're not mates. We can't be. It just doesn't make any sense."

Oh, great. He couldn't believe they were back on this subject *again*.

"I mean, think about it, I'm half demon, quarter fairy, quarter witch. Sam's a full-blooded shifter. Put the two of us together and my badness, what monsters would we create?"

She tilted her head to the side and seemed to be counting on her fingers as she attempted to do the math in her head.

"Half shifter, quarter demon, one eighth fairy, one-eighth witch?" Merry shook her head. "No, that can't be right. Eight plus eight is only sixteen. What's half of a quarter? 12.5? 12.5% fairy, 12.5% witch, 25% demon and 50% wolf?"

"Uh." Sam hesitated to bring it up, but he just couldn't keep silent on this. It was math, for goddess' sake! "You do realize that one-eighth *is* 12.5%?"

"What? No. You're just messing with me. That can't be right. That's—is it? No. Wait. A hundred divided by eight is.... 12.5. No!"

She jumped up and began pacing back and forth.

Sam, along with everyone else at the dining room table, turned to watch as she paced and counted on her fingers, muttering numbers under her breath, before finally throwing her arms wide and shouting at the ceiling, "It's too much math, damnit. I have to stop before my head explodes. Besides, who cares about the math? Math sucks!" She let out a huff, then stomped back to the table.

"What matters," she said as she yanked her chair out and sat again, "are the little devils we'd create. They'd be demon-monsters who could cast spells and shift into weird-looking wolves with wings."

"Actually, that sounds pretty cool," Max said.

"Yeah," Karl said. "Flying wolves? Who wouldn't want that?"

"I kind of have to agree," Sam said as the rest of the wolves nodded and murmured agreement.

"Are you lot crazy?" Merry exclaimed as she jumped to her feet and began to pace again. "We'd have to actually *raise* the little monsters. No way. It's just not possible." She stopped pacing and stood there, hands on hips, glaring at the floor.

Sam just watched her, grinning.

"Look, Sam." She whirled to face him. "You know I adore you, but we *can't* be mates."

"You adore me?" Sam asked, focusing on the most important thing he'd heard.

"Well, of *course*, I adore you. No one could possibly give one person that many orgasms and walk away without that person's adoration."

The room exploded with laughter.

MERRY GLANCED AROUND IN CONFUSION. "What's so funny about that?"

"Absolutely nothing." Sam hooked an arm around her waist and dragged her into his lap where he kissed her breathless.

"I'm just saying, Sam," she murmured against his lips when he finally pulled back a little, "there's no way the Fates would be that cruel."

"Yeah, you've said that before," Sam said, "but have you ever actually *met* the fates?"

"What? Well, no, of course not, but, who has?"

Karl snickered.

"Actually," Sam said, "we've got a couple friends who have met people who know the Fates, and according to them, the Fates sort of specialize in cruelty. For their own amusement, you know."

Merry's eyes narrowed. "You know people who know people who know the Fates?"

He nodded.

"The only people who know the Fates are the gods and the goddesses, and occasionally, their offspring."

"Yep. Exactly right."

"Huh." Merry stared into her wolf's eyes and

wondered what other secrets he held that she just needed time to discover. She popped a small candy bar of pure chocolate into her mouth, sucking on it slowly while staring into his eyes, then leaned forward and whispered in his ear, "I'm afraid chocolate by itself is *way* less satisfying now."

He stiffened beneath her in all the best of ways.

She leaned back and grinned at him.

Sam's eyes flared bright, and she caught a glimpse of his wolf staring back at her before he surged to his feet. "Great dinner, Mom. See you next week!"

"Sam!" Francine's voice carried over the sound of everyone else's laughter as he carried his mate back to the cabin where the hell-kitties and their future waited.

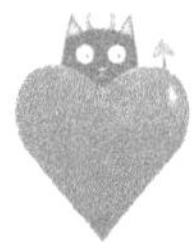

Spike and Drusilla raced around the house in celebration as their demon finally claimed her mate. When things fell silent in the bedroom, they had just finished off the very last of the chocolates Spike had found in the kitchen cabinets.

It's good to be a hell-cat, Spike said.

So good, Drusilla agreed.

Imagine not being able to eat chocolate without getting sick.

Those poor wolves. Drusilla led the way down the hall toward the bedroom.

Eh, they're dogs. They're probably dumb enough to eat the chocolate anyway. It's the earthbound kitties I feel sorry for. They'll never know the glory of chocolate.

That's a good thing, though. Drusilla stopped at the bedroom door and examined the wall to the left of it. *At least they won't get sick.*

True. Spike sniffed the wall on the right. *Shall we?*

Absolutely.

The two hell-cats stretched to their full height, set their paws just under the ceiling on either side of the bedroom door and raked their claws downward, scorching the walls in perfect lines and marking their territory.

Dropping back onto four feet, they examined their claw marks.

Perfect, Spike proclaimed.

Our best markings yet, Drusilla agreed.

Tomorrow, we'll mark the perimeter of the cabin, Spike said.

We should also mark their cars.

Definitely.

Satisfied with their plans to ensure their demon

and her shifter mate remained safe and well-protected in their territory, Spike and Drusilla sauntered into the bedroom and leapt onto the bed, shrinking into their smaller, house cat forms as they curled up together at the base of the bed and fell into a rumbling, purr-filled sleep.

Read on for an excerpt from *Satan's Kitty!*

Excerpt

THAT BYGUL'S LATEST matchmaking efforts resulted in Christmas morning dawning at the Bed & Breakfast in Hell *wasn't* his fault.

He was the top matchmaking cat at Pawsitively Purrfect Matches, for goddess' sake. He was a professional and he didn't make mistakes like that.

He blamed Soraya.

Ever since she saw Jasmine playing with the kittens at the witches' coven house in Zero, Kansas, all Soraya could talk about was matching that little girl with one of the kittens on their caseload *and* matching her mother, who was both human and single, with a mate.

Bygul kept reminding Soraya that neither Starlight nor her daughter, Jasmine, were on their caseload, but this didn't matter to Soraya.

"Witches first," Bygul kept saying, "especially after we lost weeks in Jamesville, matching Tempest's sister."

But then, catastrophe struck, no pun intended.

Jasmine wrote a letter to Santa, but before anyone could read it, the letter disappeared and Starlight went into a tizzy, begging her daughter to tell her what she'd asked Santa for.

Jasmine, being the stubborn sort, refused to share. "It's magic, Mom. Magic took the letter to Santa and Santa's gonna take care of everything, so don't worry."

The problem was that Bygul assumed Soraya had stolen the letter, so that she could get details that might help her choose the purrfect kitten for Jasmine.

Soraya assumed Tivali stole the letter for the same reason.

None of them suspected the demon hell-cat, Kyrie.

Unfortunately, being a hell-cat, Kyrie had a lot of magic herself and could pretty much zip around Zero however she pleased.

And apparently, she pleased to steal that letter.

A hell-cat leapt onto Luc's lap, startling him and making him chuckle. "Well, now, when did you get here, Kyrie? Did you get bored in the earth realm already? How's my sweet girl, Tempest, doing?"

Kyrie let out a happy meow and started making biscuits on his legs, causing Luc to yelp and laugh again.

"Okay, okay." He stroked her over and over again until her purr rumbled through the room like a freight train.

Over the next thirty minutes, one by one, Kyrie's kittens, who were no longer kitten-sized, jumped onto Luc's lap to climb all over their mother, batting at her tail and chewing on her ears, until Kyrie lost her patience, slammed a paw on the offending kitten's neck and pinning them down, groomed them to her satisfaction. Eventually, she lifted her paw and the kitten ran away, only to be replaced with another one.

Luc chuckled when he realized that some of the kittens visiting weren't Kyrie's at all. Still she tolerated their play, then groomed each one until the visits finally tapered off.

At that point, Kyrie curled up into a ball and napped for a while.

Of course, during this time, Luc had no choice but to remain motionless, frozen in his chair, a victim of feline purralysis.

Luc felt a terrible mix of both relief and profound

regret, when Kyrie finally stood, stretching leisurely before butting her head against his and jumping down.

"Thanks for visiting, Kyrie," Luc called after her. "We miss you around here."

With a swish of her tail and head held high, Kyrie sauntered from the room.

It was only when she was completely gone that Luc realized she'd left something behind. "What's this?"

An envelope sat on his lap.

It was addressed to Satan Claus, North Pole, from a Jasmine in Zero, Kansas.

Lucifer chuckled. "Haven't received one of these in a long time, now have we, kittens? Ever since the humans automated everything, most of the misspelled letters still make it to good old Mr. Claus. Well, let's see what we can do for Miss Jasmine of Zero, Kansas."

He opened the letter, scanned it and laughed. "Oh, this is going to be sooo much fun."

Start reading *Satan's Kitty today.*

Wondering about the Shenanigans crew?
Read on for an excerpt from Phoenix and Travis' story.

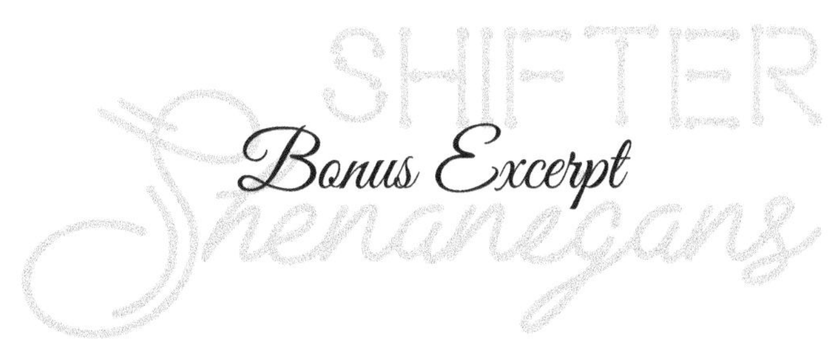

Bonus Excerpt

AS PHOENIX SMITH hid behind Shenanigans' bar, the latest in her long string of waitress gigs, she remembered the claim she'd made to her new boss when he'd hired her two days before.

He'd warned her in his gravely voice that Shenanigans "doesn't have crowds like you're used to serving."

She'd assured him that she had plenty of experience working with the roughest of customers and that she could handle whatever his bar patrons threw at her.

Famous last words.

Phoenix peeked over the top of the bar and ducked back down, horrified. The brawl was still happening. Which wasn't a big deal. She'd been in barroom brawls before. Even knocked a few heads together herself when the occasion called for it.

The problem wasn't the fight.

It wasn't the beer bottles being thrown or the bodies flung through the air. It also wasn't the sounds of tables being destroyed or chairs knocked over.

The problem was that her boss, the unbelievably sexy bartender with the gravely voice, had lunged over the top of the bar and landed in a whole different body.

And then, in that *whole new body,* had let out a roar that shook the rafters and started tossing his customers everywhere.

And as for them.

Well, they were the problem too.

Snarling and growling, snapping at each other with viciously long fangs.

Fangs.

No, not like vampires.

More like werewolves. And werecougars. Which shouldn't even be a thing.

But since it was a thing, it also meant her boss was a werebear. Or wereblackbear.

This was crazy.

But now the location of this bar, which was right in the middle of the woods, with no roads leading up to it, made perfect sense to Phoenix.

At first, it had seemed crazy that people would hike to their neighborhood bar, but then the more she'd thought about it, the more she'd realized how ingenious it was. They'd never have to worry about drunk drivers because their customers could just walk their drunk asses home.

Only now she was realizing they'd probably be walking their drunk, *furry* asses home. Because who was more comfortable in the middle of the woods than a bunch of wolves and cougars?

Certainly not her. And now she was stuck here, with an unknown number of cougars and wolves between her and the door. Not to mention her boss, the scary-ass bear. What were the chances of her getting out of here without any of them noticing her?

Surely there was a back door. She couldn't believe she hadn't explored all the exits by now. She knew better than this.

"Shit, shit, shit. Phoenix, what are you going to do? Shit, this is madness!" She clutched her hair and dragged in a deep breath.

That's when she realized the sounds of fighting had stopped.

All the growls, snarls and roars had faded.

She'd never really understood how the hair on

someone's neck could stand on end, but that's exactly what it did. Followed by a wave of ice-cold fear and a preternatural instinct that told her to run.

Only there was nowhere to go.

She'd trapped herself behind the bar.

"What's she doin' down there, Travis?" someone asked.

"Hell if I know."

Phoenix shivered at the sound of her boss's gravelly voice. If he was speaking, he had to be back in human form. Right?

She slowly raised her head and looked up.

The other two waitresses, along with the men and women they'd served that night, were all crowded around the bar, staring down at her.

While naked.

Okay, so she wasn't *positive* they were naked since the bar hid their lower halves, but everything up top was on display, so she had to assume...

"I thought you said you could handle this job," Travis growled at her as he shoved his way behind the bar. He faced her, hands on hips, a furious scowl on his face. "You told me you had experience with rough crowds. I knew I'd never heard of those bars before. They were all human bars, weren't they? You should have told me you'd never had any experience working at a shifter bar!"

Phoenix was speechless. It wasn't really what he was saying. Because she'd already pretty much processed that shifters were real and that this was a shifter bar. That had become shockingly clear when everyone in the bar went furry.

"Are you even listening to me?"

With great effort, Phoenix dragged her eyes away from the gorgeous cock bobbing in front of her and pushed to her feet. Swallowing, she looked her boss in the eye and said, "I'm sorry, what?"

"Why would you lie about your experiences? You could have been seriously hurt! At the very least, you should have shifted to give you a better chance in that brawl."

"Um, why exactly would I shift again?"

He stared at her, a perplexed look on his face, then glanced over at the customers, as if asking them for help.

"Well, usually, it's what shifters do, lass," one of the men offered.

She glanced at him. Then back at Travis.

She had no idea why they thought she was a shifter, but she wasn't about to admit the truth.

They'd probably eat her or do something worse, like throw her in prison for the rest of her life, just to keep humans from discovering their secret.

"So why didn't you shift, honey?" Cassie, one of the other waitresses, asked.

"Yeah, why?"

Several voices chimed in, wondering what kind of shifter wouldn't even bother to shift for protection in the middle of a shifter brawl.

Phoenix didn't know what to say, so she just shrugged and refused to reply.

"What kind of shifter are you, anyway?"

"Karl!" Glory, another waitress, slapped him on the back of the head. "Never ask a woman about her animal!"

"Well, I never smelled her kind before."

"Me neither."

The murmurs of agreement spread.

Had they never been around humans before? Surely that wasn't possible.

"Doesn't matter," Glory insisted. "A woman's animal is very personal." She turned to Phoenix. "Don't worry about it, honey. You'll shift with us when you feel safe. Until then, you just keep your animal a well-guarded secret. No one will fault you for it." She glared around at the rest of the room. "Right?"

Travis rolled his eyes and crossed his arms, the movement causing his cock to bounce a little. "Look. You can't work in a shifter bar if you're not willing to shift. That's just the way it is."

"That's rather prejudicial," Phoenix said, glaring at him, trying desperately to ignore his bobbing cock. It couldn't be sanitary to have all that nakedness around – well, everything. And what was she saying? She should be taking this opportunity to quit, not arguing her right to stay.

"Oh, don't listen to him," Glory said. "I'm half-owner of this bar, Travis, and I say she stays."

This was news to Phoenix, who hadn't realized the waitress who'd been pitching in occasionally was one of the owners. She should have guessed when Travis introduced her as his sister though. It made sense that they would own the bar together.

"She did a magnificent job tonight," Glory continued. "And when the fight broke out, she quite sensibly retreated behind the bar, leaving you to knock sense into the lot of them."

"She's the best waitress we've had in a while, Travis," Cassie agreed. "We need her."

Travis groaned. "Whatever."

"You know, it'd be so much easier to take you seriously if your junk wasn't all out and proud right now."

Phoenix waved a hand in the general vicinity of his cock. "Can you please put some clothes on? Or go to the other side of the bar? Or something? Nobody wants your pubes in their beer."

Groans and gagging sounds filled the air.

"Oh, my god, Travis, get away from there right now!" Glory exclaimed. "That is disgusting! I never even thought about that and now I'm going to have that vision in my head every damn time I order a beer from my own bar!"

Travis rolled his eyes. "It's not like I expected to explode out of my clothes tonight, Glory."

"Well, you should expect it," she said sharply. "It happens practically every weekend." She turned to face the customers still crowded around the bar. "All right. I think that's enough for one night. Clean up your areas, settle up your tabs and get out, the lot of you. And don't forget to tip your waitresses. *Generously.*" She glared at them.

With shuffled feet and a number of muttered, "yes, ma'ams," the customers began to assist in the clean-up and one by one, wandered over to the bar to settle their tabs with Phoenix and Cassie.

An hour later, the doors were shut behind the final customer and thirty minutes after that, Phoenix was headed out the door, officially ending the weirdest shift she'd ever worked, and that was saying *a lot*.

Start the series with *Shifter Shenanigans* today.

WELCOME TO
HELL'S B&B

Thank you for reading

CHOCOLATE

Furnanigans

Please consider leaving a review on your favorite book site.

If you would like to be notified of

Pepper's new releases, please sign up here:

www.peppermcgraw.com/newsletter

Join Pepper's reader groups on Facebook:

Matchmaking Cats of the Goddesses

The Shenanigans Crew

Other Books by Pepper

BLACKTHORN ACADEMY

Monster's Reward

Monster's Madness

MATCHMAKING CATS OF THE GODDESSES

Catnapped

The Real McCat

Unbearably Cute

A Catmas to Remember

This Cat's for You

Santa Kitty

Hocus Purrcus

Abra-CAT-Abra

Tridents & Tails

Her Purrfect Familiar

Chocolate Furnanigans

Satan's Kitty

Valen-Cats

Catanic Rituals

A Beautiful Catship

Going Catty

Grave Cattitude

MURRYSVILLE COALITION

The Crazy Cheetah Lady

One Sad Kitty

SHENANIGANS

Shifter Shenanigans

Witchy Shenanigans

Full Moon Shenanigans

Hotel Shenanigans

Dragon Shenanigans

Undercover Shenanigans

Spooky Shenanigans

Holiday Shenanigans

Valentine Shenanigans

Lucky Shenanigans

STORIES OF THE VEIL

Guardians of the Veil

Astra

Glory

Luna

Zara

Guardians of the Realms

WICKED

No Rest for the Wicked

Wicked Is As Wicked Does

Anthologies & Collections

MATCHMAKING CATS OF THE GODDESSES BUNDLES

The Cat's Meow

Holly Jolly Pawliday

Familiar Meowgic

The Devil's in the Cattails

SHENANIGANS ANTHOLOGIES

Crazed

Amazed

Holidazed

STORIES OF THE VEIL

The Unveiled

The Veiled

COMPLETE SERIES COLLECTIONS

Shenanigans

The Veil

Wicked

amazon.com/author/peppermcgraw

bookbub.com/authors/pepper-mcgraw

facebook.com/ShenanigansSeries

goodreads.com/peppermcgraw

instagram.com/peppermcgraw_author

tiktok.com/@peppermcgraw

x.com/peppermcgraw